Westfield Memorial Librar
Westfield, New Jersey

P9-DDK-890

Lewis Trondheim & Fabrice Parme

Westfield Memorial Library
Westfield, New Jersey

Tiny Tyrant

Translated by Alexis Siegel

First Second
New York & London

Contents

The Ethelbertosaurus

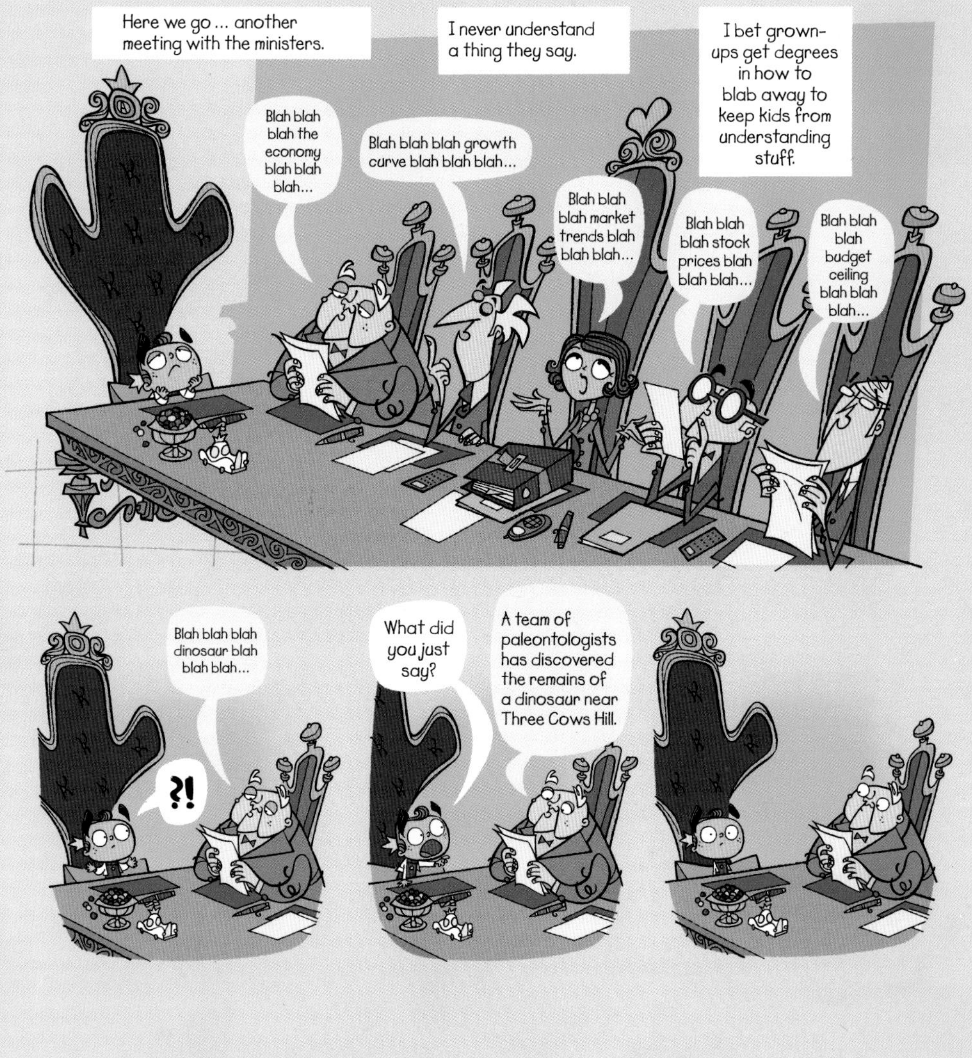

Here we go ... another meeting with the ministers.
I never understand a thing they say.
I bet grown-ups get degrees in how to blab away to keep kids from understanding stuff.
Blah blah blah the economy blah blah blah...
Blah blah blah growth curve blah blah blah...
Blah blah blah market trends blah blah blah...
Blah blah blah stock prices blah blah blah...
Blah blah blah budget ceiling blah blah blah...
Blah blah blah dinosaur blah blah blah...
?!
What did you just say?
A team of paleontologists has discovered the remains of a dinosaur near Three Cows Hill.

Faster!!

I want to see MY dinosaur!

I'll call it the **portocristosaurus!**

No, even better: the **ethelbertosaurus!**

So where is it? Where is it?

Where is it?

Ah, Your Majesty, good morning!

Allow me to introduce myself. I am Professor Tibia, and I have just discovered what I have named the **tibiatosaurus.**

You mean the ethelbertosaurus?

Why no, er—

—I mean, yes, of course...

Your Majesty is correct

So, show me the monster!

This way, Your Majesty.

A beautiful specimen, isn't it? This little Jurassic herbivore is almost completely intact.

The ethelbertosaurus is a colossal discovery.

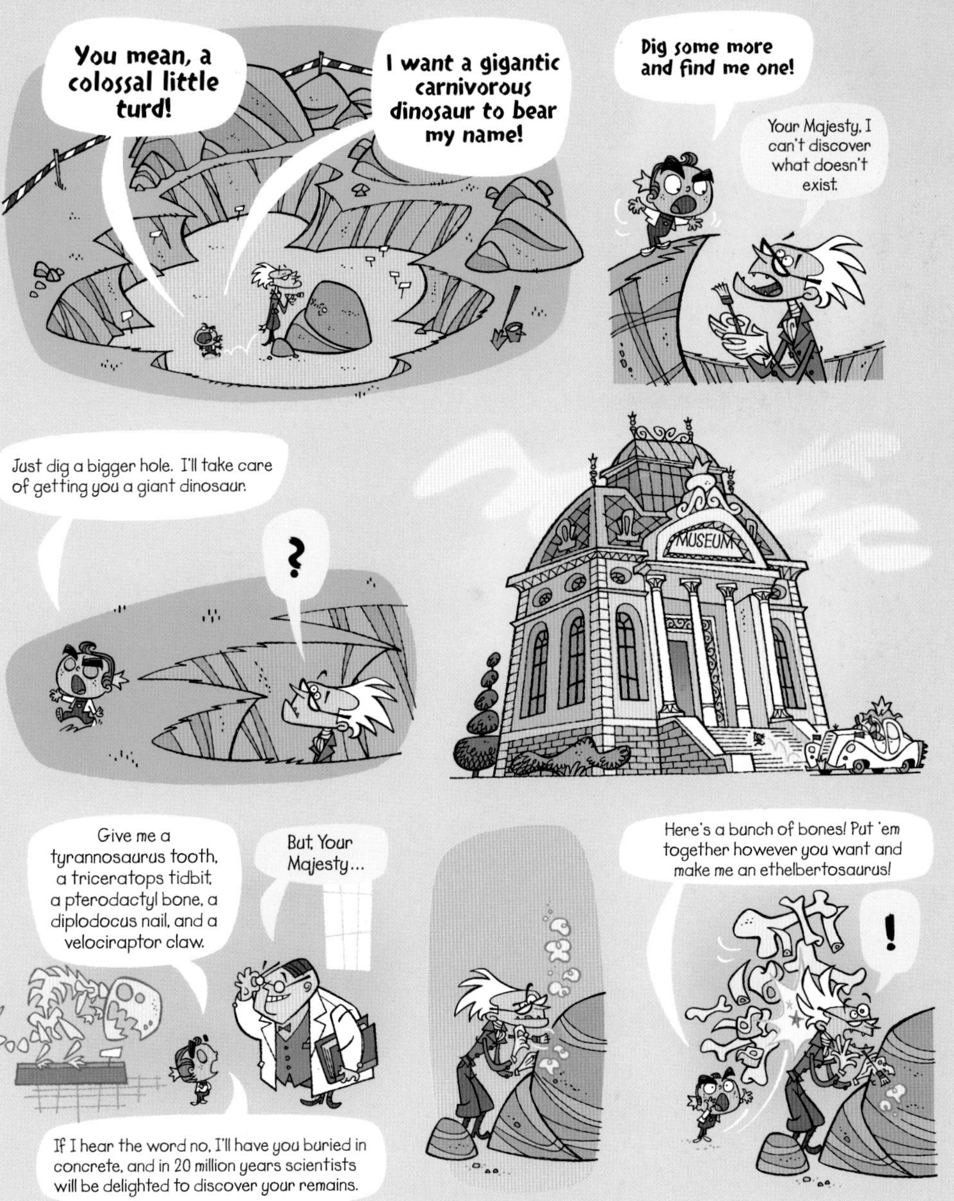

You mean, a colossal little turd!
I want a gigantic carnivorous dinosaur to bear my name!
Dig some more and find me one!
Your Majesty, I can't discover what doesn't exist.
Just dig a bigger hole. I'll take care of getting you a giant dinosaur.
?
MUSEUM
Give me a tyrannosaurus tooth, a triceratops tidbit, a pterodactyl bone, a diplodocus nail, and a velociraptor claw.
But, Your Majesty...
If I hear the word no, I'll have you buried in concrete, and in 20 million years scientists will be delighted to discover your remains.
Here's a bunch of bones! Put 'em together however you want and make me an ethelbertosaurus!
!

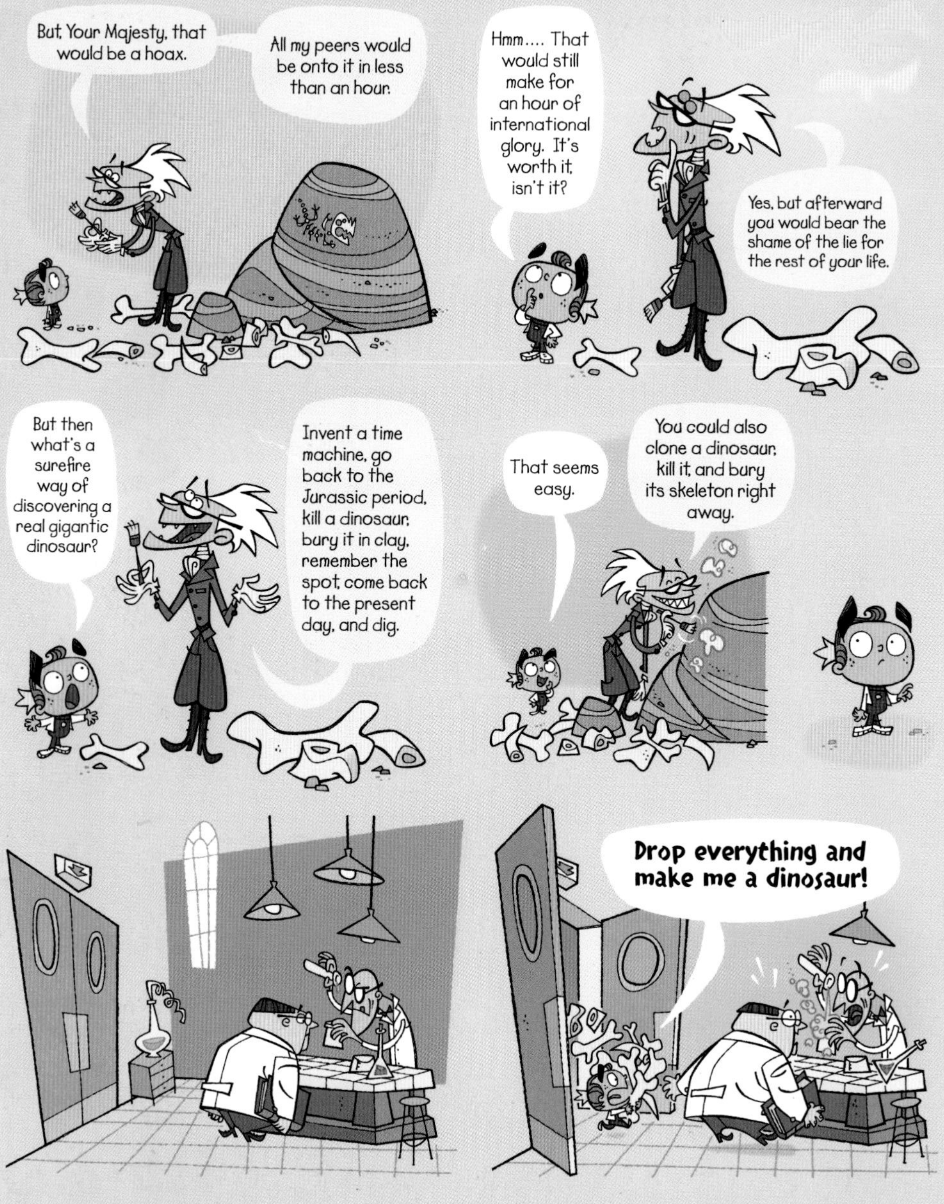

But, Your Majesty, that would be a hoax.
All my peers would be onto it in less than an hour.
Hmm.... That would still make for an hour of international glory. It's worth it, isn't it?
Yes, but afterward you would bear the shame of the lie for the rest of your life.
But then what's a surefire way of discovering a real gigantic dinosaur?
Invent a time machine, go back to the Jurassic period, kill a dinosaur, bury it in clay, remember the spot, come back to the present day, and dig.
That seems easy.
You could also clone a dinosaur, kill it, and bury its skeleton right away.
Drop everything and make me a dinosaur!

Here's a bunch of bones! Clone me one on the double!
Uh ... yes, Your Majesty.
Right away, Your Majesty!
Hurry up! Faster! Stop dithering around!
I've organized a press conference at 7 tonight to show journalists from around the world my discovery!
But Your Majesty, we will need at least 20 or 30 years of work to perfect this cloning process.
No way! In movies they just mix a whole bunch of stuff together and it works. Like this!
Then they zap it with some gamma, beta, and omega rays...
And a bolt from a laser enhanced by a good hard kick.
BOP

Look! It's moving!
Indeed.... Fascinating!
Let's write down the procedure and not touch anything else!
Are you kidding? We have to throw in a few pick-me-ups, some vitamins, and a drop of every pretty-colored chemical you have.
Your Majesty! Life does not result from chance and randomness.
Or perhaps it does?
An egg!
Get me a hammer to crack it!
We don't have a hammer, Sire, but might I suggest an incubator?
Don't worry, I'll use the floor.
Krak
YES!!
Look how fast the little creature's growing! Get me a rifle so I can kill it!

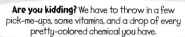

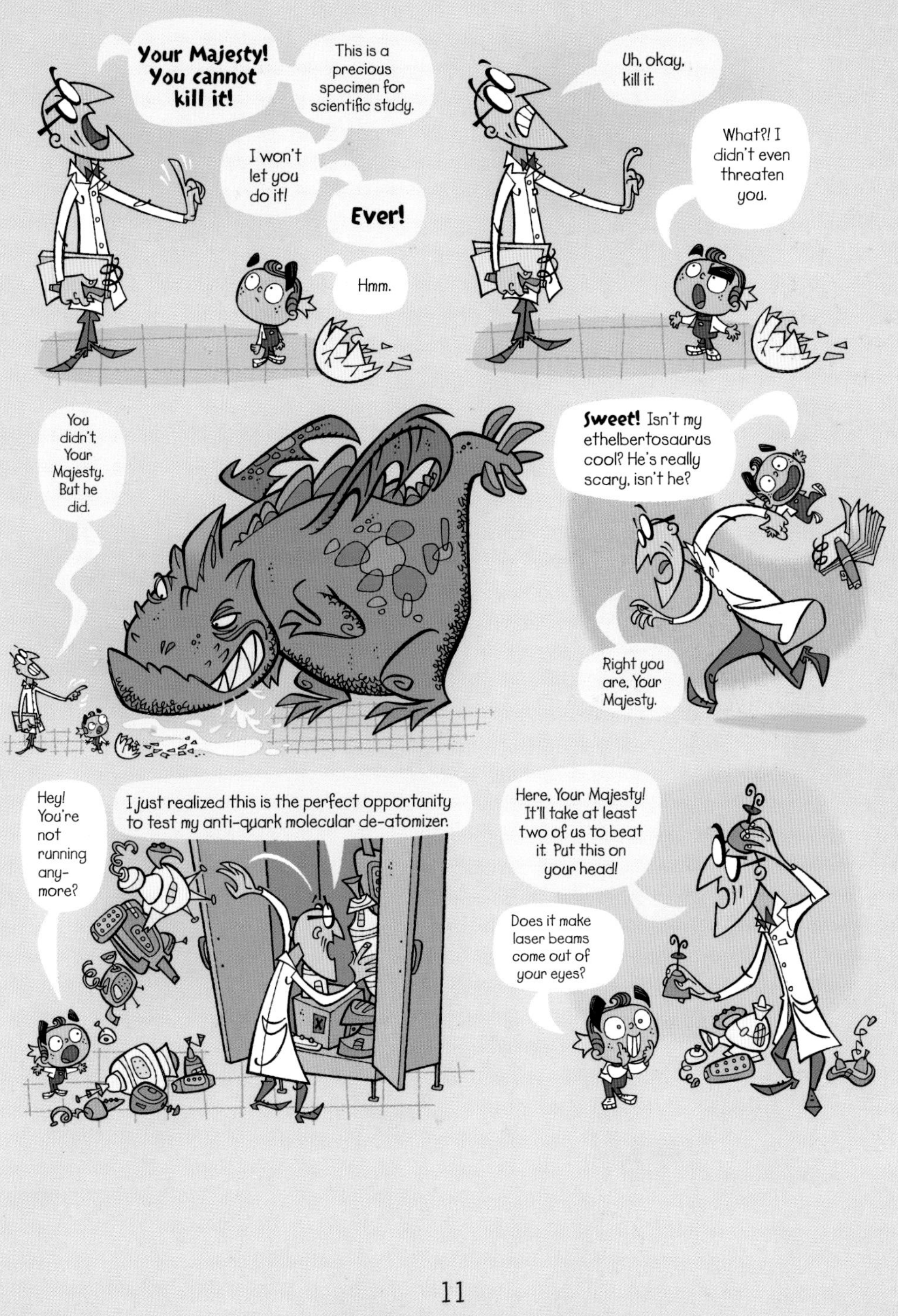

Your Majesty! You cannot kill it!
This is a precious specimen for scientific study.
I won't let you do it!
Ever!
Hmm.
Uh, okay, kill it.
What?! I didn't even threaten you.
You didn't, Your Majesty. But he did.
Sweet! Isn't my ethelbertosaurus cool? He's really scary, isn't he?
Right you are, Your Majesty.
Hey! You're not running any-more?
I just realized this is the perfect opportunity to test my anti-quark molecular de-atomizer.
Here, Your Majesty! It'll take at least two of us to beat it. Put this on your head!
Does it make laser beams come out of your eyes?

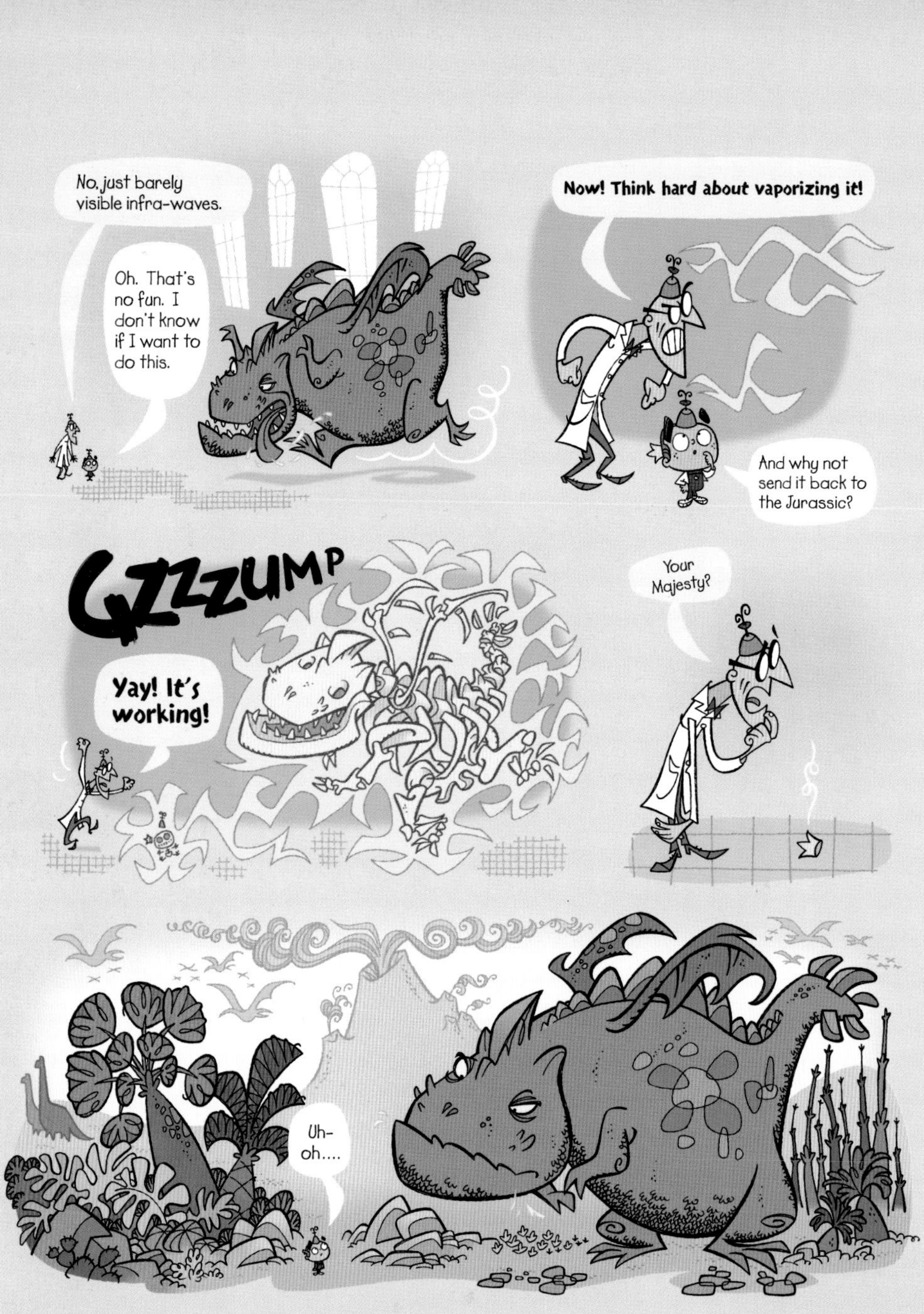
No, just barely visible infra-waves.
Oh. That's no fun. I don't know if I want to do this.
Now! Think hard about vaporizing it!
And why not send it back to the Jurassic?
GZZZUMP
Yay! It's working!
Your Majesty?
Uh-oh....

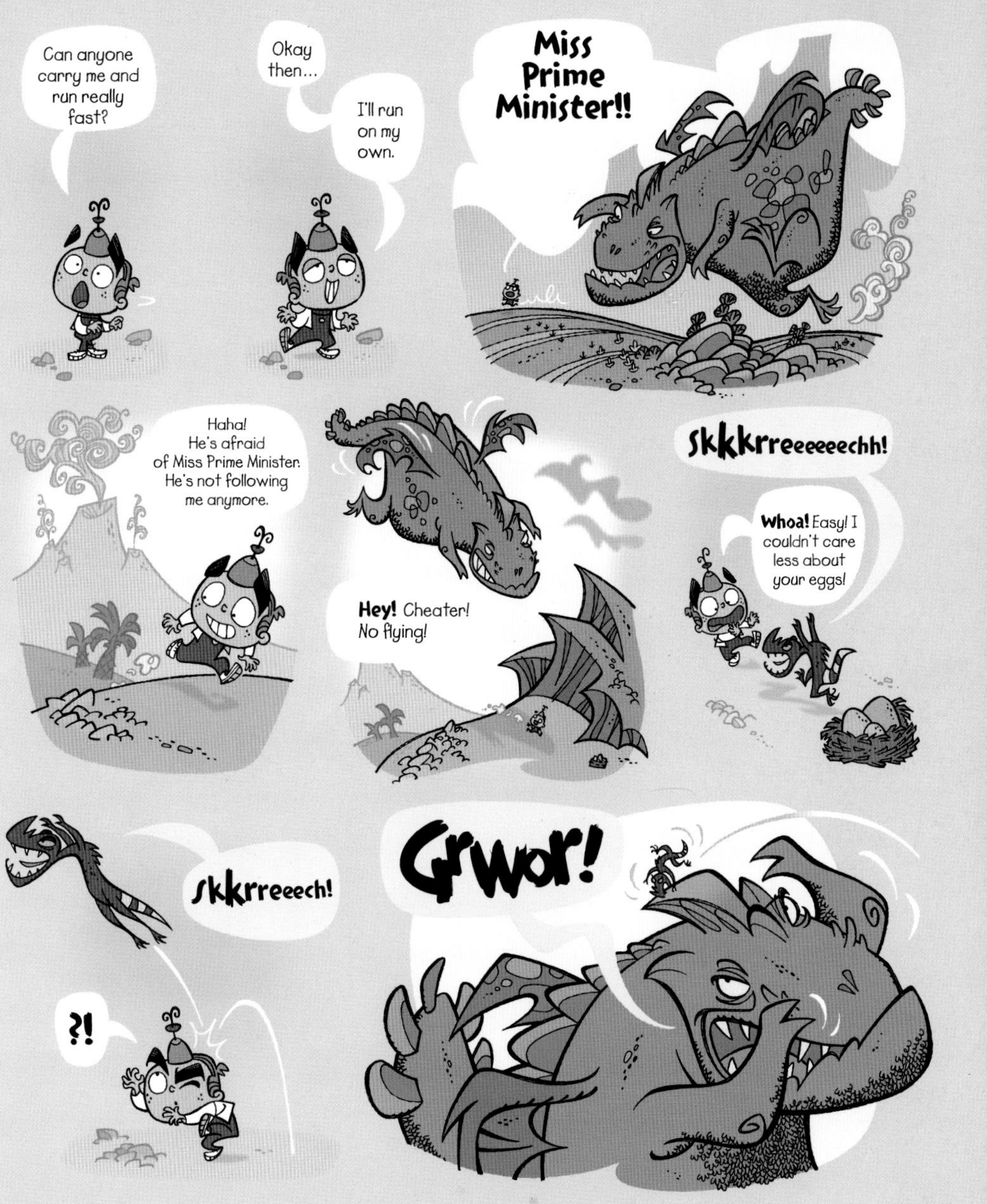
Can anyone carry me and run really fast?
Okay then...
I'll run on my own.
Miss Prime Minister!!
Haha! He's afraid of Miss Prime Minister. He's not following me anymore.
Hey! Cheater! No flying!
skkkrreeeeeechh!
Whoa! Easy! I couldn't care less about your eggs!
skkrreeech!
?!
Grwor!

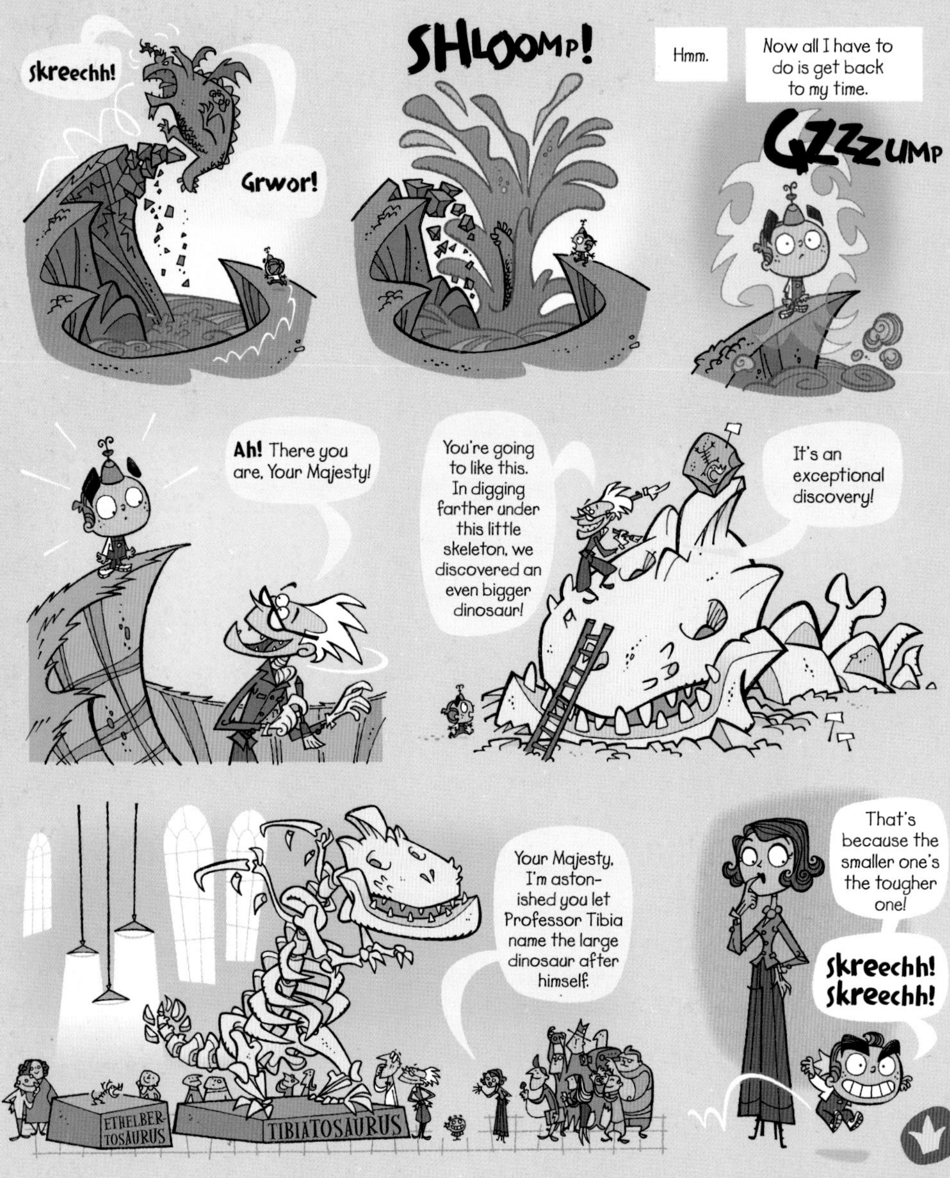
Skreechh!
Grwor!
SHLOOMP!
Hmm.
Now all I have to do is get back to my time.
GZZZUMP
Ah! There you are, Your Majesty!
You're going to like this. In digging farther under this little skeleton, we discovered an even bigger dinosaur!
It's an exceptional discovery!
ETHELBER-TOSAURUS
TIBIATOSAURUS
Your Majesty, I'm aston-ished you let Professor Tibia name the large dinosaur after himself.
That's because the smaller one's the tougher one!
Skreechh! Skreechh!

Safety First

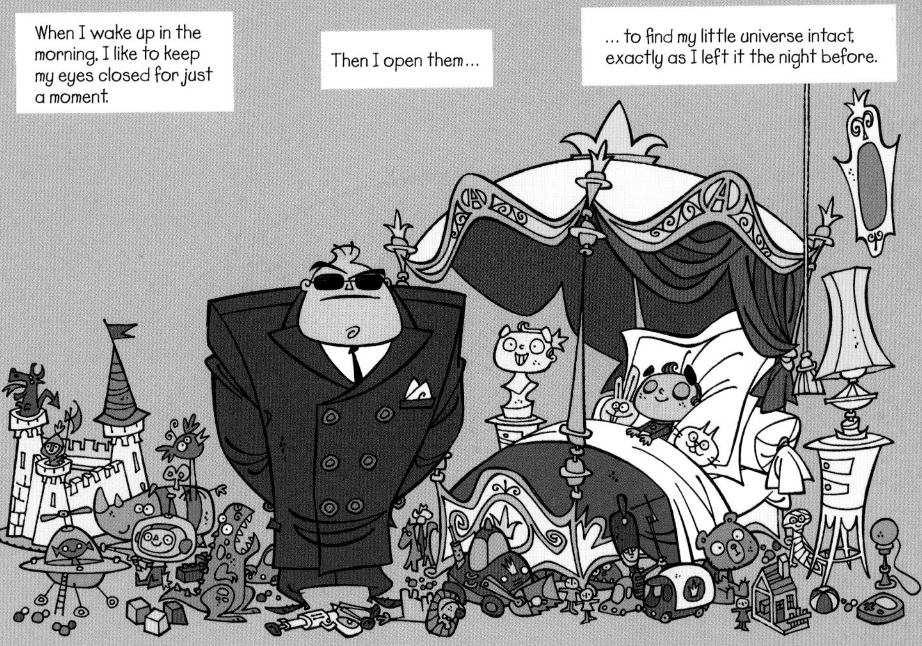
When I wake up in the morning, I like to keep my eyes closed for just a moment.
Then I open them...
... to find my little universe intact, exactly as I left it the night before.

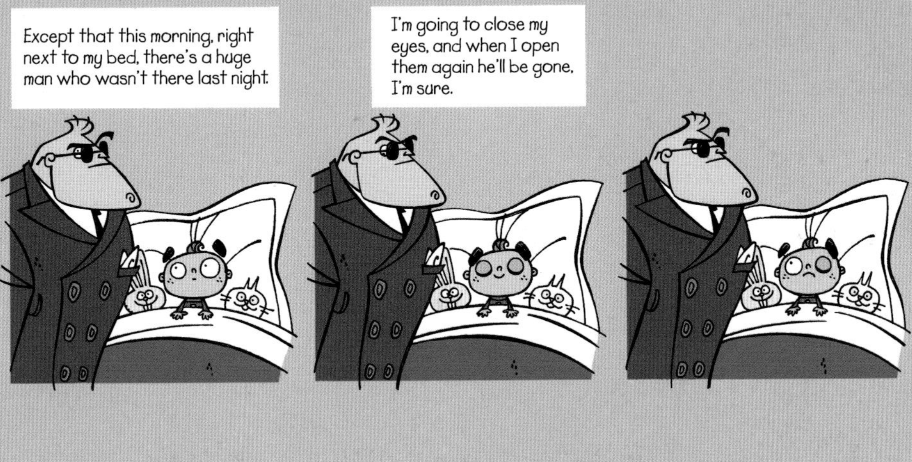
Except that this morning, right next to my bed, there's a huge man who wasn't there last night.
I'm going to close my eyes, and when I open them again he'll be gone, I'm sure.

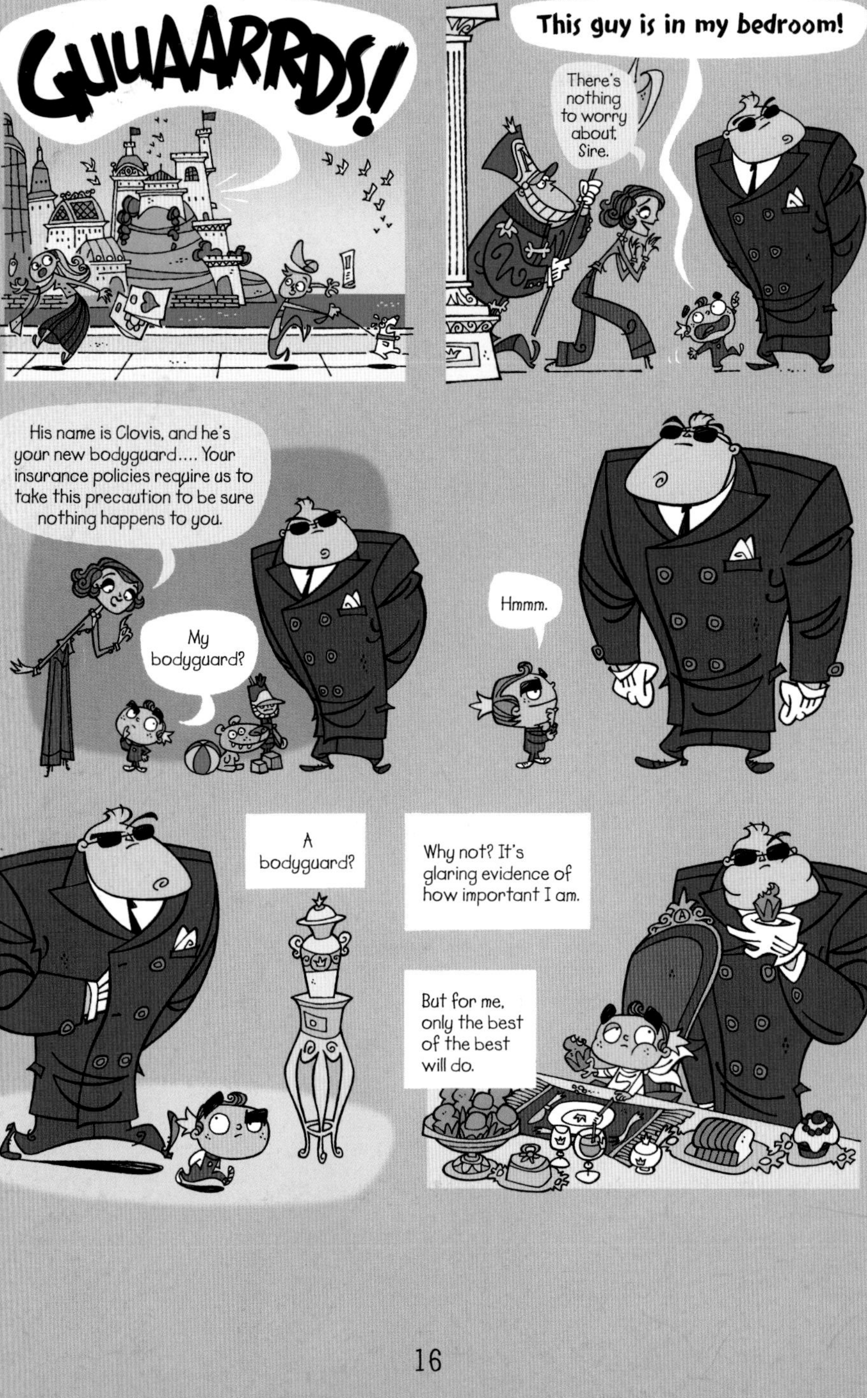
GUUAARRDS!
This guy is in my bedroom!
There's nothing to worry about, Sire.
His name is Clovis, and he's your new bodyguard.... Your insurance policies require us to take this precaution to be sure nothing happens to you.
My bodyguard?
Hmmm.
A bodyguard?
Why not? It's glaring evidence of how important I am.
But for me, only the best of the best will do.

Do you have any references, Clovis?

I can hit a fly from half a mile away. I've fought in eight wars. Was a secret agent for seventeen years. Saved thirteen presidents and prevented twenty-nine assassinations. Foiled thirty-one coup attempts and received seventy-four medals of honor.

Wow!

He can hit a fly from half a mile away...

But perhaps I should test his abilities *myself*.

Oh, no! A draft just swept me out the window!

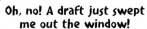

Eh... that was too easy. He was standing right there.

Would you mind walking to the other end of the room, please?

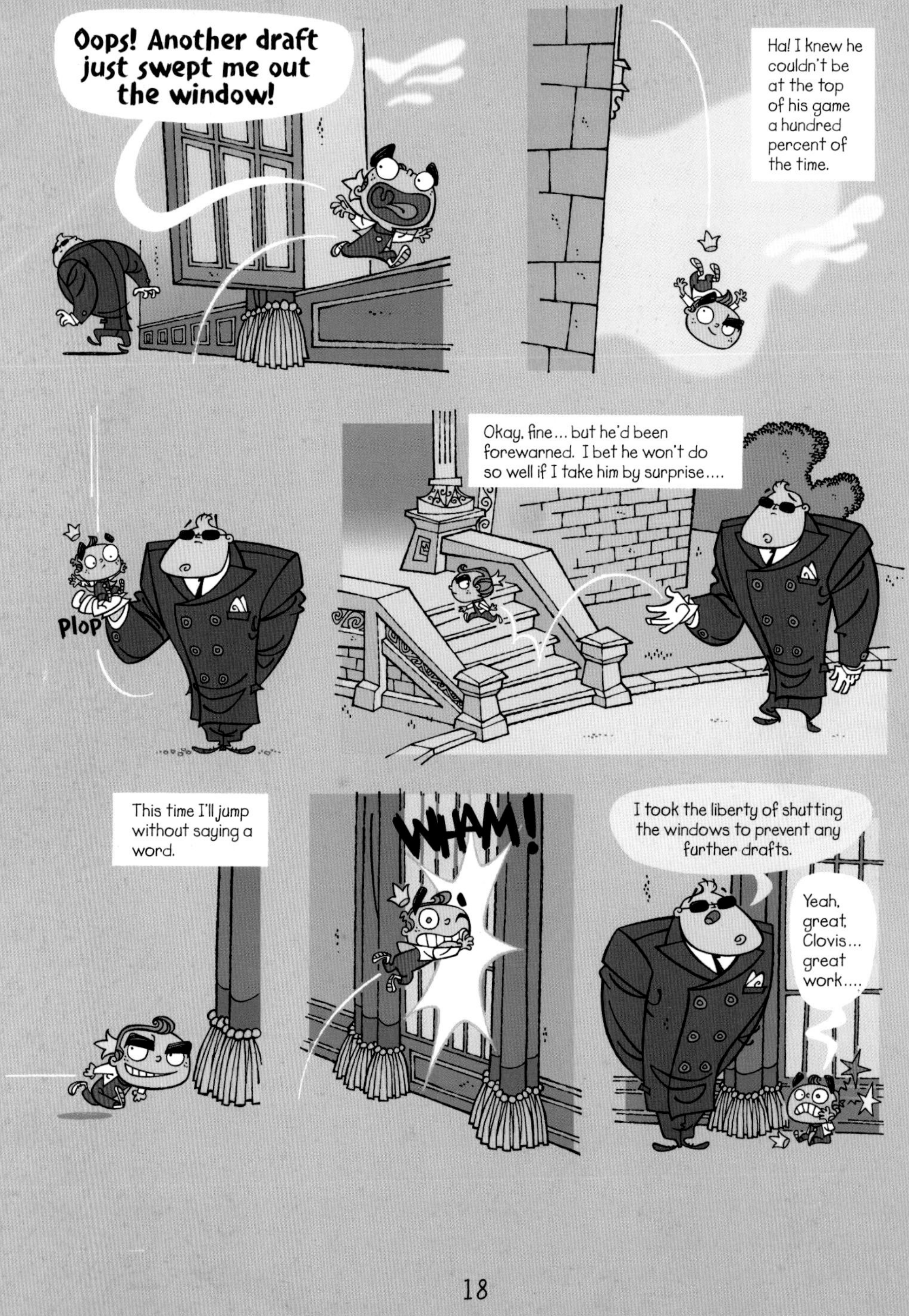

Oops! Another draft just swept me out the window!
Ha! I knew he couldn't be at the top of his game a hundred percent of the time.
PLOP
Okay, fine... but he'd been forewarned. I bet he won't do so well if I take him by surprise....
This time I'll jump without saying a word.
WHAM!
I took the liberty of shutting the windows to prevent any further drafts.
Yeah, great, Clovis... great work....

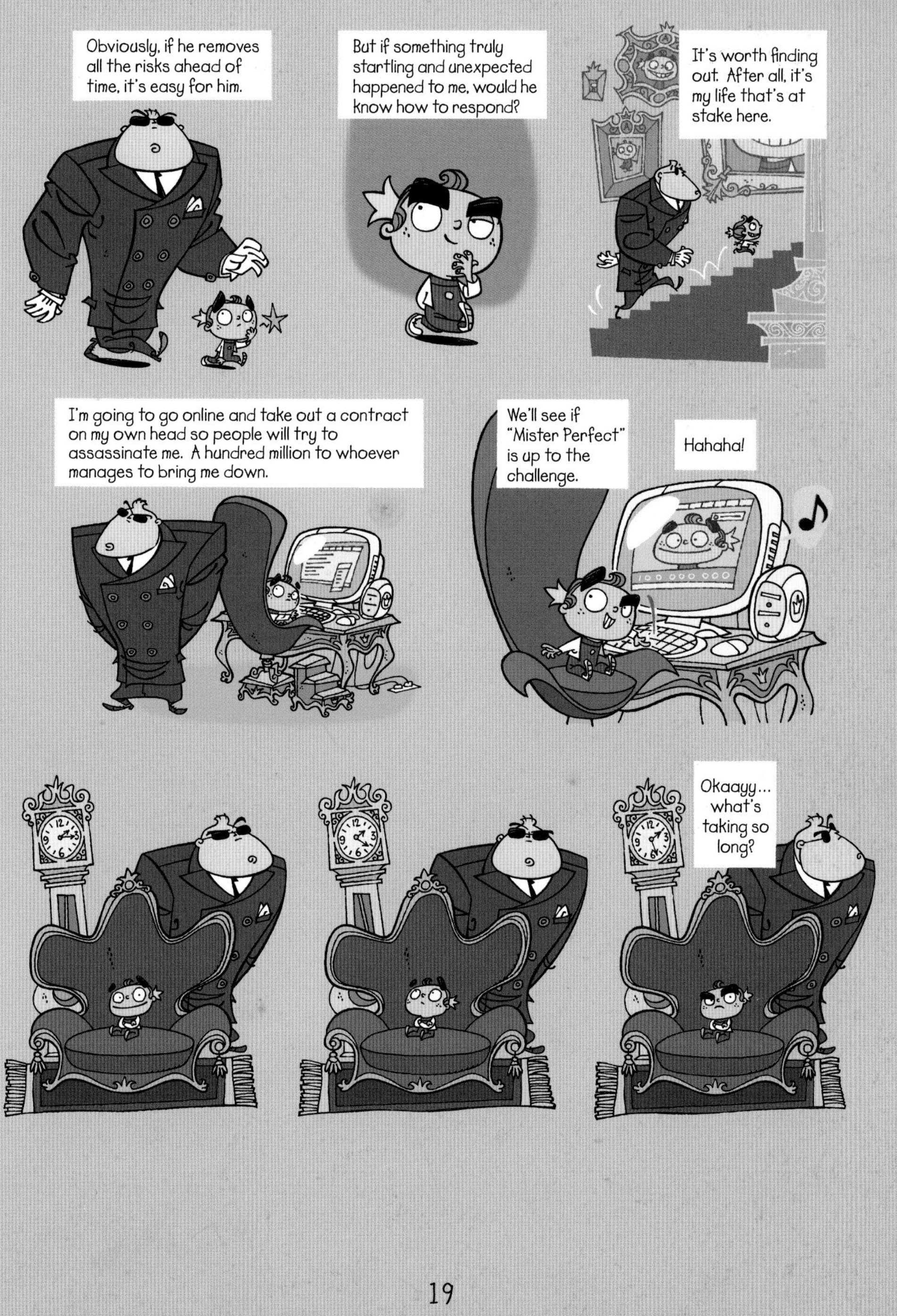
Obviously, if he removes all the risks ahead of time, it's easy for him.
But if something truly startling and unexpected happened to me, would he know how to respond?
It's worth finding out. After all, it's my life that's at stake here.
I'm going to go online and take out a contract on my own head so people will try to assassinate me. A hundred million to whoever manages to bring me down.
We'll see if "Mister Perfect" is up to the challenge.
Hahaha!
Okaayy... what's taking so long?

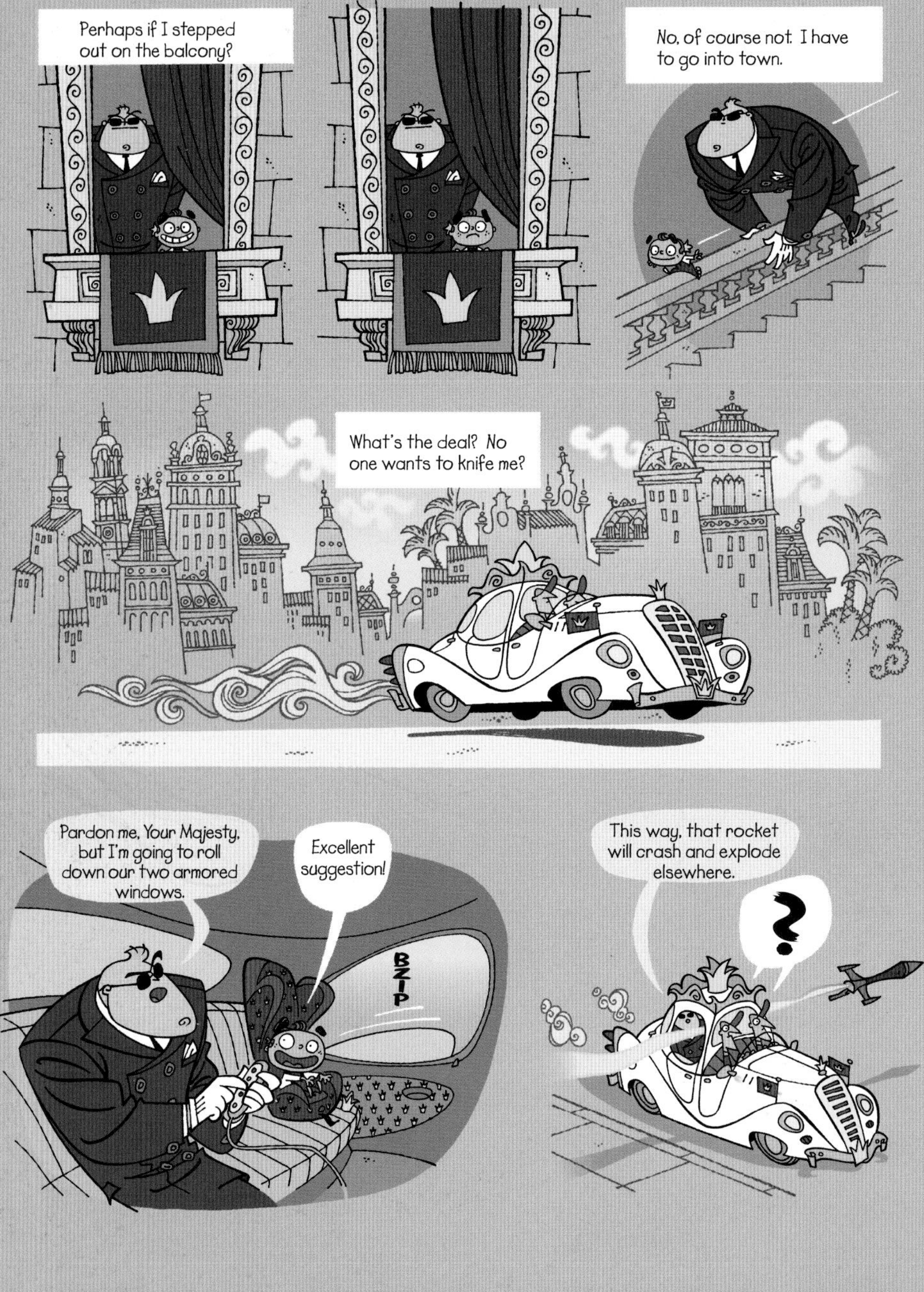
Perhaps if I stepped out on the balcony?
No, of course not. I have to go into town.
What's the deal? No one wants to knife me?
Pardon me, Your Majesty, but I'm going to roll down our two armored windows.
Excellent suggestion!
BZIP
This way, that rocket will crash and explode elsewhere.
?

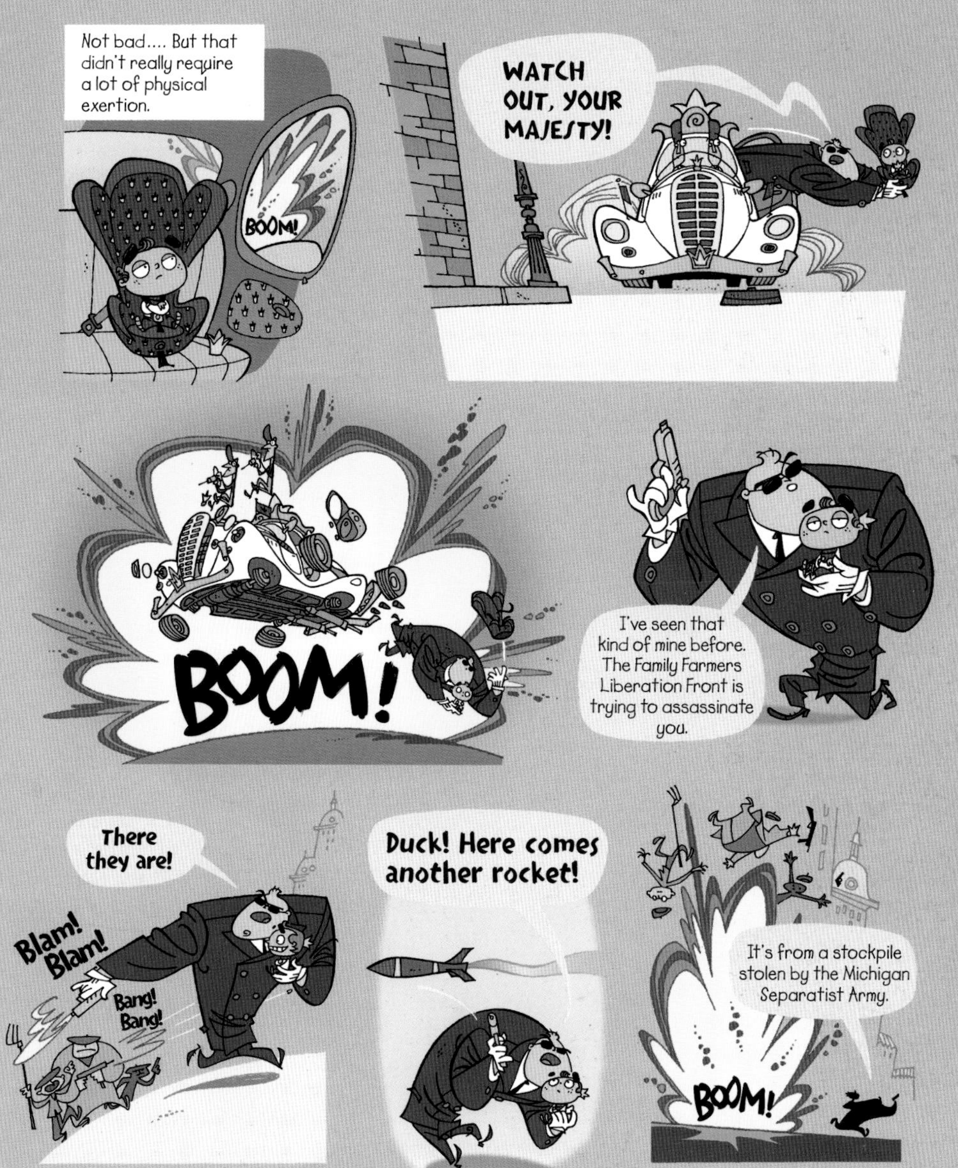
Not bad.... But that didn't really require a lot of physical exertion.
BOOM!
WATCH OUT, YOUR MAJESTY!
BOOM!
I've seen that kind of mine before. The Family Farmers Liberation Front is trying to assassinate you.
There they are!
Blam! Blam!
Bang! Bang!
Duck! Here comes another rocket!
It's from a stockpile stolen by the Michigan Separatist Army.
BOOM!

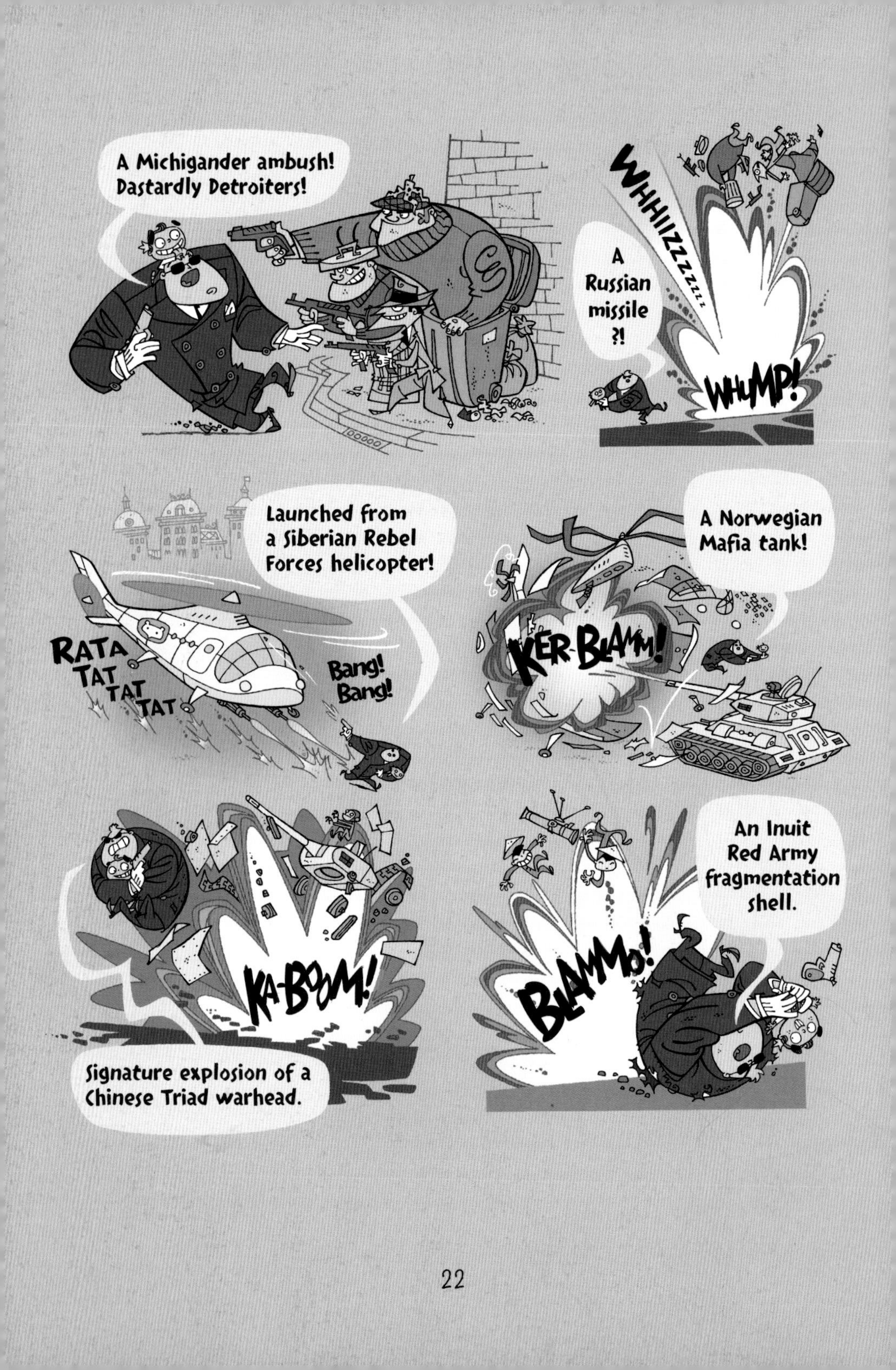

A Michigander ambush!
Dastardly Detroiters!
WHHIIZZZzzzz
A Russian missile ?!
WHUMP!
Launched from a Siberian Rebel Forces helicopter!
RATA TAT TAT TAT
Bang! Bang!
A Norwegian Mafia tank!
KER-BLAMM!
KA-BOOM!
Signature explosion of a Chinese Triad warhead.
An Inuit Red Army fragmentation shell.
BLAMMO!

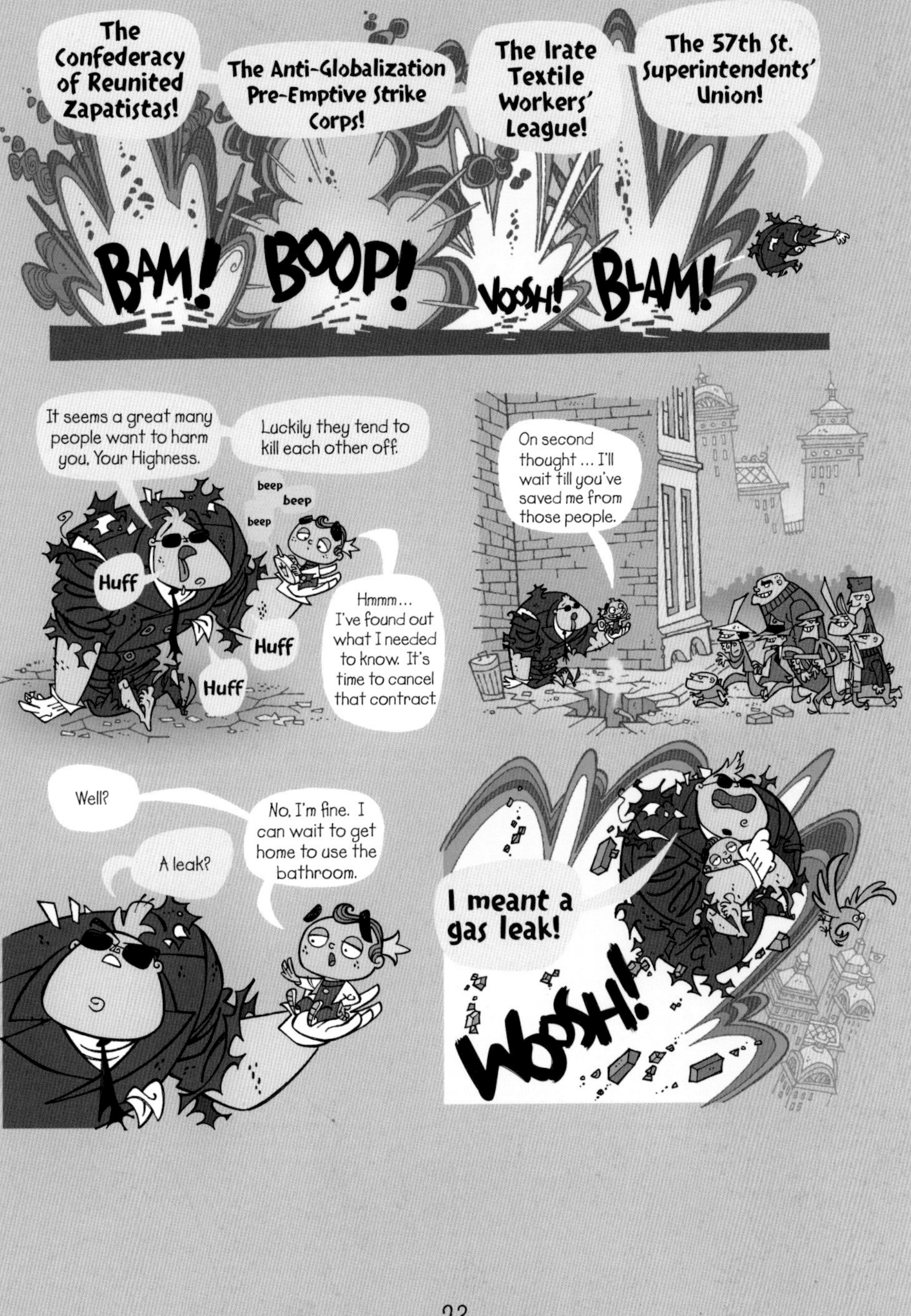
The Confederacy of Reunited Zapatistas!
The Anti-Globalization Pre-Emptive Strike Corps!
The Irate Textile Workers' League!
The 57th St. Superintendents' Union!
BAM!
BOOP!
VOOSH!
BLAM!
It seems a great many people want to harm you, Your Highness.
Luckily they tend to kill each other off.
beep
beep
beep
Huff
Huff
Huff
Hmmm... I've found out what I needed to know. It's time to cancel that contract.
On second thought ... I'll wait till you've saved me from those people.
Well?
No, I'm fine. I can wait to get home to use the bathroom.
A leak?
I meant a gas leak!
WOOSH!

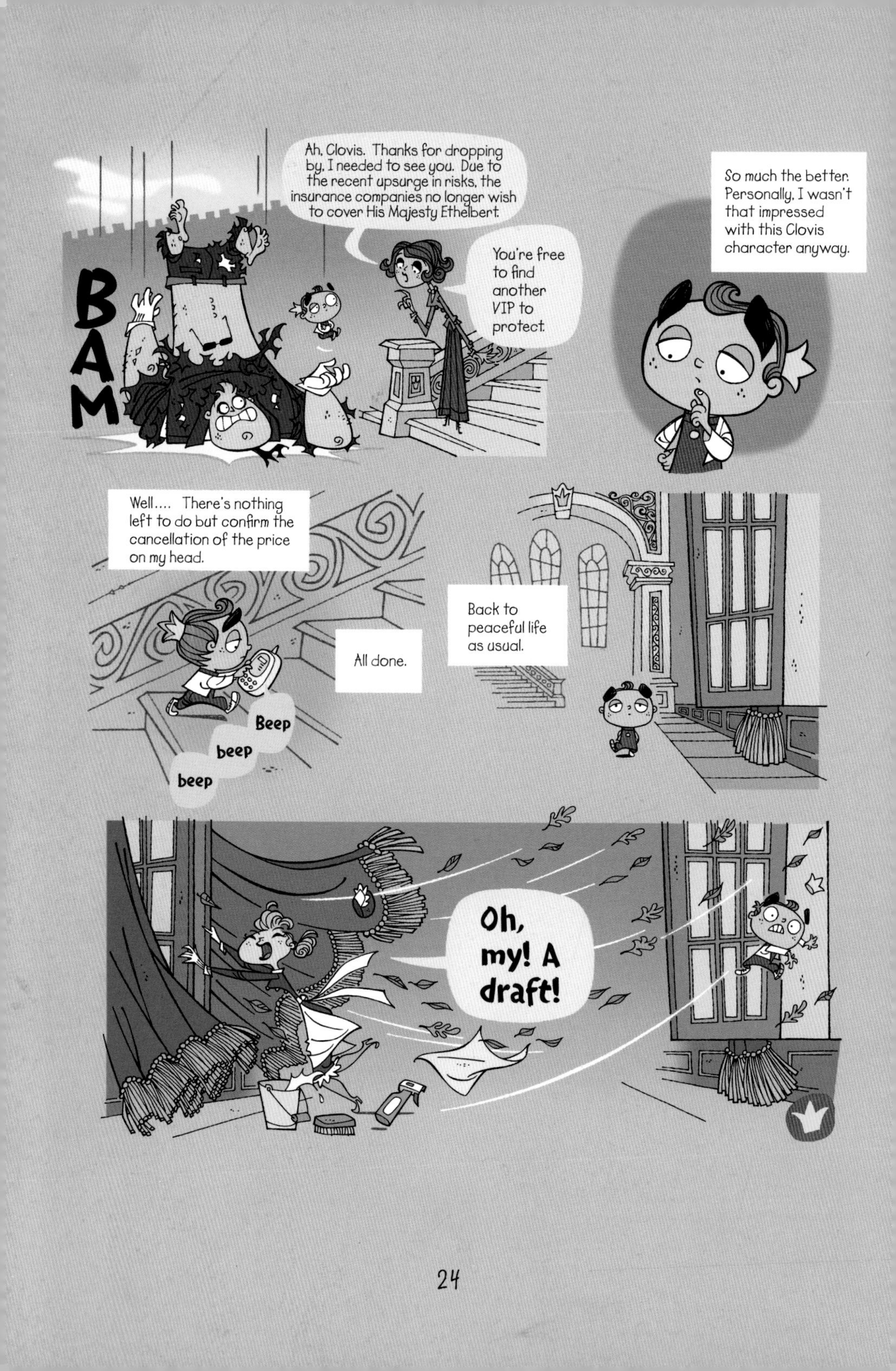

BAM
Ah, Clovis. Thanks for dropping by, I needed to see you. Due to the recent upsurge in risks, the insurance companies no longer wish to cover His Majesty Ethelbert.
You're free to find another VIP to protect.
So much the better. Personally, I wasn't that impressed with this Clovis character anyway.
Well.... There's nothing left to do but confirm the cancellation of the price on my head.
Beep
beep
beep
All done.
Back to peaceful life as usual.
Oh, my! A draft!

The Great Love Race

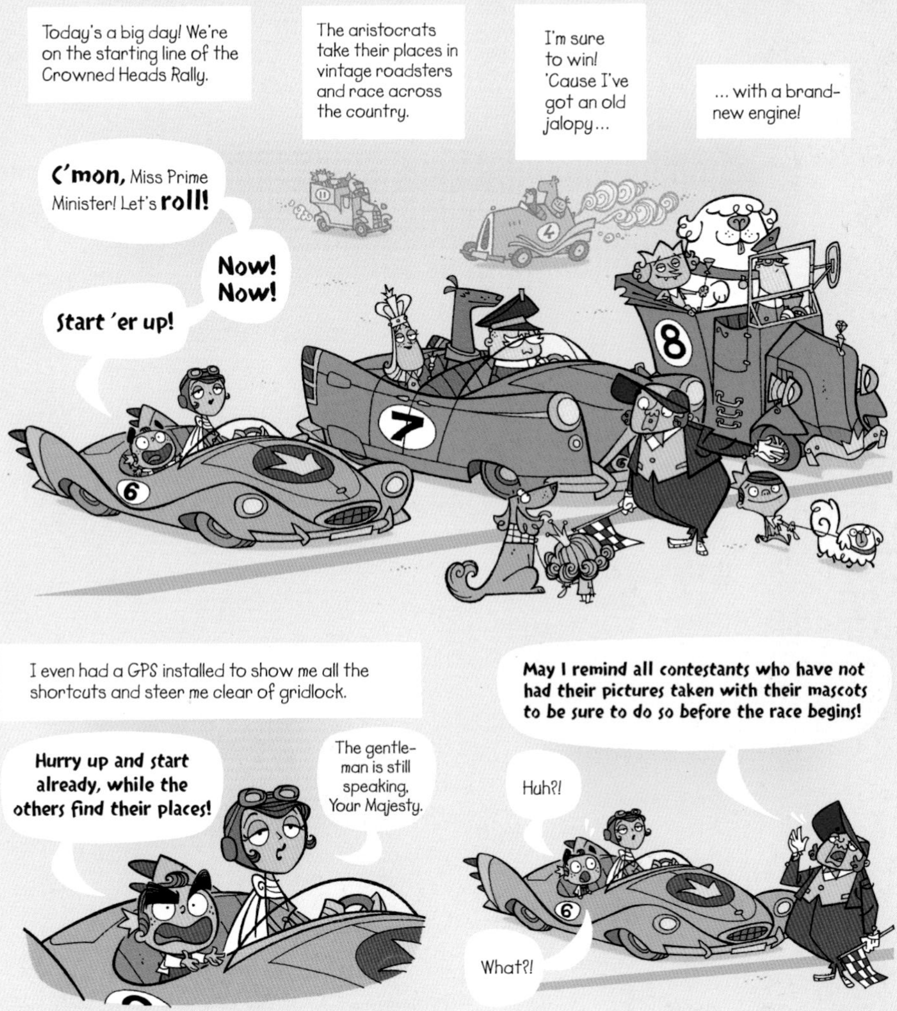
Today's a big day! We're on the starting line of the Crowned Heads Rally.
The aristocrats take their places in vintage roadsters and race across the country.
I'm sure to win! 'Cause I've got an old jalopy...
... with a brand-new engine!
C'mon, Miss Prime Minister! Let's roll!
Now! Now!
Start 'er up!
8
7
6
I even had a GPS installed to show me all the shortcuts and steer me clear of gridlock.
Hurry up and start already, while the others find their places!
The gentle-man is still speaking, Your Majesty.
May I remind all contestants who have not had their pictures taken with their mascots to be sure to do so before the race begins!
Huh?!
What?!
6

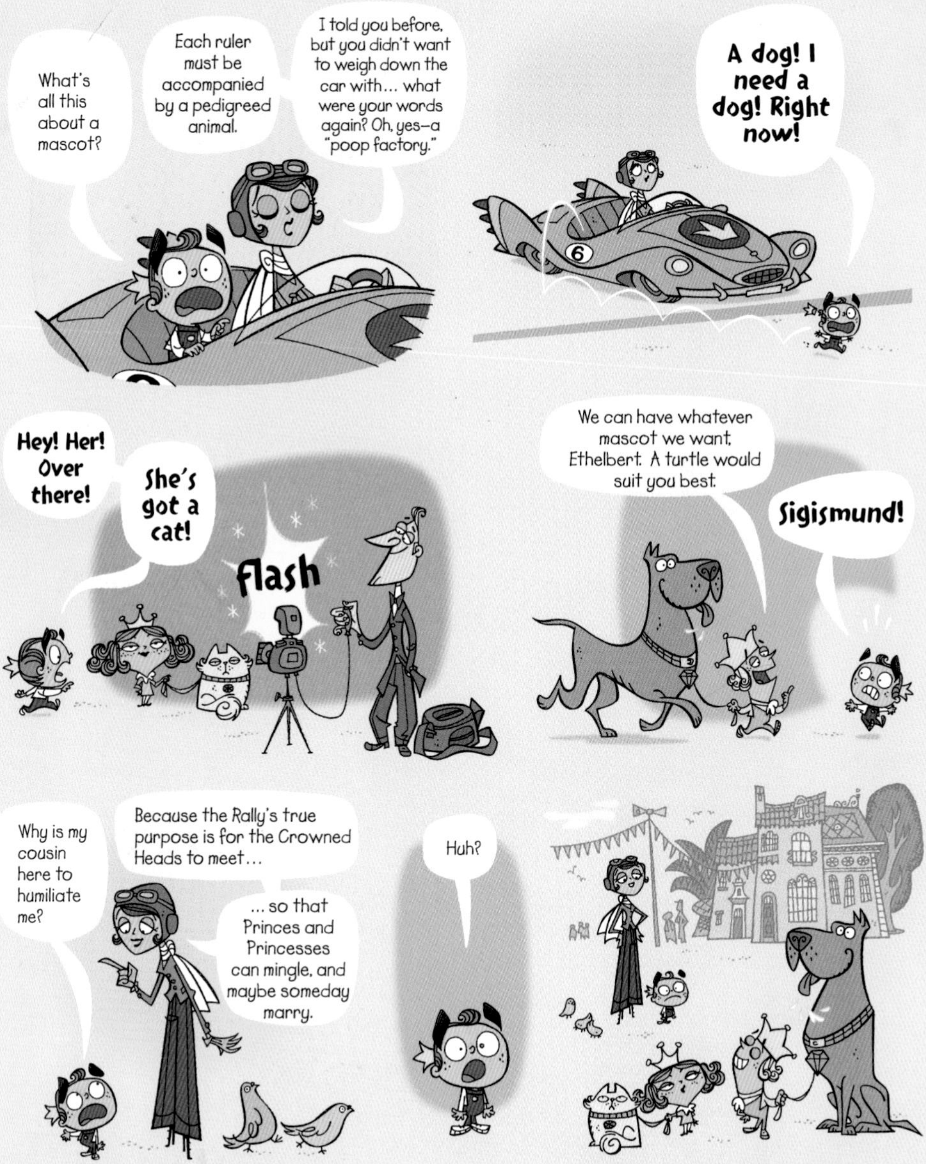
What's all this about a mascot?
Each ruler must be accompanied by a pedigreed animal.
I told you before, but you didn't want to weigh down the car with... what were your words again? Oh, yes—a "poop factory."
A dog! I need a dog! Right now!
Hey! Her! Over there!
She's got a cat!
Flash
We can have whatever mascot we want, Ethelbert. A turtle would suit you best.
Sigismund!
Why is my cousin here to humiliate me?
Because the Rally's true purpose is for the Crowned Heads to meet...
... so that Princes and Princesses can mingle, and maybe someday marry.
Huh?

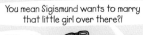

You mean Sigismund wants to marry that little girl over there?!

The "little girl over there" is none other than Princess Hildegardina, who happens to be three times as rich as you.

Yeah, yeah, I get it.

If Sigismund marries her, he'll be even richer.

Unless I...

Hello, Princess Whatsyerface! My name's Ethelbert. I'm the King of Portocristo!

Yes, of course... the kinglet of the minuscule castle perched atop a puny rock.

And what might your mascot be? Perhaps a flea lodged in your sock?

I need an animal! There's no way I'm letting Sigismund get any richer!

Look! This way, Sire!

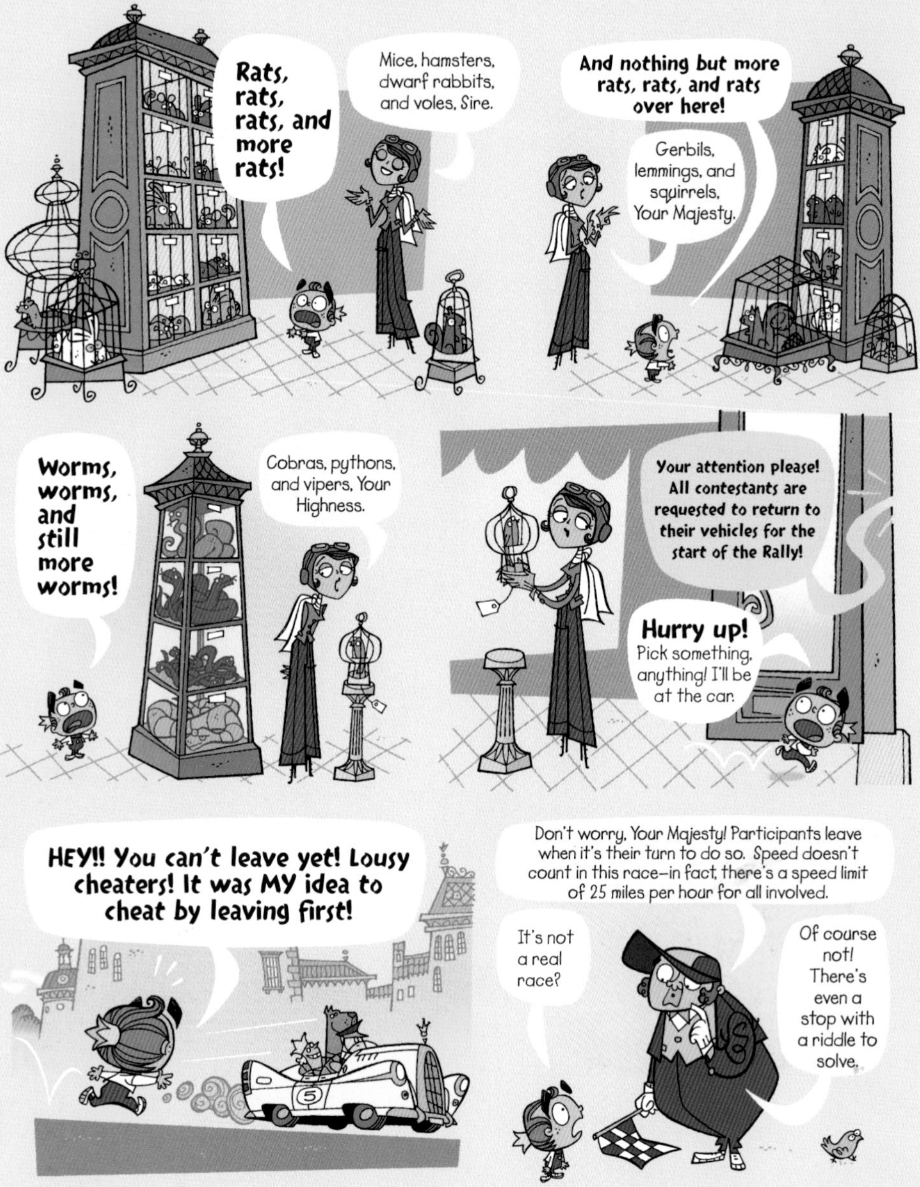
Rats, rats, rats, and more rats!
Mice, hamsters, dwarf rabbits, and voles, Sire.
And nothing but more rats, rats, and rats over here!
Gerbils, lemmings, and squirrels, Your Majesty.
Worms, worms, and still more worms!
Cobras, pythons, and vipers, Your Highness.
Your attention please! All contestants are requested to return to their vehicles for the start of the Rally!
Hurry up! Pick something, anything! I'll be at the car.
HEY!! You can't leave yet! Lousy cheaters! It was MY idea to cheat by leaving first!
Don't worry, Your Majesty! Participants leave when it's their turn to do so. Speed doesn't count in this race—in fact, there's a speed limit of 25 miles per hour for all involved.
It's not a real race?
Of course not! There's even a stop with a riddle to solve.

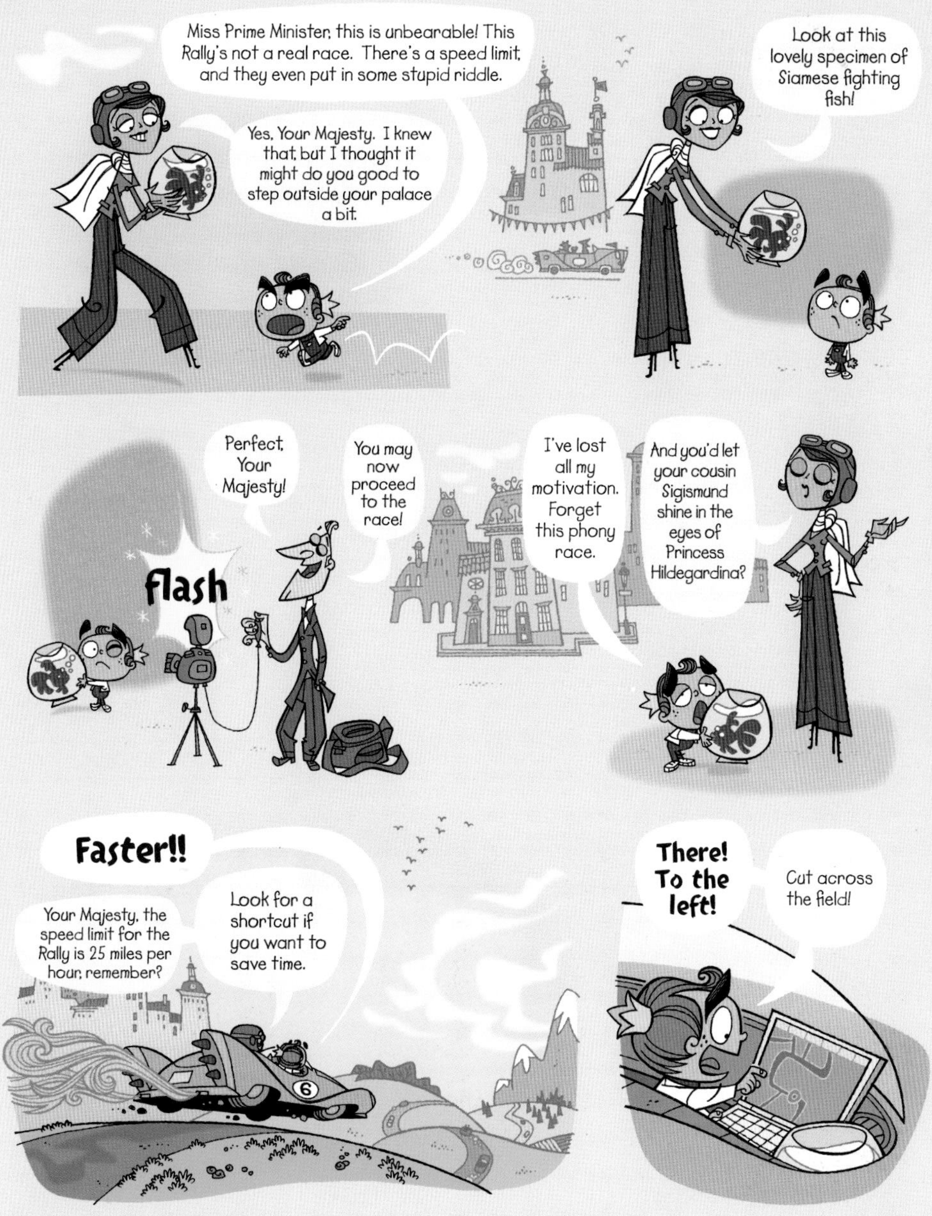
Miss Prime Minister, this is unbearable! This Rally's not a real race. There's a speed limit, and they even put in some stupid riddle.
Yes, Your Majesty. I knew that, but I thought it might do you good to step outside your palace a bit.
Look at this lovely specimen of Siamese fighting fish!
Flash
Perfect, Your Majesty!
You may now proceed to the race!
I've lost all my motivation. Forget this phony race.
And you'd let your cousin Sigismund shine in the eyes of Princess Hildegardina?
Faster!!
Your Majesty, the speed limit for the Rally is 25 miles per hour, remember?
Look for a shortcut if you want to save time.
6
There! To the left!
Cut across the field!

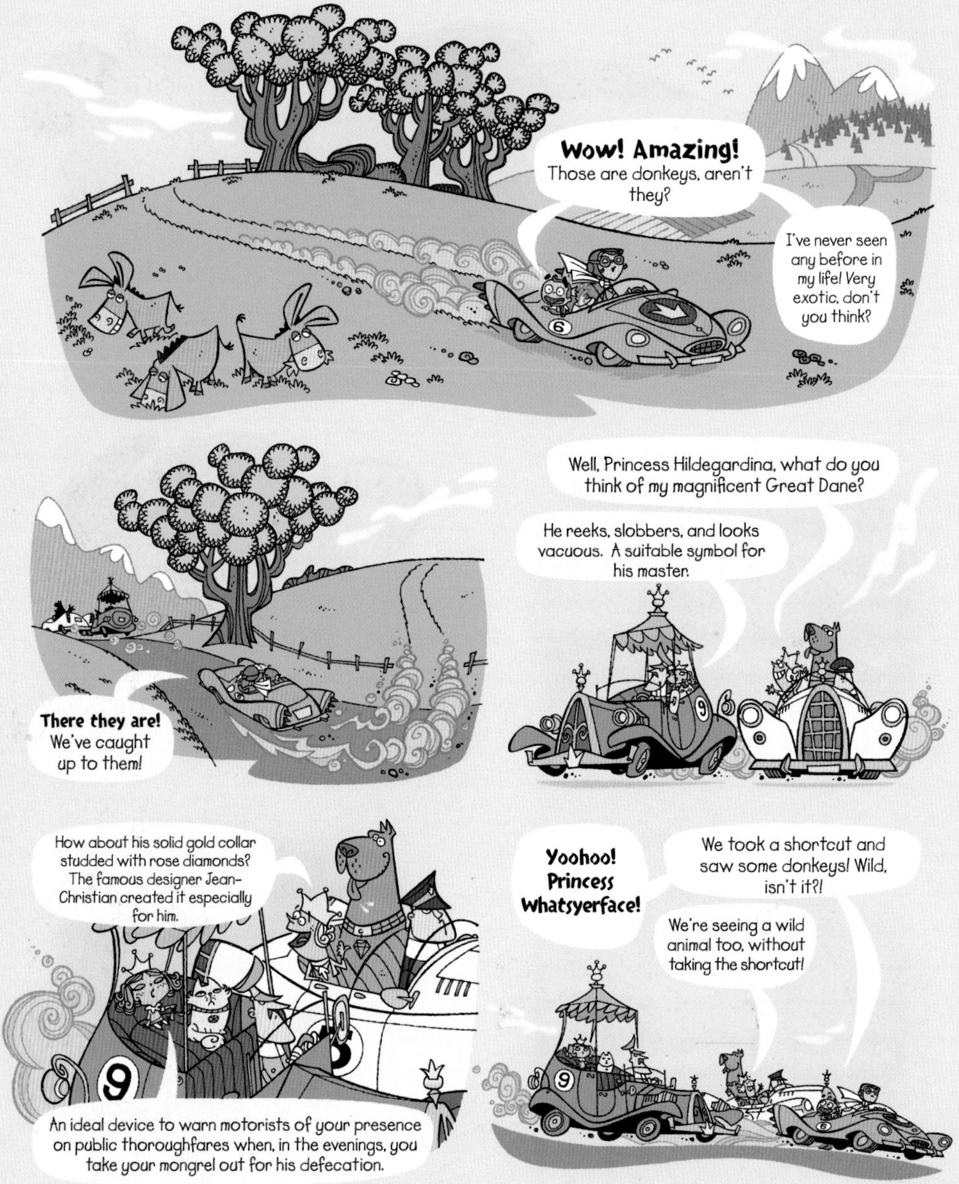
Wow! Amazing! Those are donkeys, aren't they?
I've never seen any before in my life! Very exotic, don't you think?
There they are! We've caught up to them!
Well, Princess Hildegardina, what do you think of my magnificent Great Dane?
He reeks, slobbers, and looks vacuous. A suitable symbol for his master.
How about his solid gold collar studded with rose diamonds? The famous designer Jean-Christian created it especially for him.
An ideal device to warn motorists of your presence on public thoroughfares when, in the evenings, you take your mongrel out for his defecation.
Yoohoo! Princess Whatsyerface!
We took a shortcut and saw some donkeys! Wild, isn't it?!
We're seeing a wild animal too, without taking the shortcut!

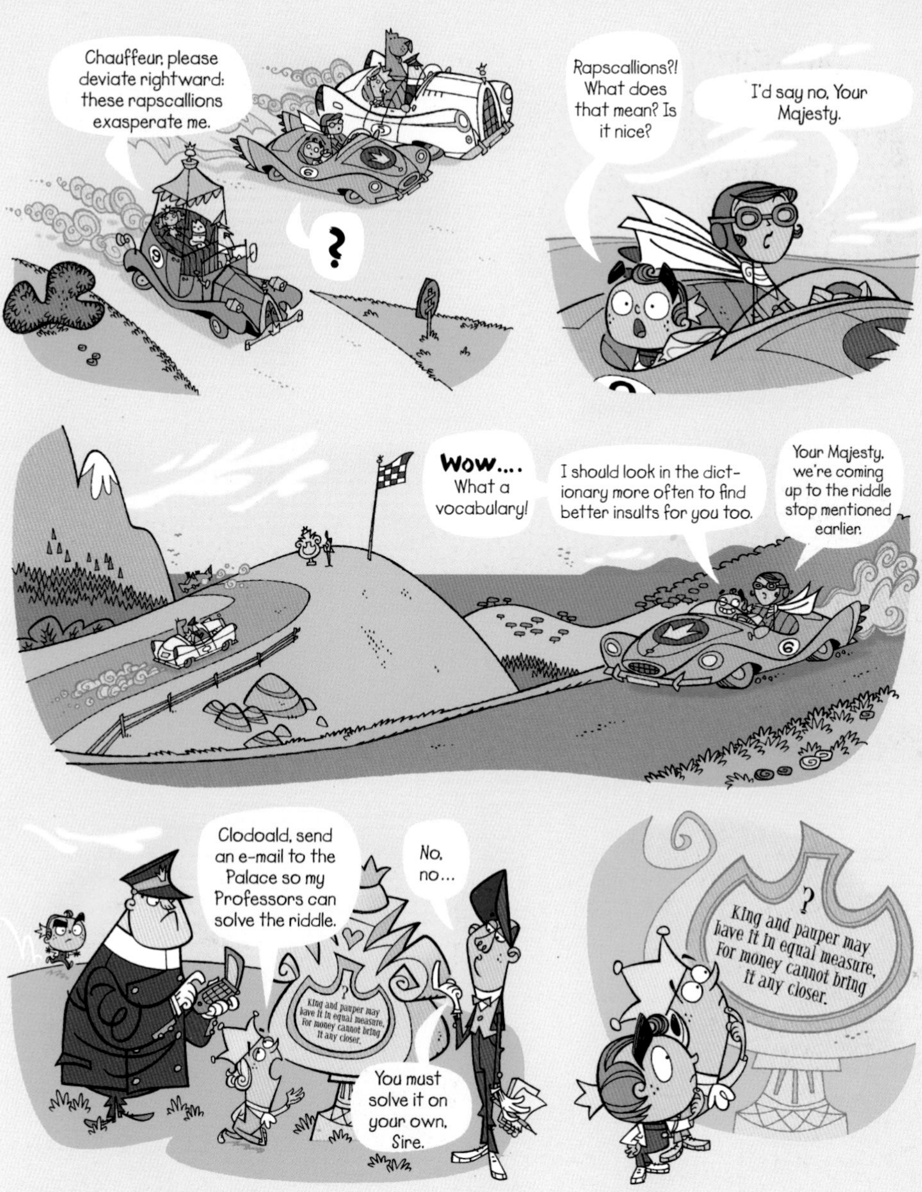

Chauffeur, please deviate rightward: these rapscallions exasperate me.
?
Rapscallions?! What does that mean? Is it nice?
I'd say no, Your Majesty.
WOW.... What a vocabulary!
I should look in the dictionary more often to find better insults for you too.
Your Majesty, we're coming up to the riddle stop mentioned earlier.
Clodoald, send an e-mail to the Palace so my Professors can solve the riddle.
No, no...
You must solve it on your own, Sire.
?
King and pauper may have it in equal measure, For money cannot bring it any closer.

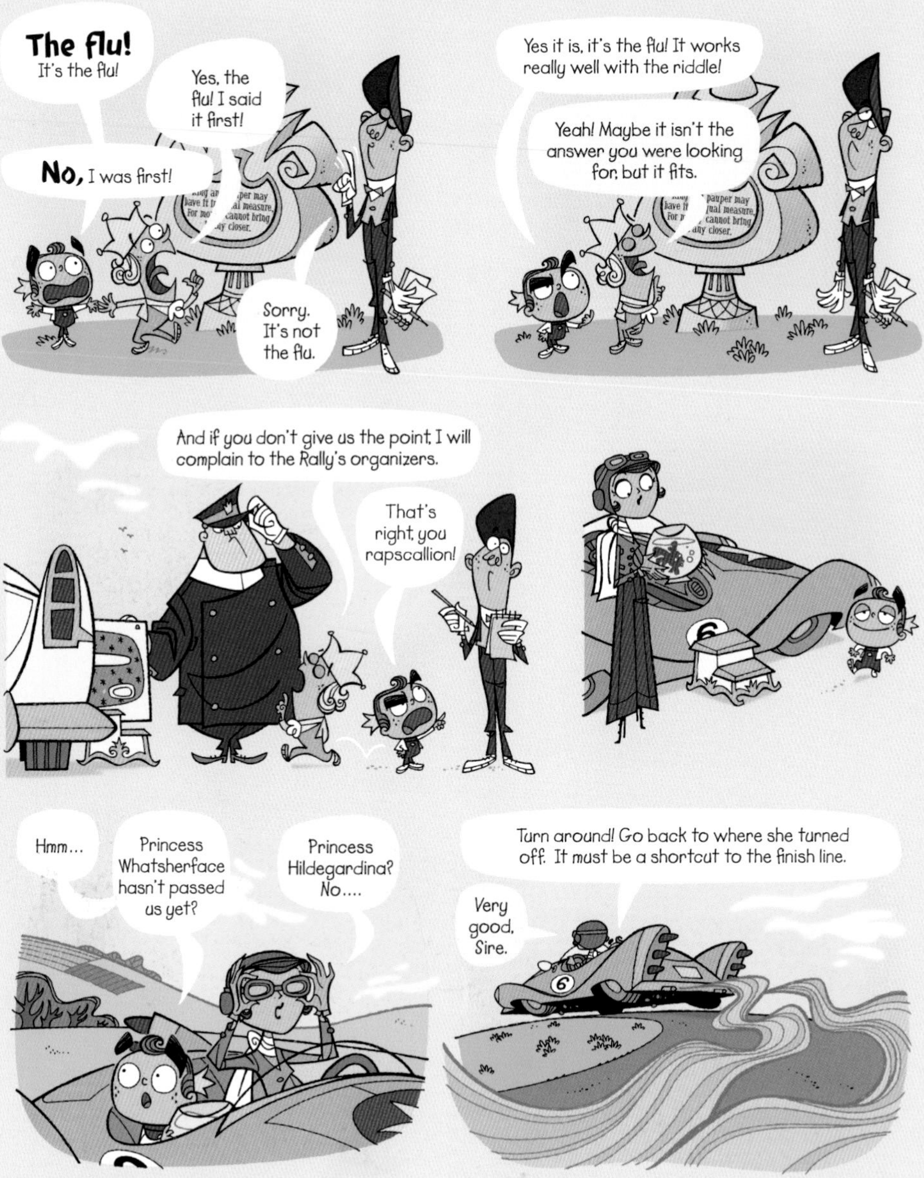

The flu!
It's the flu!
Yes, the flu! I said it first!
No, I was first!
Sorry. It's not the flu.
Yes it is, it's the flu! It works really well with the riddle!
Yeah! Maybe it isn't the answer you were looking for, but it fits.
And if you don't give us the point, I will complain to the Rally's organizers.
That's right, you rapscallion!
Hmm...
Princess Whatsherface hasn't passed us yet?
Princess Hildegardina? No....
Turn around! Go back to where she turned off. It must be a shortcut to the finish line.
Very good, Sire.

HEY! Over there! Look! Look!

What are they called again? What are they called?

Sheep, Sire.

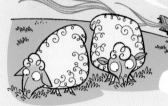

Awesome! And what are sheep good for?

We eat them and use their fleece for wool.

Oh yeah.... And wool, what's that good for?

Uh... to have wool.

Oh, my! Look, Your Majesty.

Over here! Help!

Just my luck! Her shortcut ends in a puddle of mud.

Okay, hang a U-turn.

Perhaps we might help them, Sire? It would make us look good with the Princess.

Whatever, I don't care about that. But it'd be a shame to let such a nice car sink....

Grab on! We'll send a tow truck back for your car when we reach the finish line.

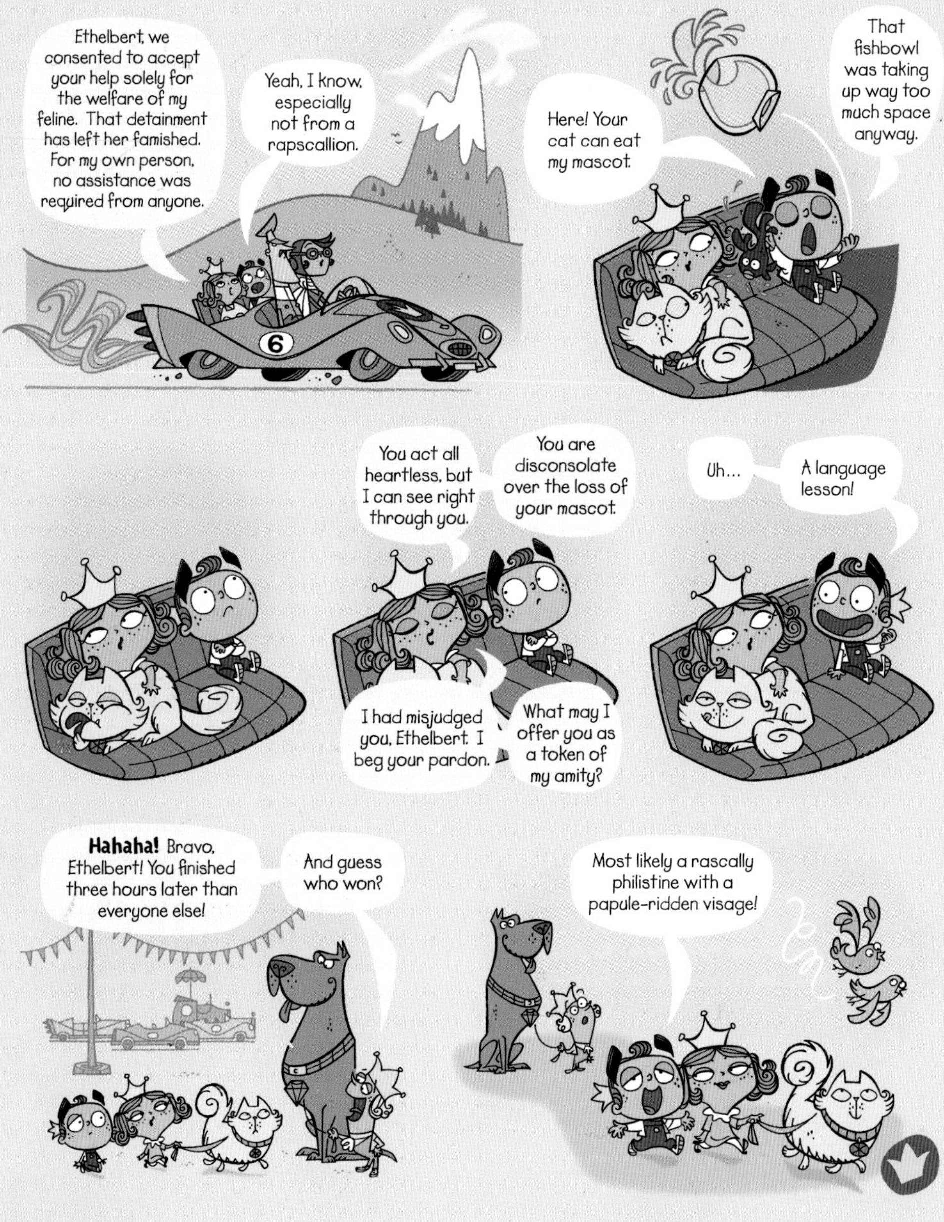

Ethelbert, we consented to accept your help solely for the welfare of my feline. That detainment has left her famished. For my own person, no assistance was required from anyone.
Yeah, I know, especially not from a rapscallion.
6
Here! Your cat can eat my mascot.
That fishbowl was taking up way too much space anyway.
You act all heartless, but I can see right through you.
You are disconsolate over the loss of your mascot.
I had misjudged you, Ethelbert. I beg your pardon.
What may I offer you as a token of my amity?
Uh...
A language lesson!
Hahaha! Bravo, Ethelbert! You finished three hours later than everyone else!
And guess who won?
Most likely a rascally philistine with a papule-ridden visage!

The Magic of Christmas

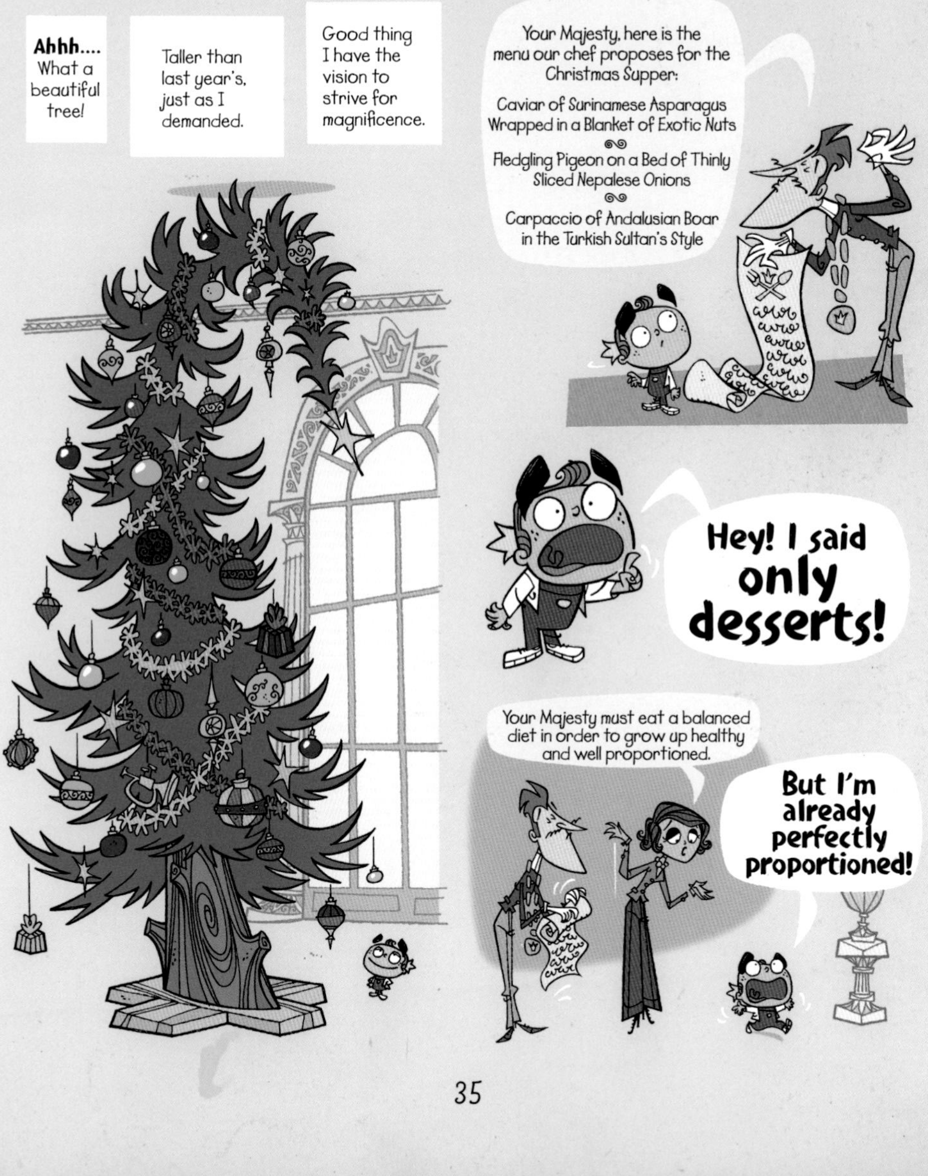
Ahhh.... What a beautiful tree!
Taller than last year's, just as I demanded.
Good thing I have the vision to strive for magnificence.
Your Majesty, here is the menu our chef proposes for the Christmas Supper:
Caviar of Surinamese Asparagus Wrapped in a Blanket of Exotic Nuts
Fledgling Pigeon on a Bed of Thinly Sliced Nepalese Onions
Carpaccio of Andalusian Boar in the Turkish Sultan's Style
Hey! I said only desserts!
Your Majesty must eat a balanced diet in order to grow up healthy and well proportioned.
But I'm already perfectly proportioned!

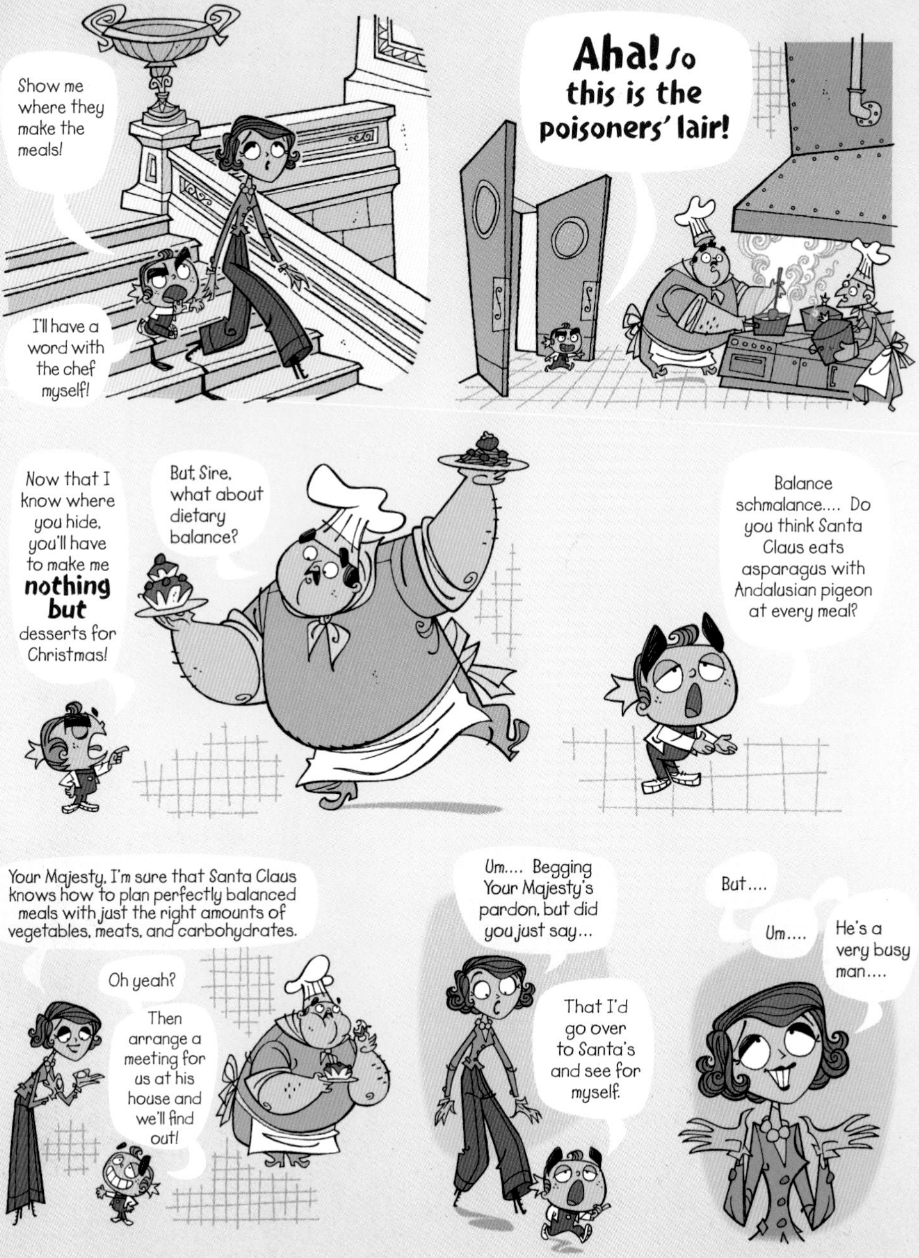
Show me where they make the meals!
I'll have a word with the chef myself!
Aha! So this is the poisoners' lair!
Now that I know where you hide, you'll have to make me **nothing but** desserts for Christmas!
But, Sire, what about dietary balance?
Balance schmalance.... Do you think Santa Claus eats asparagus with Andalusian pigeon at every meal?
Your Majesty, I'm sure that Santa Claus knows how to plan perfectly balanced meals with just the right amounts of vegetables, meats, and carbohydrates.
Oh yeah?
Then arrange a meeting for us at his house and we'll find out!
Um.... Begging Your Majesty's pardon, but did you just say...
That I'd go over to Santa's and see for myself.
But....
Um....
He's a very busy man....

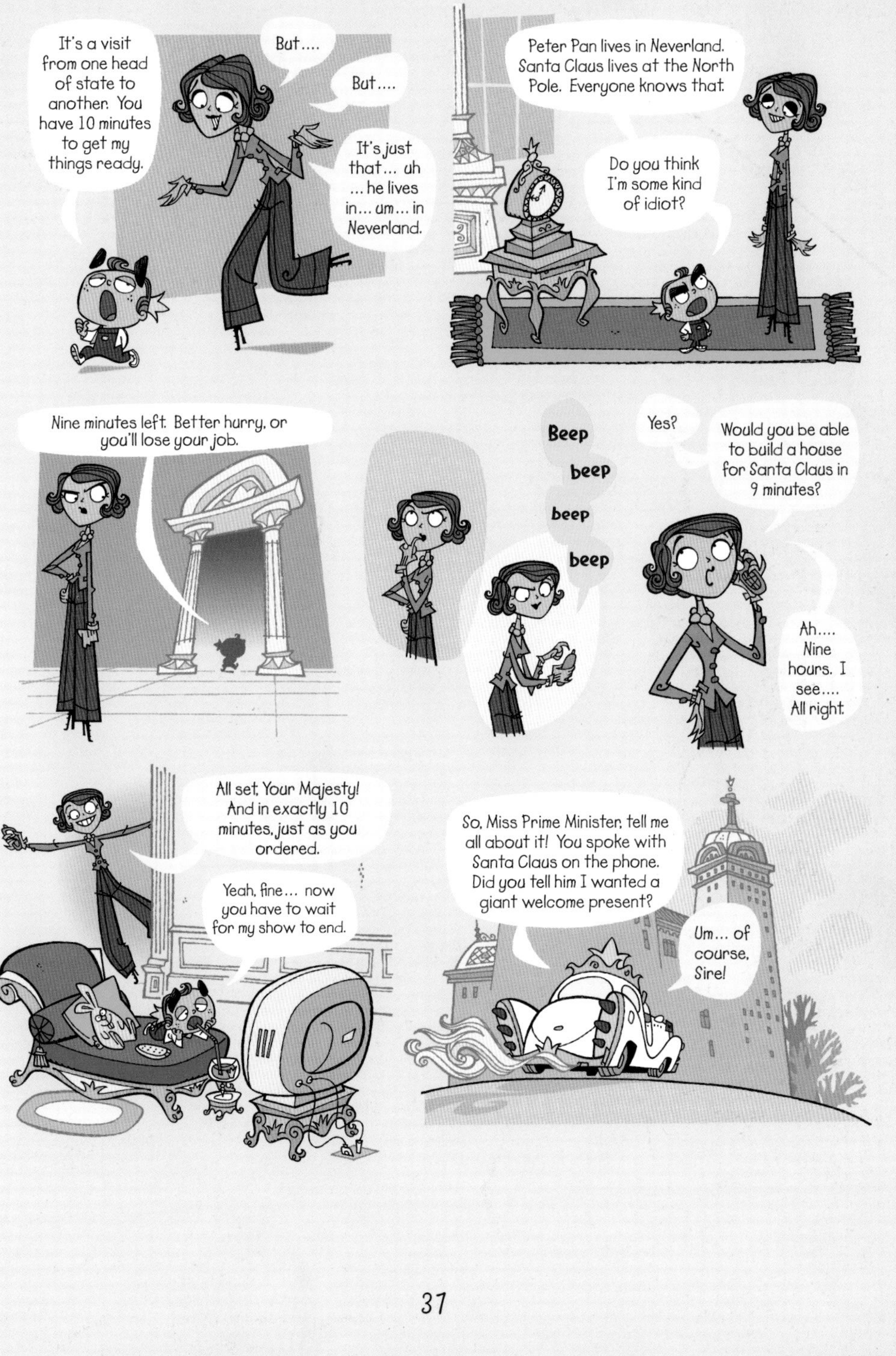
It's a visit from one head of state to another. You have 10 minutes to get my things ready.
But....
But....
It's just that... uh ... he lives in... um... in Neverland.
Peter Pan lives in Neverland. Santa Claus lives at the North Pole. Everyone knows that.
Do you think I'm some kind of idiot?
Nine minutes left. Better hurry, or you'll lose your job.
Beep
beep
beep
beep
Yes?
Would you be able to build a house for Santa Claus in 9 minutes?
Ah.... Nine hours. I see.... All right.
All set, Your Majesty! And in exactly 10 minutes, just as you ordered.
Yeah, fine... now you have to wait for my show to end.
So, Miss Prime Minister, tell me all about it! You spoke with Santa Claus on the phone. Did you tell him I wanted a giant welcome present?
Um... of course, Sire!

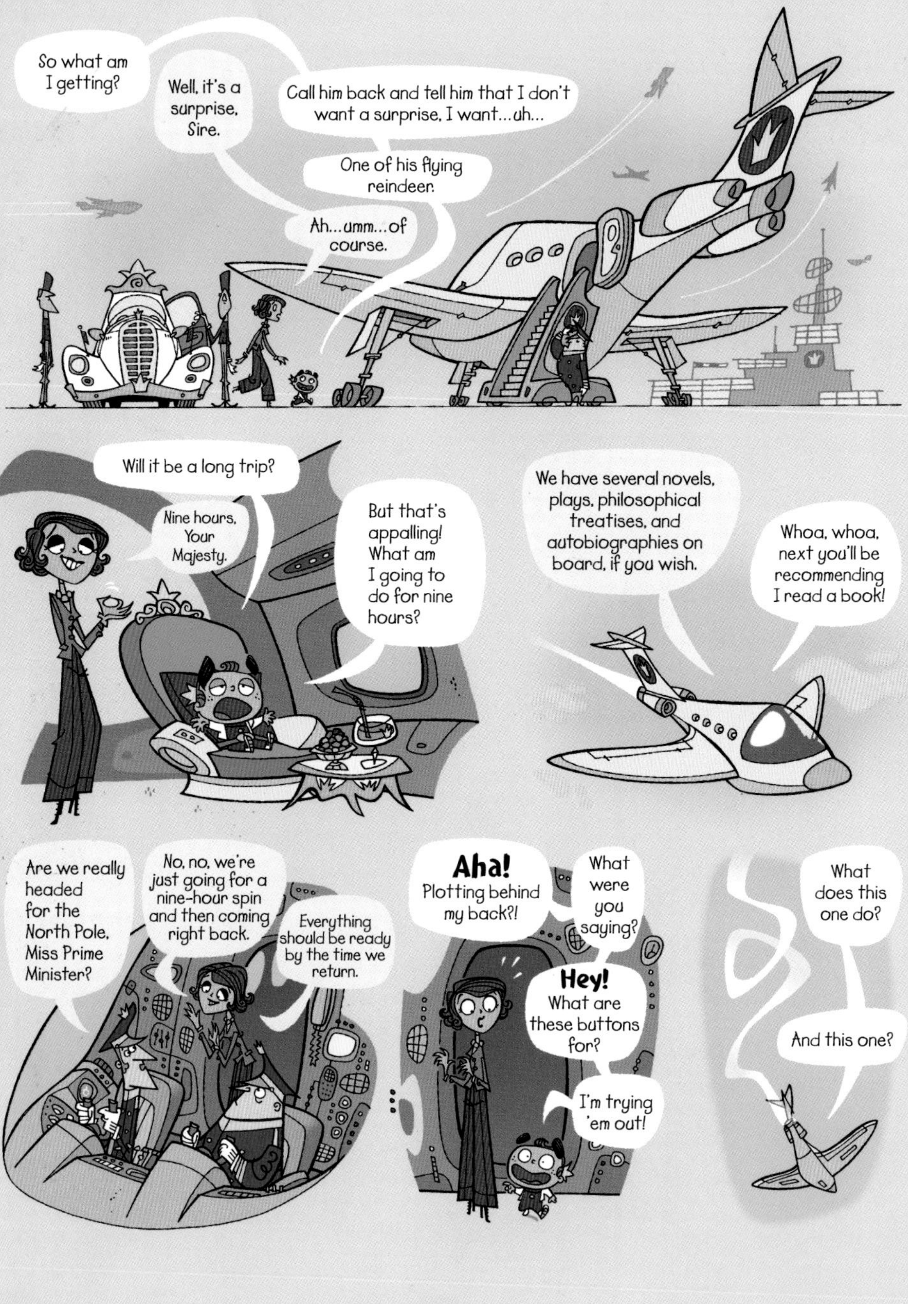
So what am I getting?
Well, it's a surprise, Sire.
Call him back and tell him that I don't want a surprise, I want...uh...
One of his flying reindeer.
Ah...umm...of course.
Will it be a long trip?
Nine hours, Your Majesty.
But that's appalling! What am I going to do for nine hours?
We have several novels, plays, philosophical treatises, and autobiographies on board, if you wish.
Whoa, whoa, next you'll be recommending I read a book!
Are we really headed for the North Pole, Miss Prime Minister?
No, no, we're just going for a nine-hour spin and then coming right back.
Everything should be ready by the time we return.
Aha! Plotting behind my back?!
What were you saying?
Hey! What are these buttons for?
I'm trying 'em out!
What does this one do?
And this one?

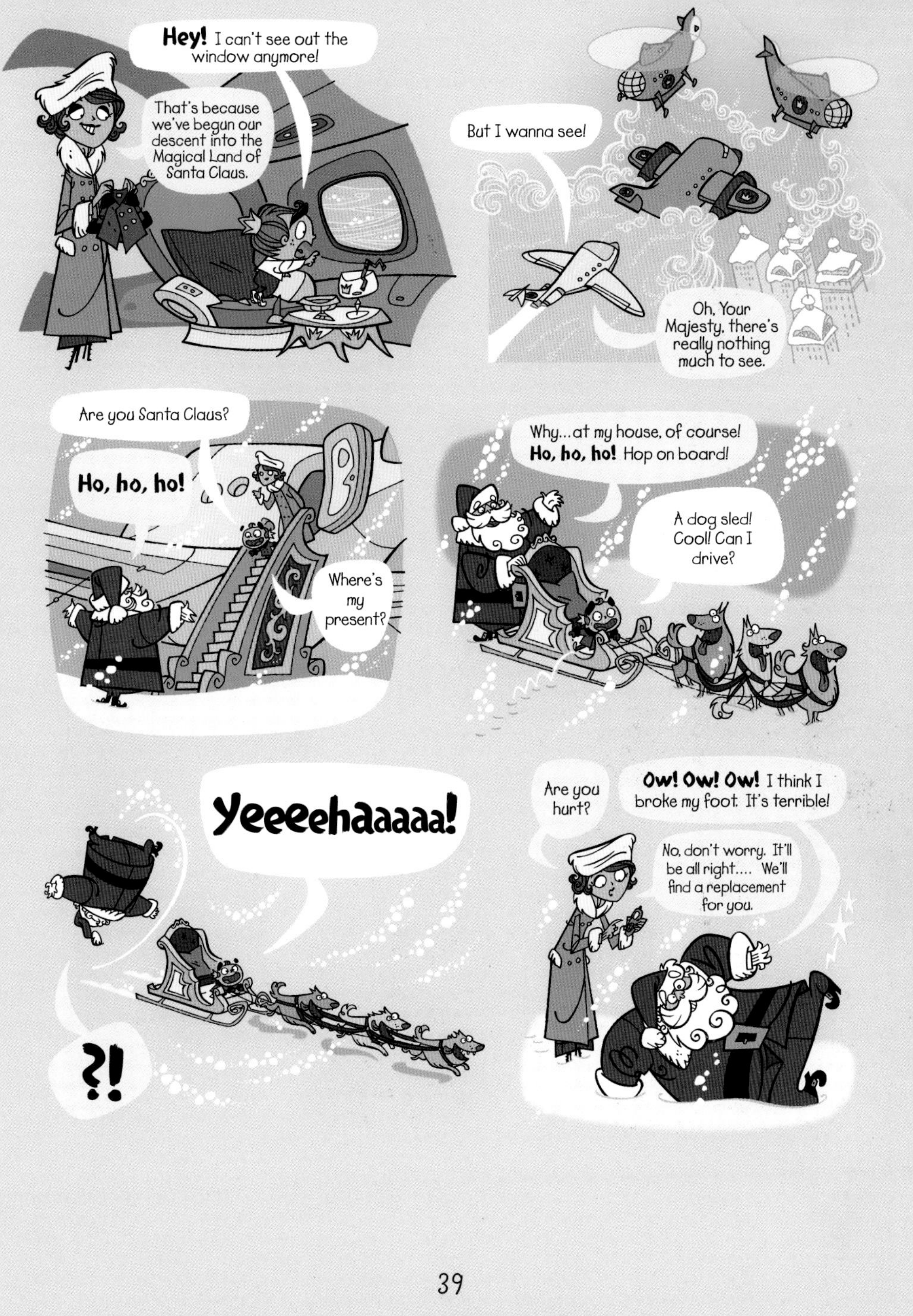
Hey! I can't see out the window anymore!
That's because we've begun our descent into the Magical Land of Santa Claus.
But I wanna see!
Oh, Your Majesty, there's really nothing much to see.
Are you Santa Claus?
Ho, ho, ho!
Where's my present?
Why...at my house, of course! Ho, ho, ho! Hop on board!
A dog sled! Cool! Can I drive?
Yeeeehaaaaa!
?!
Are you hurt?
Ow! Ow! Ow! I think I broke my foot. It's terrible!
No, don't worry. It'll be all right.... We'll find a replacement for you.

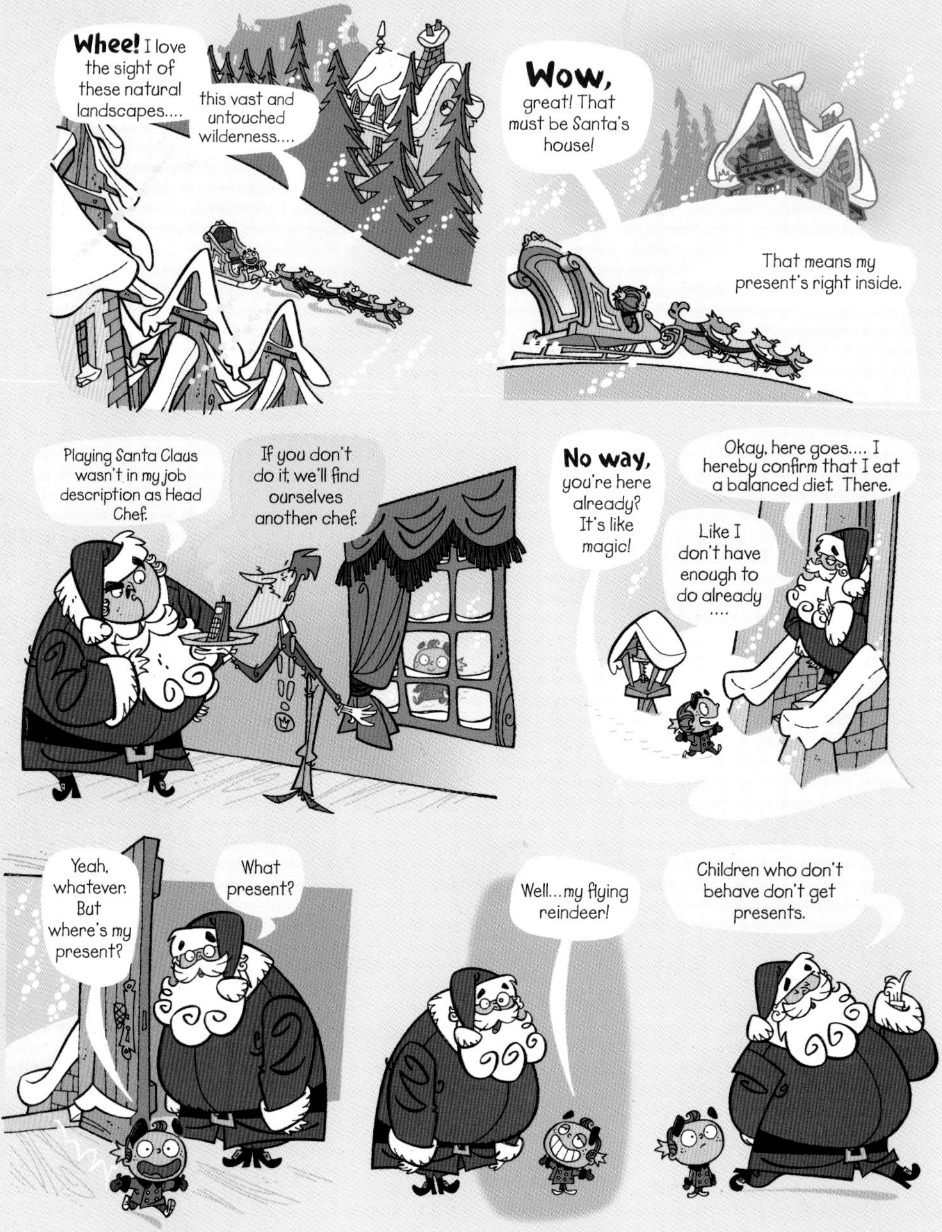
Whee! I love the sight of these natural landscapes....
this vast and untouched wilderness....
Wow, great! That must be Santa's house!
That means my present's right inside.
Playing Santa Claus wasn't in my job description as Head Chef.
If you don't do it, we'll find ourselves another chef.
No way, you're here already? It's like magic!
Okay, here goes.... I hereby confirm that I eat a balanced diet. There.
Like I don't have enough to do already ....
Yeah, whatever. But where's my present?
What present?
Well...my flying reindeer!
Children who don't behave don't get presents.

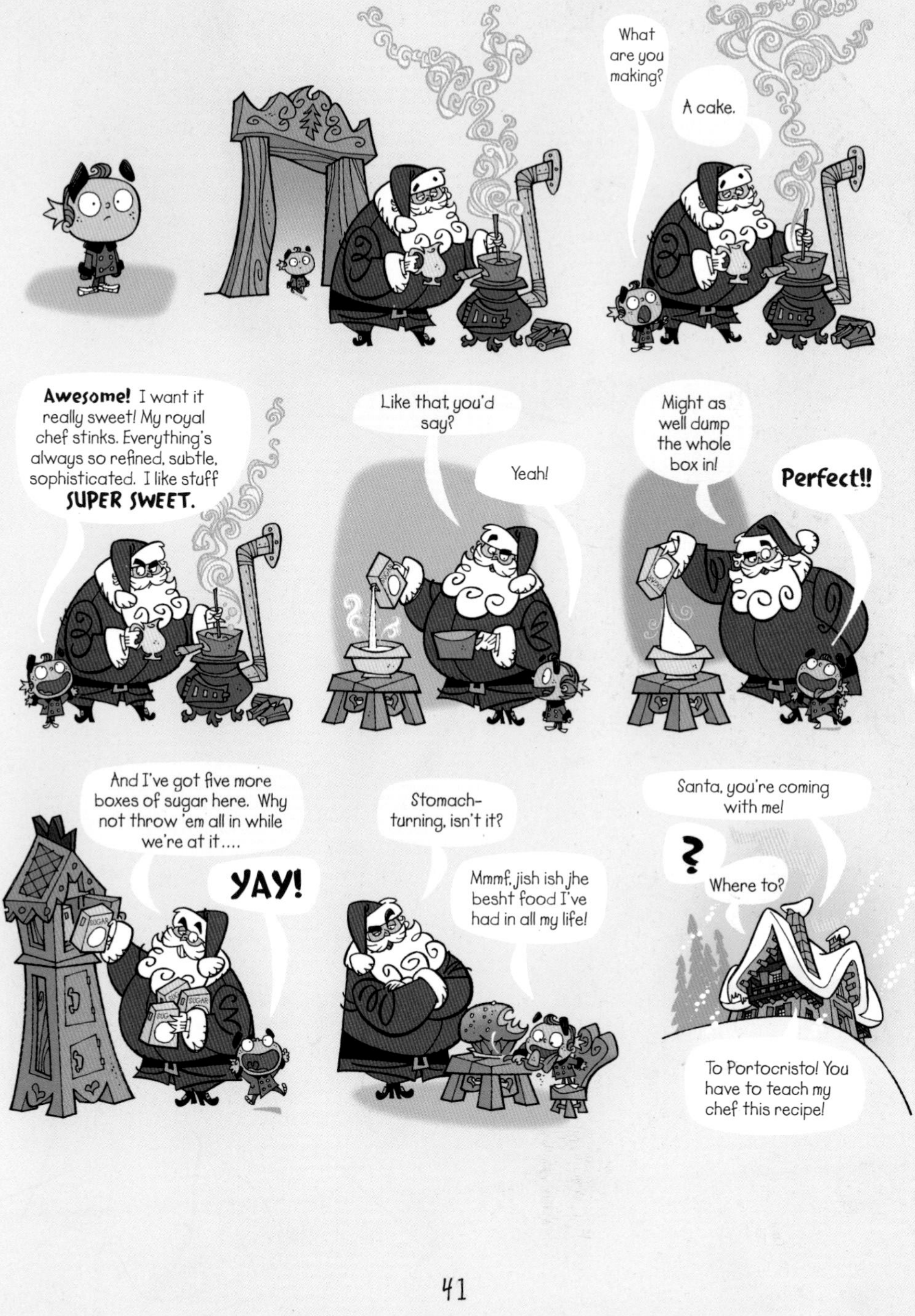
What are you making?
A cake.
Awesome! I want it really sweet! My royal chef stinks. Everything's always so refined, subtle, sophisticated. I like stuff SUPER SWEET.
Like that, you'd say?
Yeah!
Might as well dump the whole box in!
Perfect!!
And I've got five more boxes of sugar here. Why not throw 'em all in while we're at it....
YAY!
SUGAR
Stomach-turning, isn't it?
Mmmf, jish ish jhe besht food I've had in all my life!
Santa, you're coming with me!
?
Where to?
To Portocristo! You have to teach my chef this recipe!

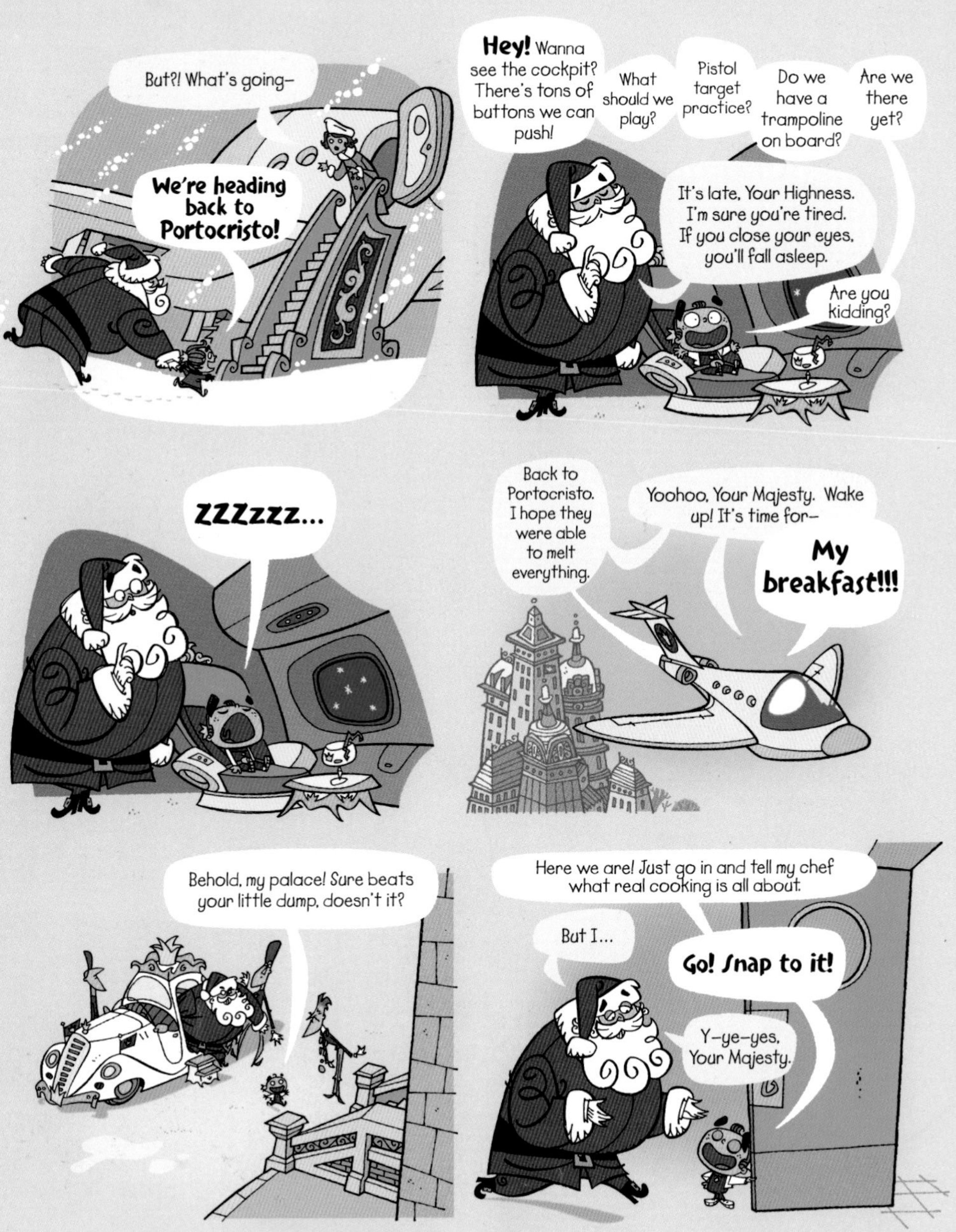
But?! What's going–
We're heading back to Portocristo!
Hey! Wanna see the cockpit? There's tons of buttons we can push!
What should we play?
Pistol target practice?
Do we have a trampoline on board?
Are we there yet?
It's late, Your Highness. I'm sure you're tired. If you close your eyes, you'll fall asleep.
Are you kidding?
ZZZzzz...
Back to Portocristo. I hope they were able to melt everything.
Yoohoo, Your Majesty. Wake up! It's time for–
My breakfast!!!
Behold, my palace! Sure beats your little dump, doesn't it?
Here we are! Just go in and tell my chef what real cooking is all about.
But I...
Go! Snap to it!
Y–ye–yes, Your Majesty.

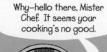 Why—hello there, Mister Chef. It seems your cooking's no good.

No good? What do you mean? Taste for yourself!

Mmmf! Delifuf!

It'sh much better jhan my own cooking.

You shimply musht show me how to make jish, Chef!

Hey, that's not what's supposed to happen!

Here's the recipe, Santa Claus.

Hey! Santa Claus!!

What was that about? Are you stupid or what? You were supposed to teach him how to cook!

Oh, no! His cooking was too delightful.

And a kick in your backside, is that delightful?

Move your whale blubber and do as you're told!

Please, Your Majesty! You're speaking to Santa Claus!

That's true, as a matter of fact....

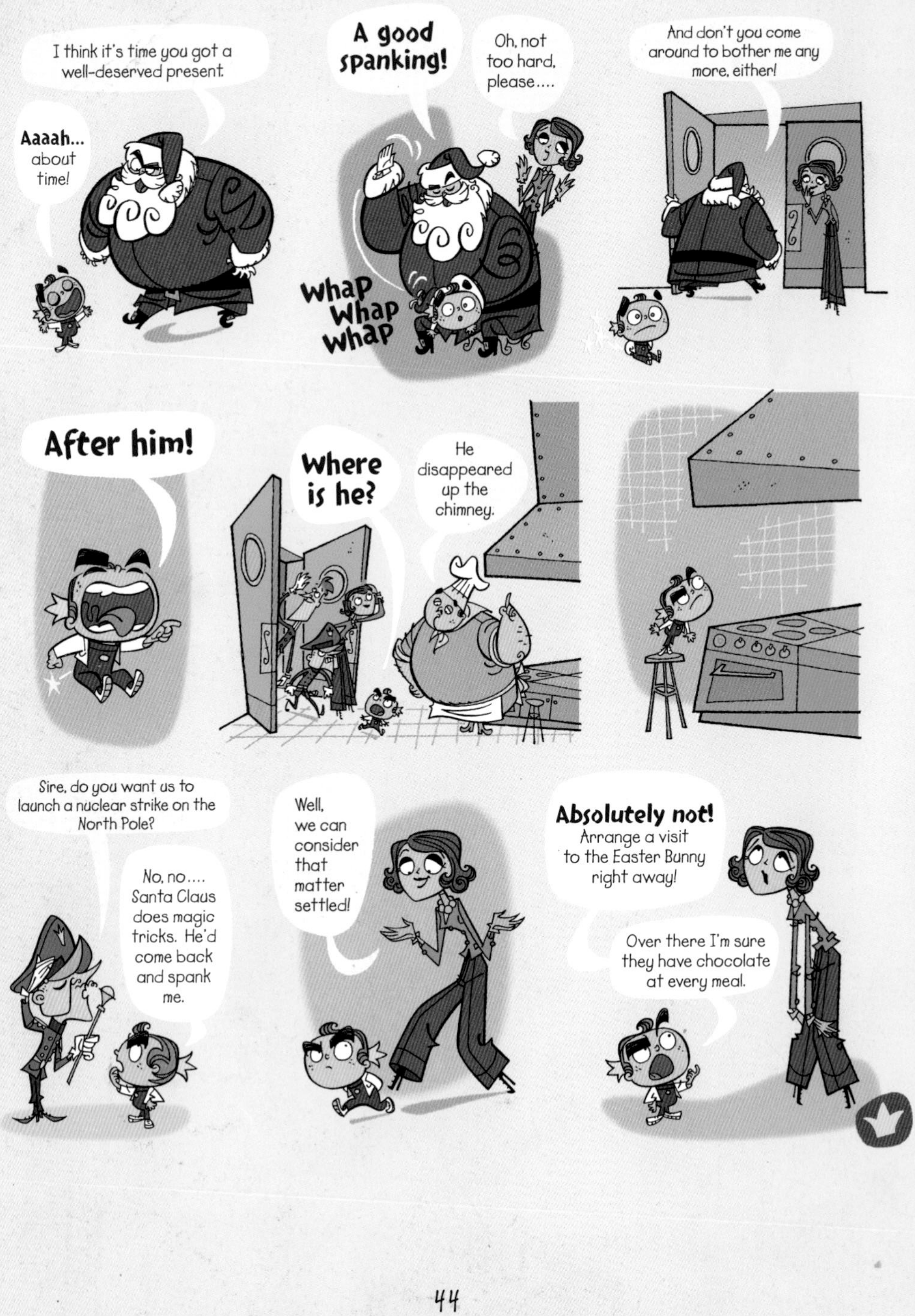
I think it's time you got a well-deserved present.
Aaaah... about time!
A good spanking!
Oh, not too hard, please....
Whap Whap Whap
And don't you come around to bother me any more, either!
After him!
Where is he?
He disappeared up the chimney.
Sire, do you want us to launch a nuclear strike on the North Pole?
No, no.... Santa Claus does magic tricks. He'd come back and spank me.
Well, we can consider that matter settled!
Absolutely not! Arrange a visit to the Easter Bunny right away!
Over there I'm sure they have chocolate at every meal.

Books are Our Friends

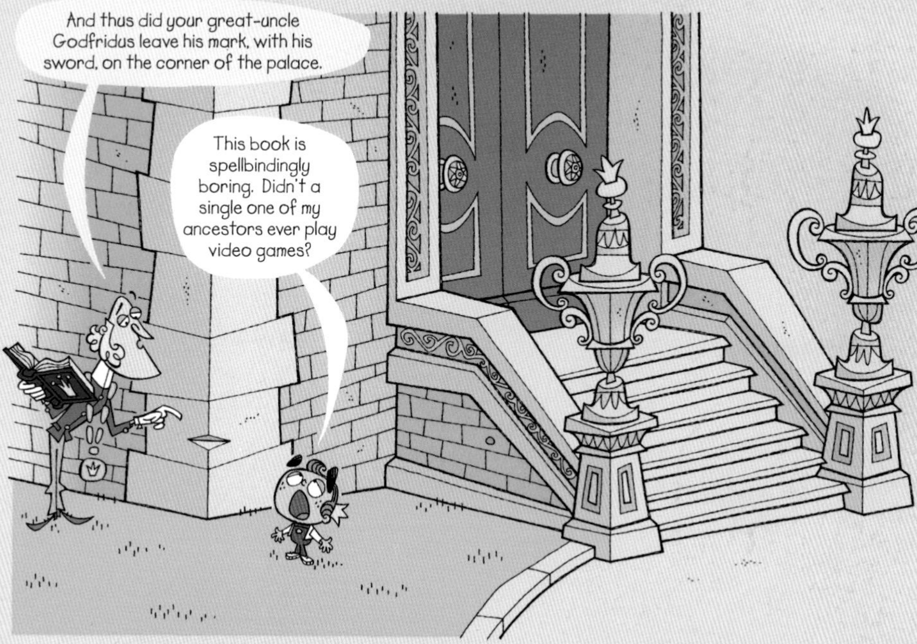
And thus did your great-uncle Godfridus leave his mark, with his sword, on the corner of the palace.
This book is spellbindingly boring. Didn't a single one of my ancestors ever play video games?

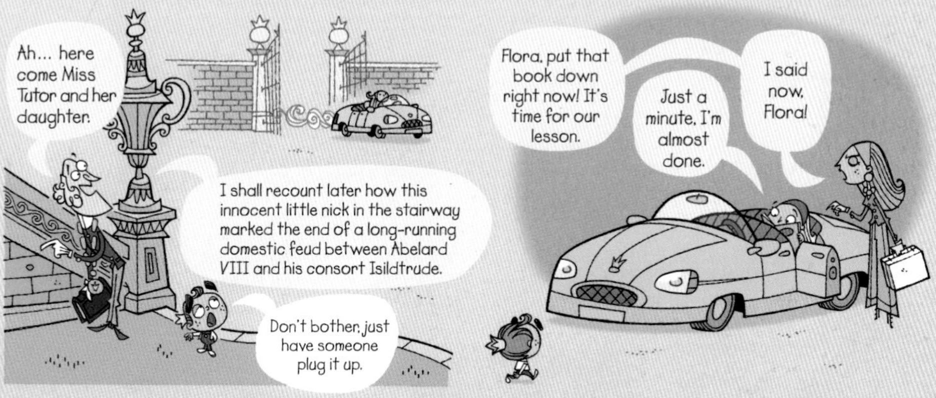
Ah... here come Miss Tutor and her daughter.
I shall recount later how this innocent little nick in the stairway marked the end of a long-running domestic feud between Abelard VIII and his consort Isildtrude.
Don't bother, just have someone plug it up.
Flora, put that book down right now! It's time for our lesson.
Just a minute, I'm almost done.
I said now, Flora!

Oh, please! It's just too good!
I'm counting to one.
Zero...
Zero and a half...
Okay, okay, zero and three quarters, I'm coming.
Oh, how do you do, Your Majesty? I hadn't seen you arrive.
What's that book?
It's called Bigobango. It's a comic book that's very popular with children.
How come I don't have one?
Most likely because it has no place in Your Royal Curriculum.... We have better things to study, Sire.
I want that comic!
No! It's mine!
I'll give you one hundred dollars for it!
You're nuts—you can get it for $12.95 in the store.
I'll give you twenty!
Sold.

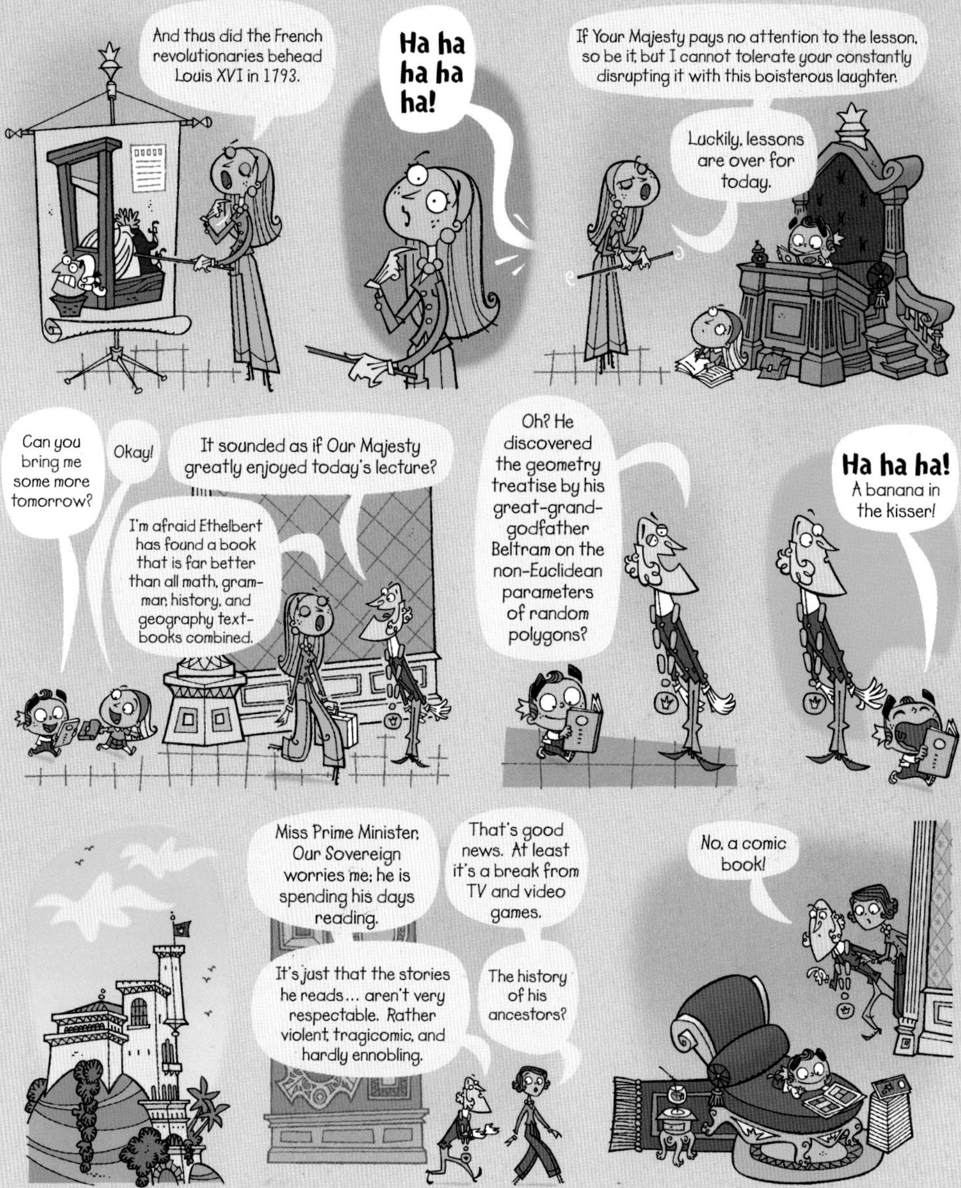
And thus did the French revolutionaries behead Louis XVI in 1793.
Ha ha ha ha ha!
If Your Majesty pays no attention to the lesson, so be it, but I cannot tolerate your constantly disrupting it with this boisterous laughter.
Luckily, lessons are over for today.
Can you bring me some more tomorrow?
Okay!
It sounded as if Our Majesty greatly enjoyed today's lecture?
I'm afraid Ethelbert has found a book that is far better than all math, grammar, history, and geography textbooks combined.
Oh? He discovered the geometry treatise by his great-grand-godfather Beltram on the non-Euclidean parameters of random polygons?
Ha ha ha! A banana in the kisser!
Miss Prime Minister, Our Sovereign worries me; he is spending his days reading.
That's good news. At least it's a break from TV and video games.
It's just that the stories he reads... aren't very respectable. Rather violent, tragicomic, and hardly ennobling.
The history of his ancestors?
No, a comic book!

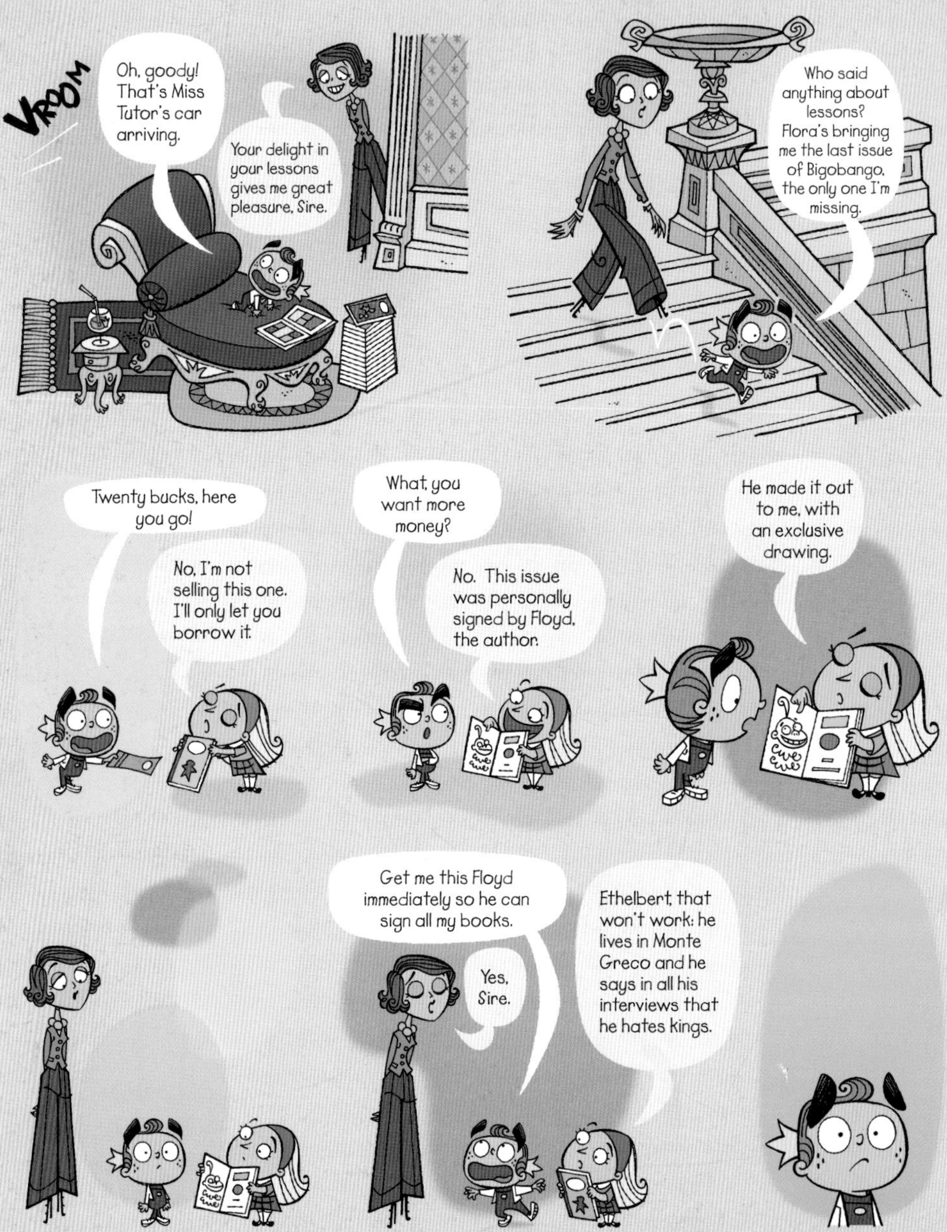
VROOM
Oh, goody! That's Miss Tutor's car arriving.
Your delight in your lessons gives me great pleasure, Sire.
Who said anything about lessons? Flora's bringing me the last issue of Bigobango, the only one I'm missing.
Twenty bucks, here you go!
No, I'm not selling this one. I'll only let you borrow it.
What, you want more money?
No. This issue was personally signed by Floyd, the author.
He made it out to me, with an exclusive drawing.
Get me this Floyd immediately so he can sign all my books.
Yes, Sire.
Ethelbert, that won't work: he lives in Monte Greco and he says in all his interviews that he hates kings.

I can't believe someone so brilliant can hate me without even having met me. Get in touch with Floyd and invite him to Portocristo!

Yes, Your Majesty.

BEEP

For today, Sire, I've prepared a special lesson called "Books Through the Centuries."

The first papyrus books date from the time of the Pharaohs in ancient Egypt.

Your Majesty, Mr. Floyd's secretary has confirmed that Mr. Floyd will never travel for a king.

However, Mr. Floyd is attending a book signing today in Montegrecoville.

Nobody move!

I'll be back!

Did you bring all my books?

Yes, Your Majesty.

To stay inconspicuous, you might want to take off your crown and wear this baseball cap instead.

What's this, a palace revolution?

If you show up as a king, Floyd won't sign anything for you.

Give me a mirror. I'll practice looking like a poor deprived kid no one can resist.

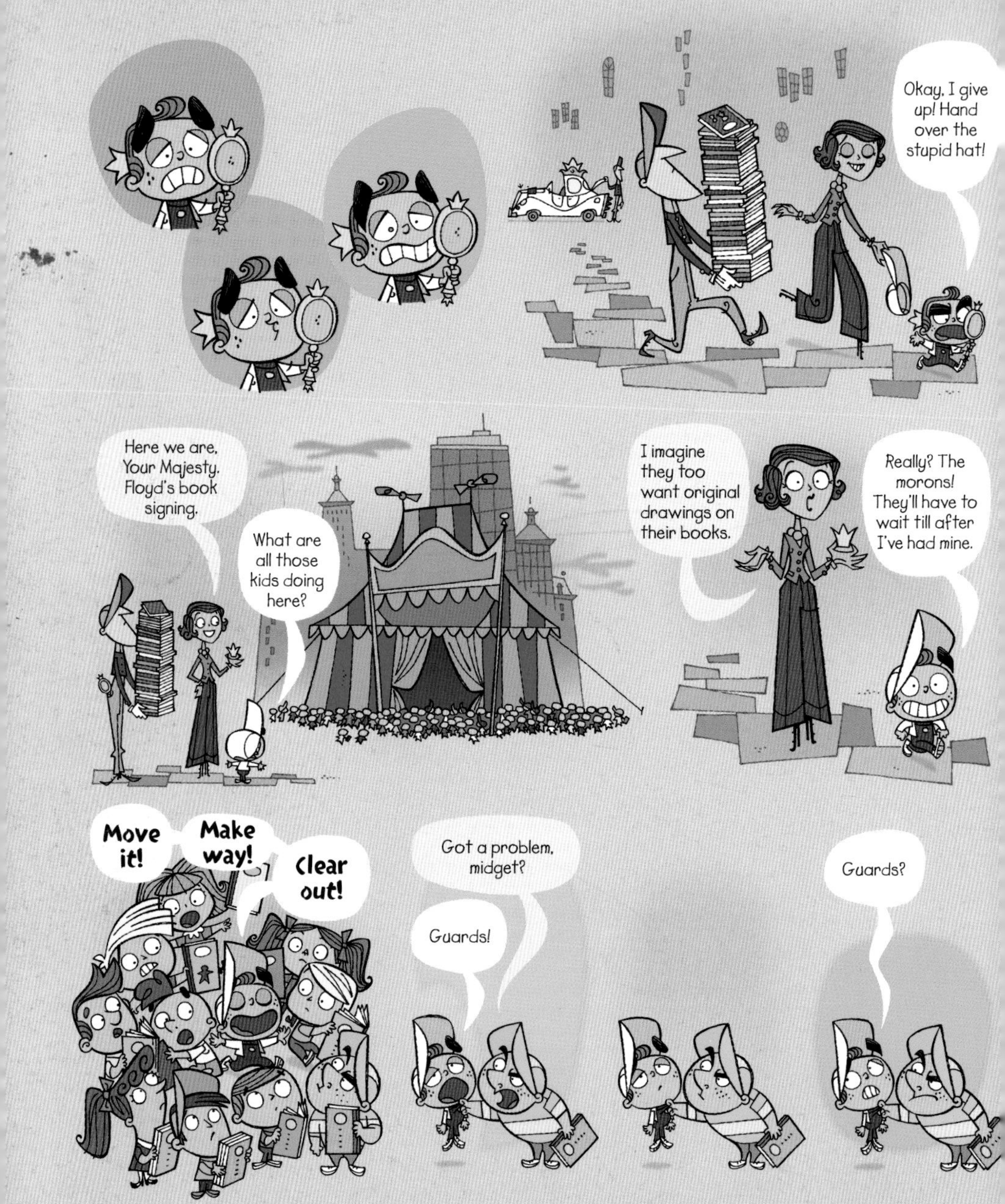

Okay, I give up! Hand over the stupid hat!
Here we are, Your Majesty. Floyd's book signing.
What are all those kids doing here?
I imagine they too want original drawings on their books.
Really? The morons! They'll have to wait till after I've had mine.
Move it!
Make way!
Clear out!
Got a problem, midget?
Guards!
Guards?

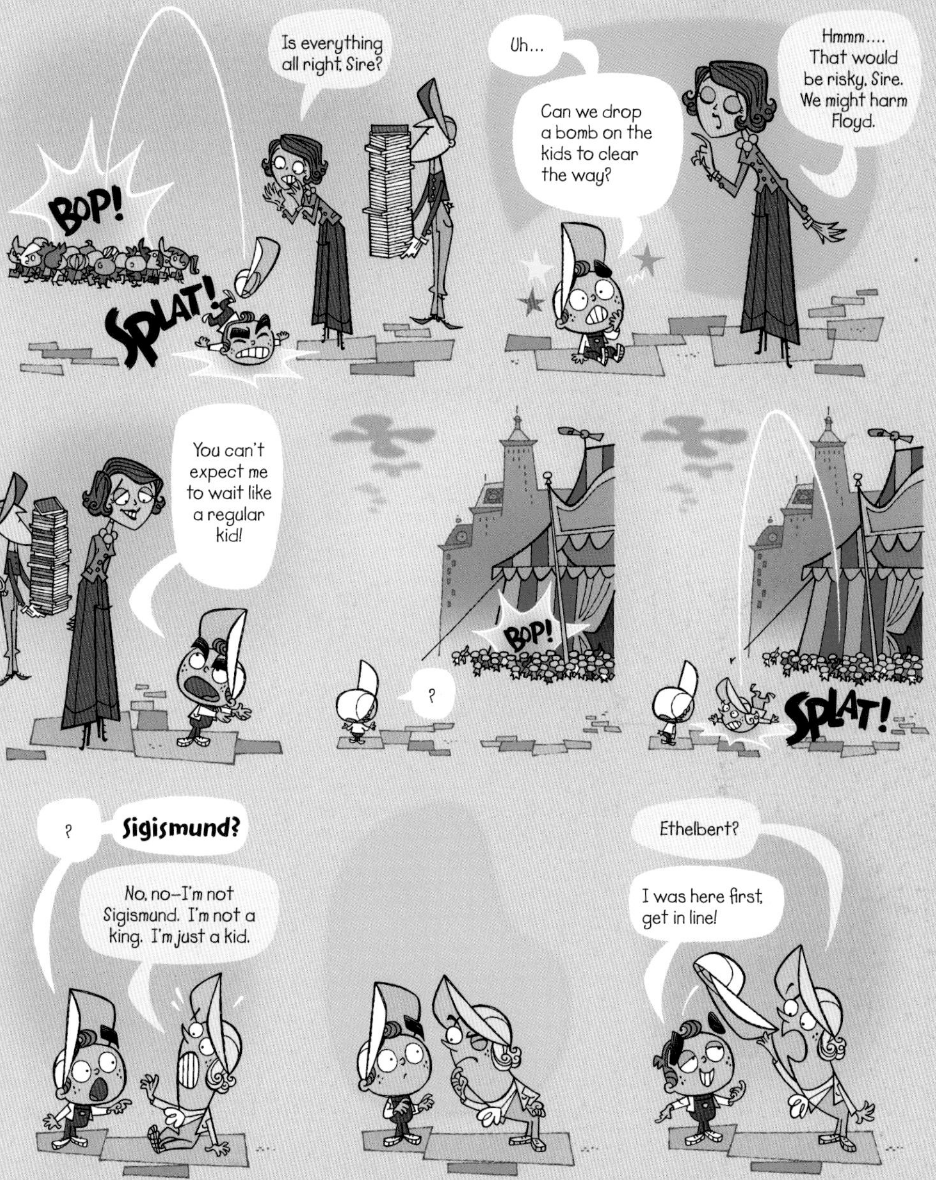
BOP!
SPLAT!
Is everything all right, Sire?
Uh...
Can we drop a bomb on the kids to clear the way?
Hmmm.... That would be risky, Sire. We might harm Floyd.
You can't expect me to wait like a regular kid!
BOP!
?
SPLAT!
?
Sigismund?
No, no—I'm not Sigismund. I'm not a king. I'm just a kid.
Ethelbert?
I was here first, get in line!

"Sigh" We've been here for hours. The line's hardly moving and I've read every book forty times.

I don't even find them that funny anymore.

So go home!

And give you my spot? **Never!**

Dear boys and girls, Floyd's signing today is coming to an end. He will now choose two readers at random from the crowd for his two final sketches.

Me!

Me!

Me!

Me!

Me!

Jessica and Kevin are the lucky winners! Thank you everyone for coming, and see you next time!

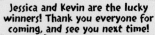

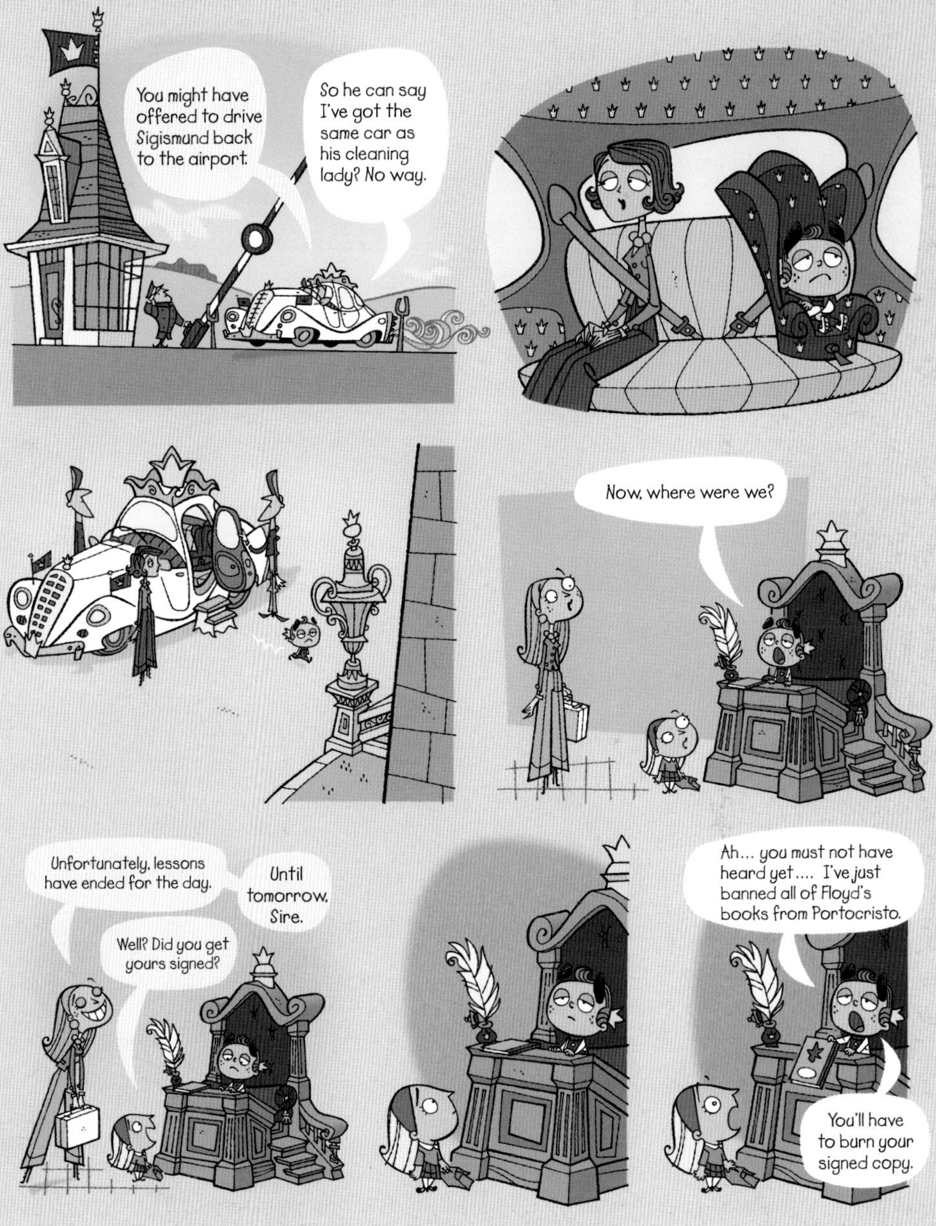
You might have offered to drive Sigismund back to the airport.
So he can say I've got the same car as his cleaning lady? No way.
Now, where were we?
Unfortunately, lessons have ended for the day.
Until tomorrow, Sire.
Well? Did you get yours signed?
Ah... you must not have heard yet.... I've just banned all of Floyd's books from Portocristo.
You'll have to burn your signed copy.

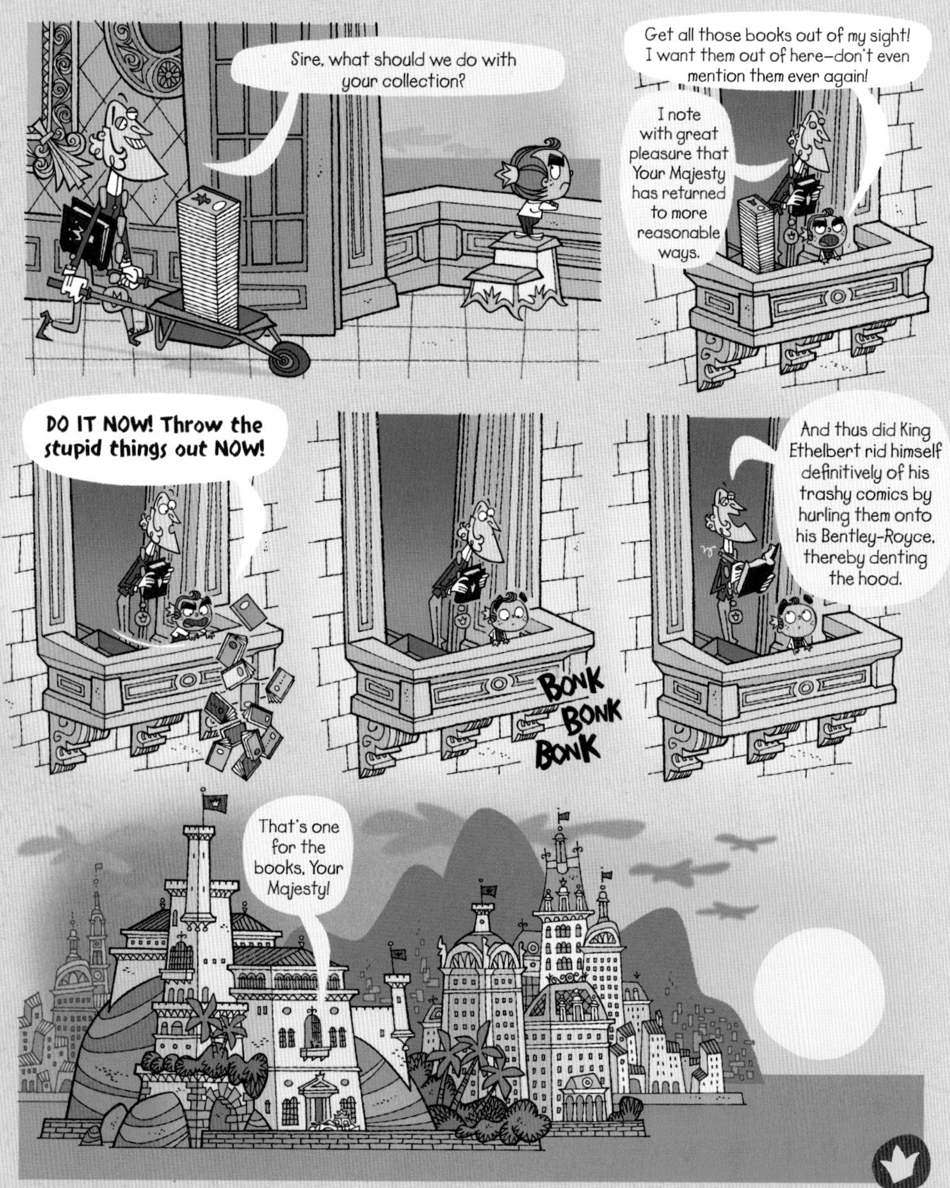
Sire, what should we do with your collection?
Get all those books out of my sight! I want them out of here—don't even mention them ever again!
I note with great pleasure that Your Majesty has returned to more reasonable ways.
DO IT NOW! Throw the stupid things out NOW!
BONK
BONK
BONK
And thus did King Ethelbert rid himself definitively of his trashy comics by hurling them onto his Bentley-Royce, thereby denting the hood.
That's one for the books, Your Majesty!

Picture-Perfect Children

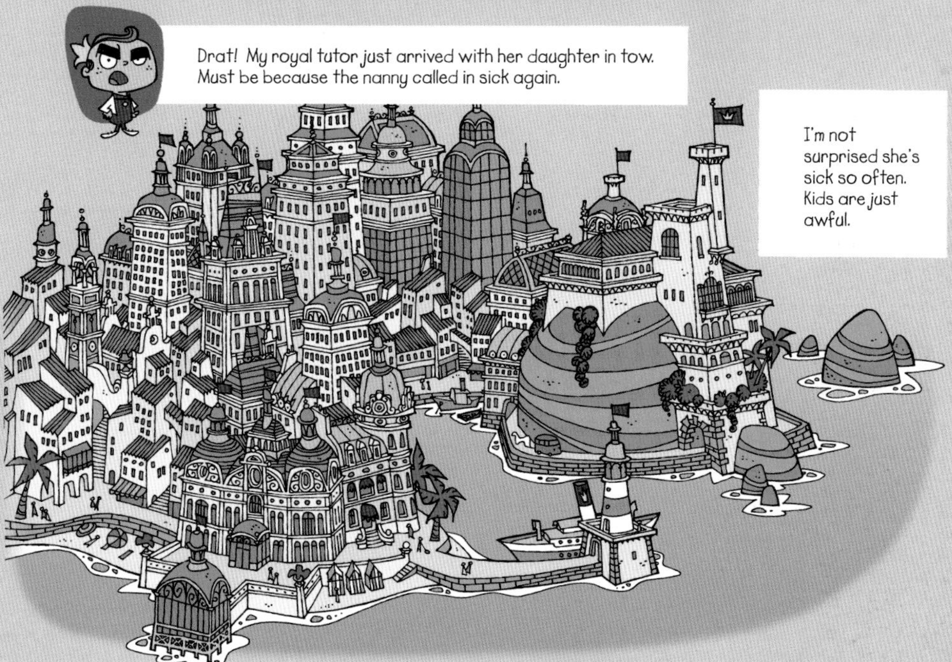
Drat! My royal tutor just arrived with her daughter in tow. Must be because the nanny called in sick again.
I'm not surprised she's sick so often. Kids are just awful.

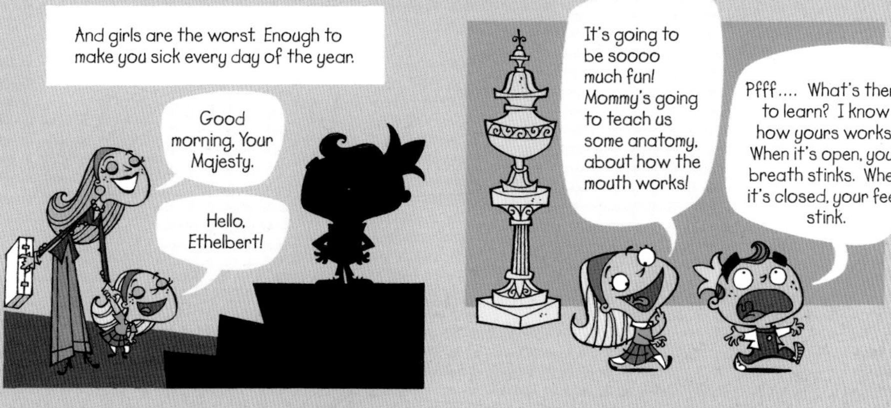
And girls are the worst. Enough to make you sick every day of the year.
Good morning, Your Majesty.
Hello, Ethelbert!
It's going to be soooo much fun! Mommy's going to teach us some anatomy, about how the mouth works!
Pfff.... What's there to learn? I know how yours works. When it's open, your breath stinks. When it's closed, your feet stink.

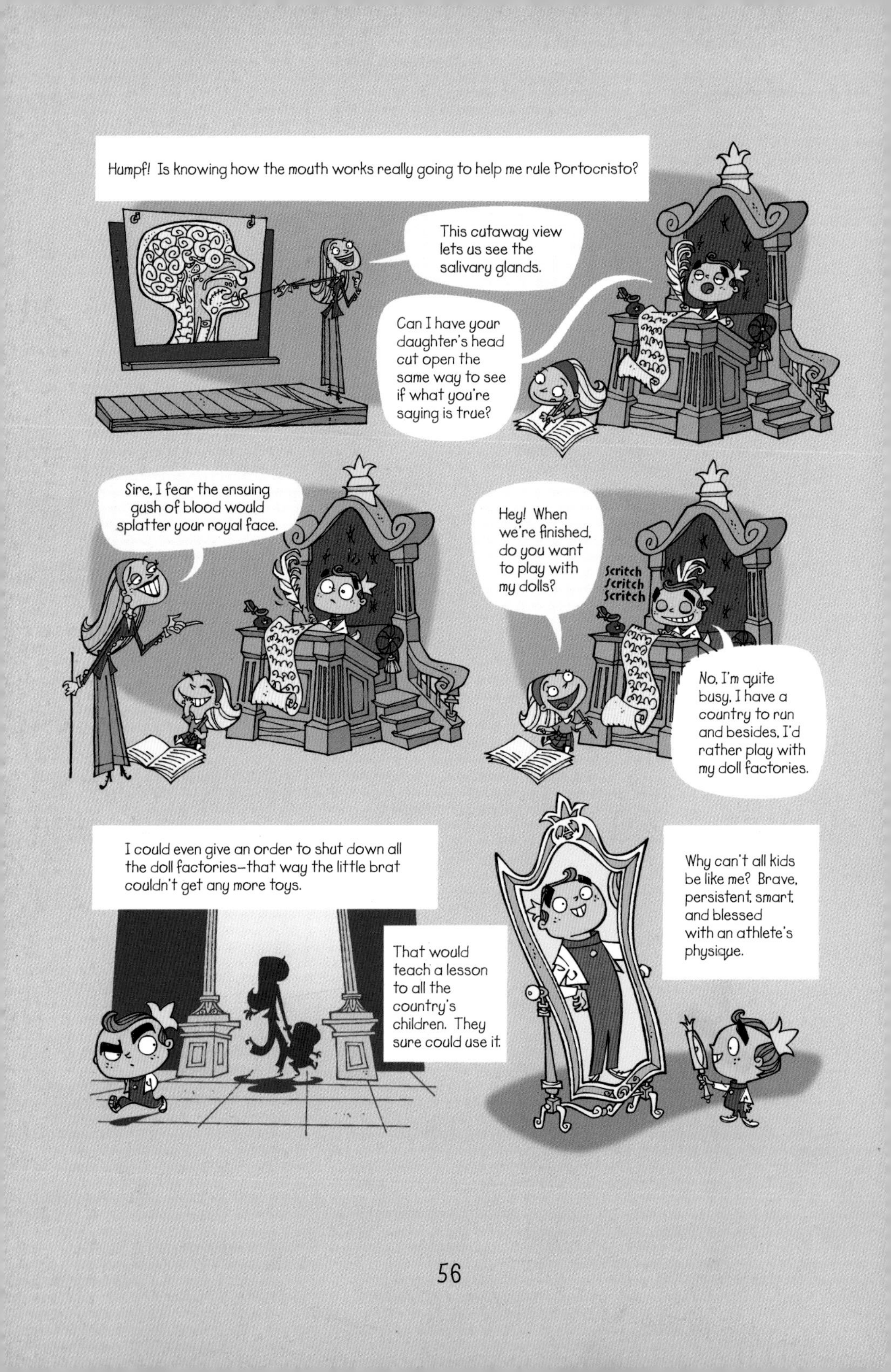

Humpf! Is knowing how the mouth works really going to help me rule Portocristo?
This cutaway view lets us see the salivary glands.
Can I have your daughter's head cut open the same way to see if what you're saying is true?
Sire, I fear the ensuing gush of blood would splatter your royal face.
Hey! When we're finished, do you want to play with my dolls?
Scritch Scritch Scritch
No, I'm quite busy. I have a country to run and besides, I'd rather play with my doll factories.
I could even give an order to shut down all the doll factories—that way the little brat couldn't get any more toys.
That would teach a lesson to all the country's children. They sure could use it.
Why can't all kids be like me? Brave, persistent, smart, and blessed with an athlete's physique.

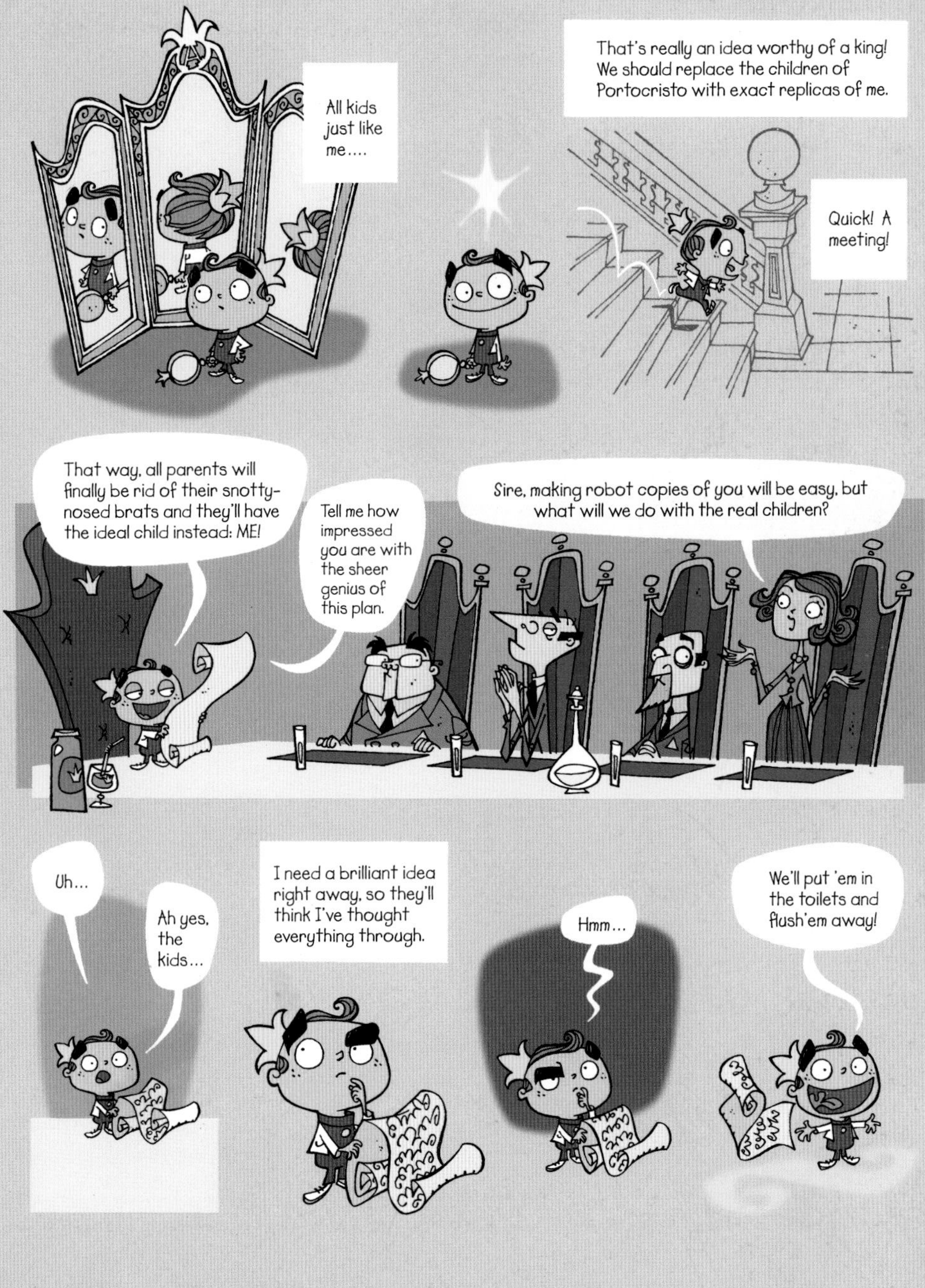
All kids just like me....
That's really an idea worthy of a king! We should replace the children of Portocristo with exact replicas of me.
Quick! A meeting!
That way, all parents will finally be rid of their snotty-nosed brats and they'll have the ideal child instead: ME!
Tell me how impressed you are with the sheer genius of this plan.
Sire, making robot copies of you will be easy, but what will we do with the real children?
Uh...
Ah yes, the kids...
I need a brilliant idea right away, so they'll think I've thought everything through.
Hmm...
We'll put 'em in the toilets and flush'em away!

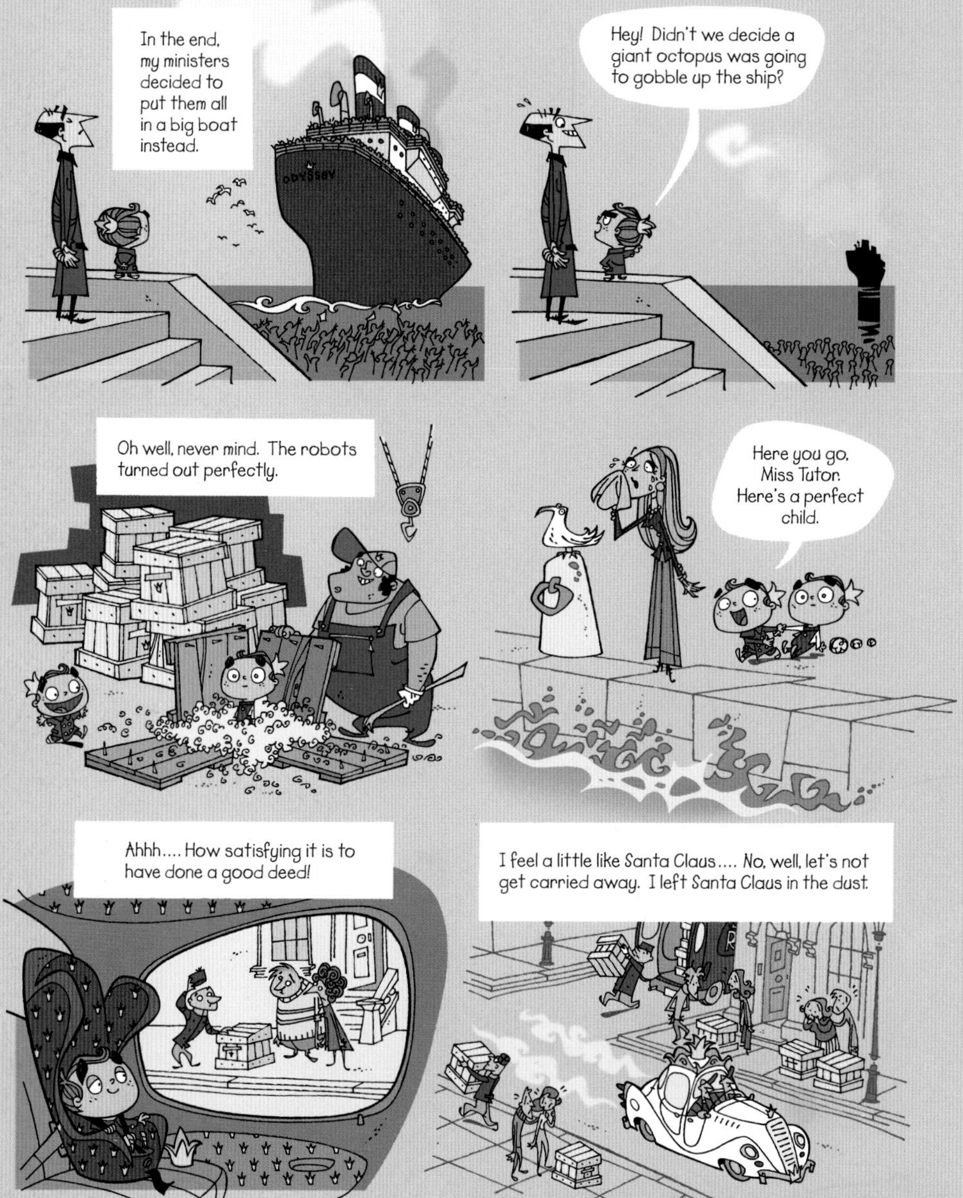

In the end, my ministers decided to put them all in a big boat instead.
ODYSSEY
Hey! Didn't we decide a giant octopus was going to gobble up the ship?
Oh well, never mind. The robots turned out perfectly.
Here you go, Miss Tutor. Here's a perfect child.
Ahhh.... How satisfying it is to have done a good deed!
I feel a little like Santa Claus.... No, well, let's not get carried away. I left Santa Claus in the dust.

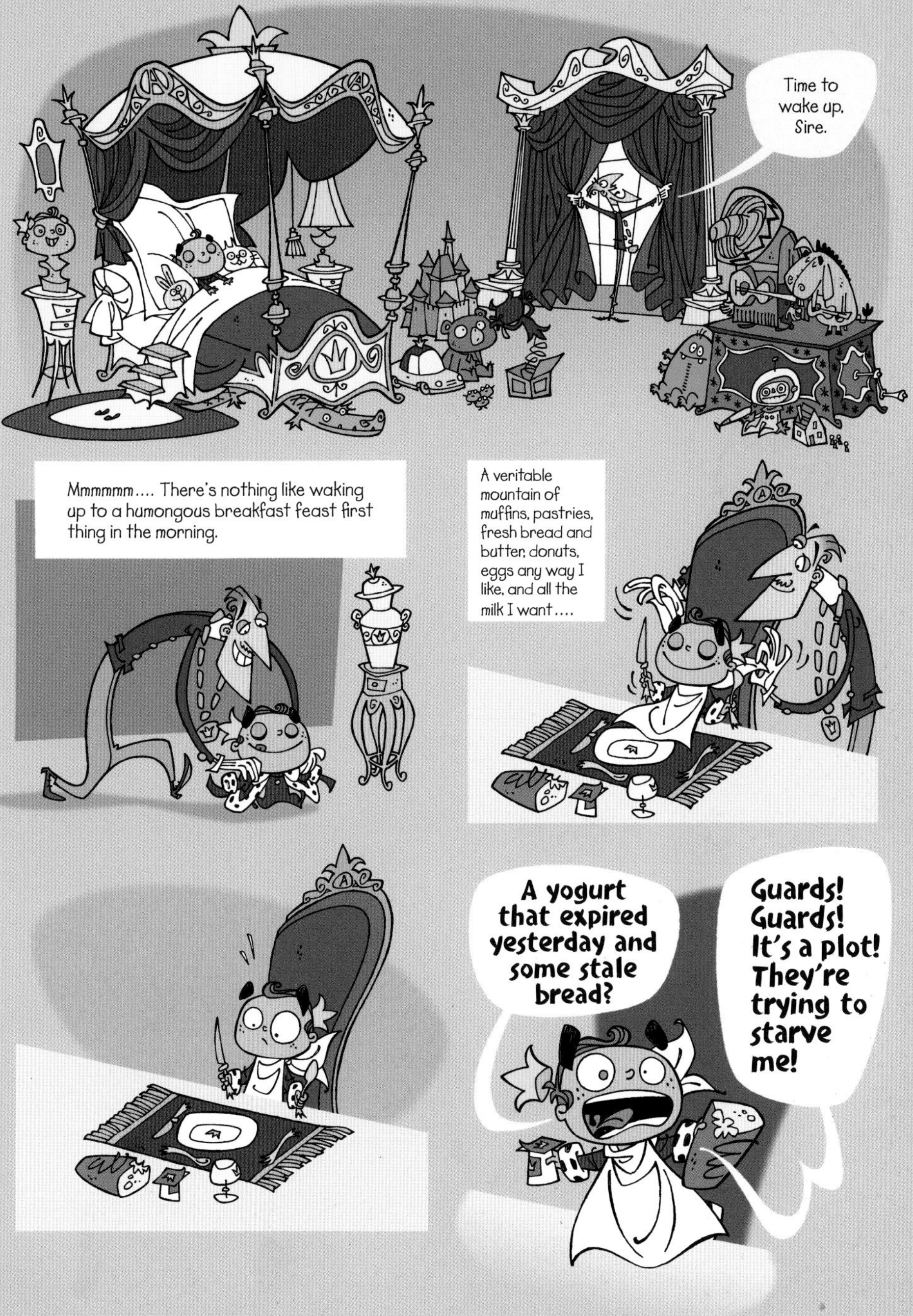
Time to wake up, Sire.
Mmmmmm.... There's nothing like waking up to a humongous breakfast feast first thing in the morning.
A veritable mountain of muffins, pastries, fresh bread and butter, donuts, eggs any way I like, and all the milk I want....
A yogurt that expired yesterday and some stale bread?
Guards! Guards! It's a plot! They're trying to starve me!

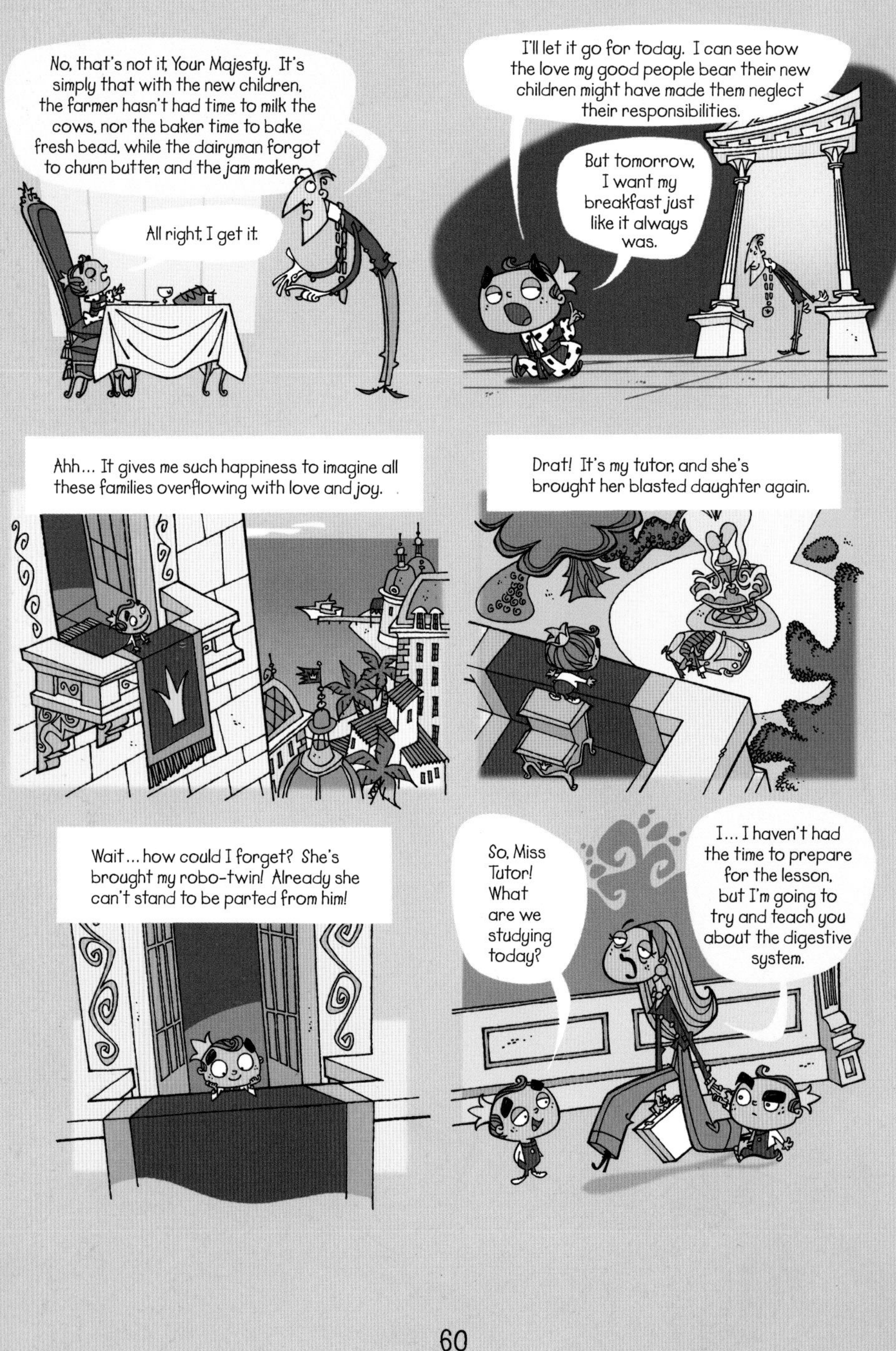
No, that's not it, Your Majesty. It's simply that with the new children, the farmer hasn't had time to milk the cows, nor the baker time to bake fresh bead, while the dairyman forgot to churn butter, and the jam maker...
All right, I get it.
I'll let it go for today. I can see how the love my good people bear their new children might have made them neglect their responsibilities.
But tomorrow, I want my breakfast just like it always was.
Ahh... It gives me such happiness to imagine all these families overflowing with love and joy.
Drat! It's my tutor, and she's brought her blasted daughter again.
Wait... how could I forget? She's brought my robo-twin! Already she can't stand to be parted from him!
So, Miss Tutor! What are we studying today?
I... I haven't had the time to prepare for the lesson, but I'm going to try and teach you about the digestive system.

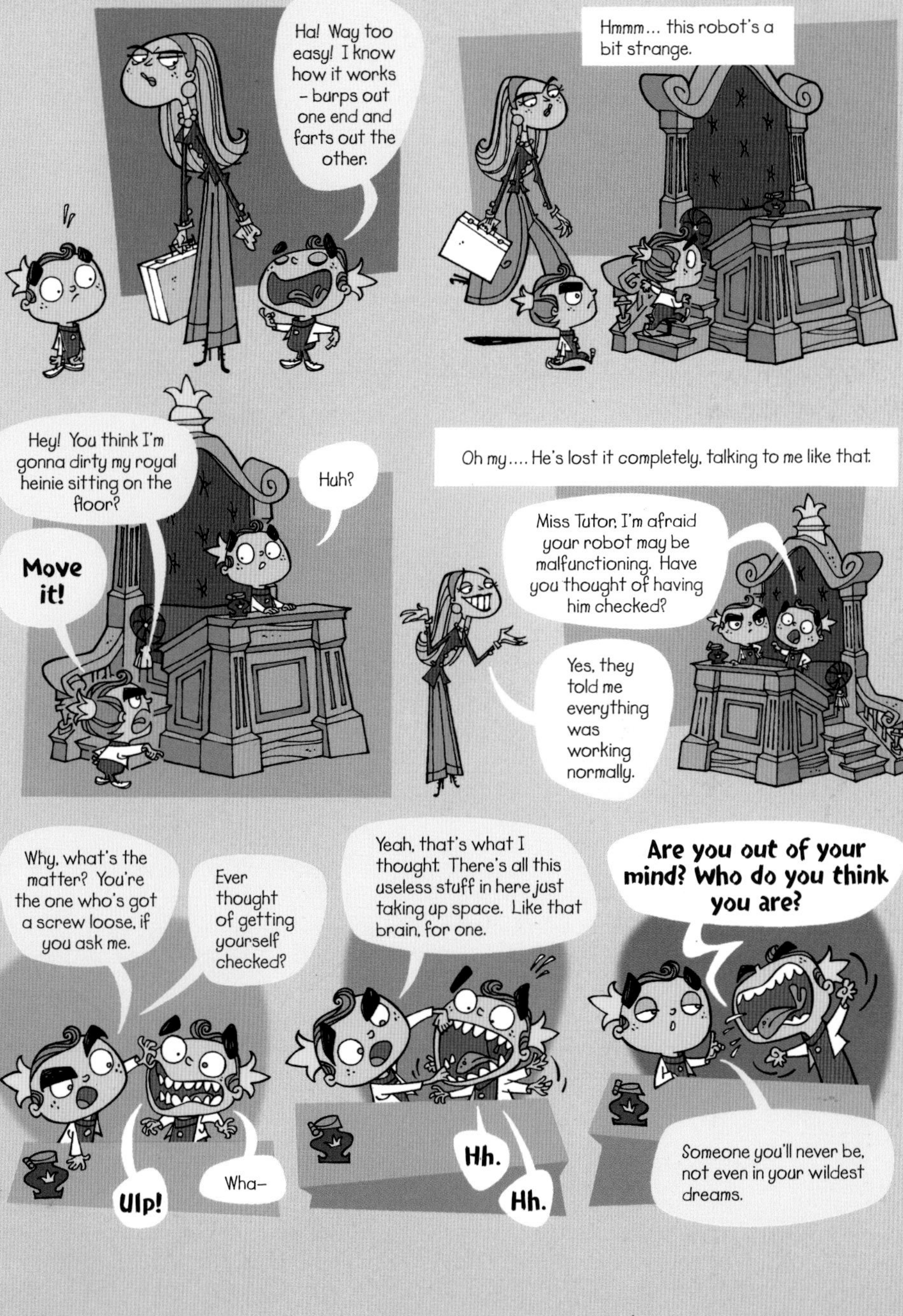
Ha! Way too easy! I know how it works – burps out one end and farts out the other.
Hmmm... this robot's a bit strange.
Hey! You think I'm gonna dirty my royal heinie sitting on the floor?
Move it!
Huh?
Oh my.... He's lost it completely, talking to me like that.
Miss Tutor, I'm afraid your robot may be malfunctioning. Have you thought of having him checked?
Yes, they told me everything was working normally.
Why, what's the matter? You're the one who's got a screw loose, if you ask me.
Ever thought of getting yourself checked?
Ulp!
Wha–
Yeah, that's what I thought. There's all this useless stuff in here just taking up space. Like that brain, for one.
Hh.
Hh.
Are you out of your mind? Who do you think you are?
Someone you'll never be, not even in your wildest dreams.

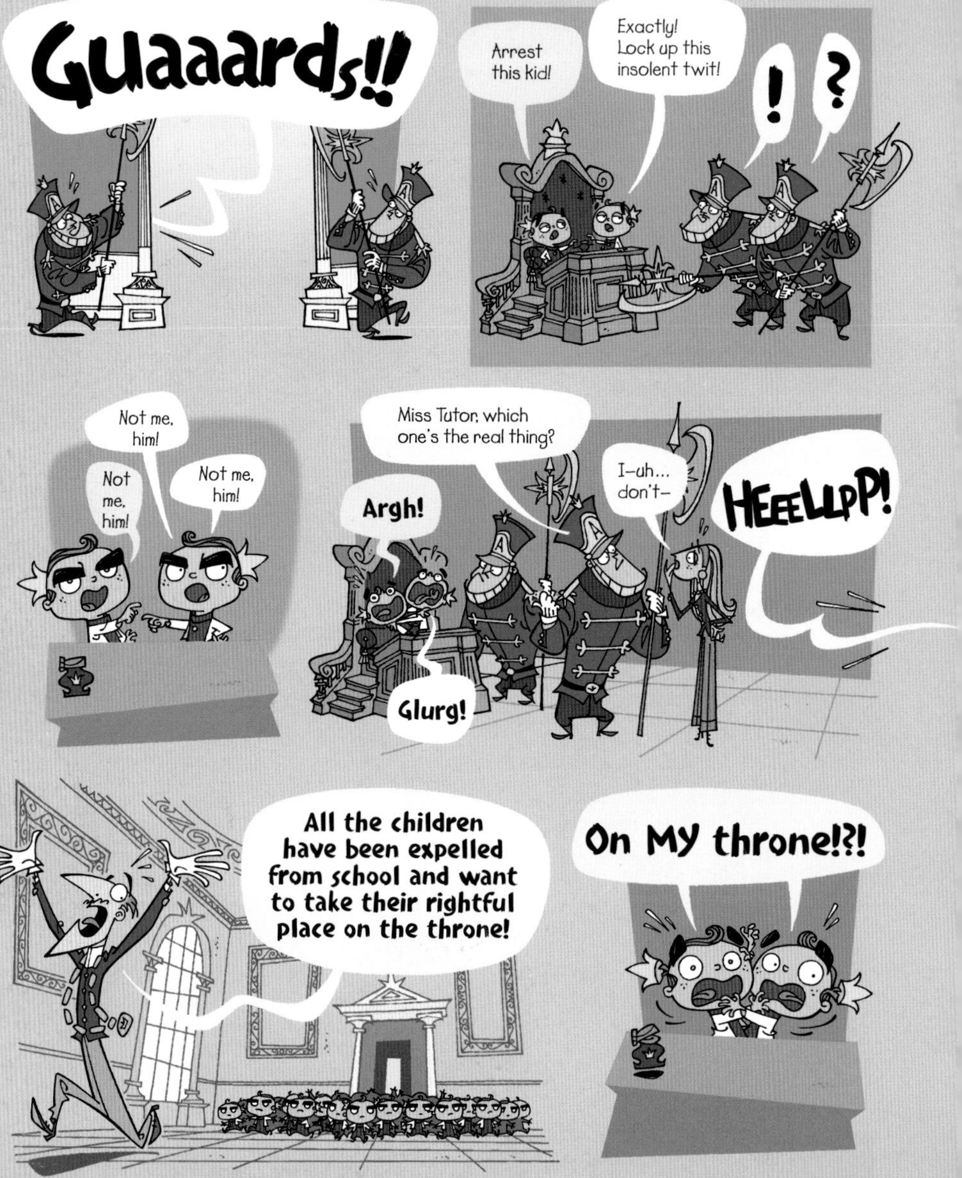
Guaaards!!
Arrest this kid!
Exactly! Lock up this insolent twit!
!
?
Not me, him!
Not me, him!
Not me, him!
Miss Tutor, which one's the real thing?
Argh!
I—uh... don't—
HEEELLPP!
Glurg!
All the children have been expelled from school and want to take their rightful place on the throne!
On MY throne!?!

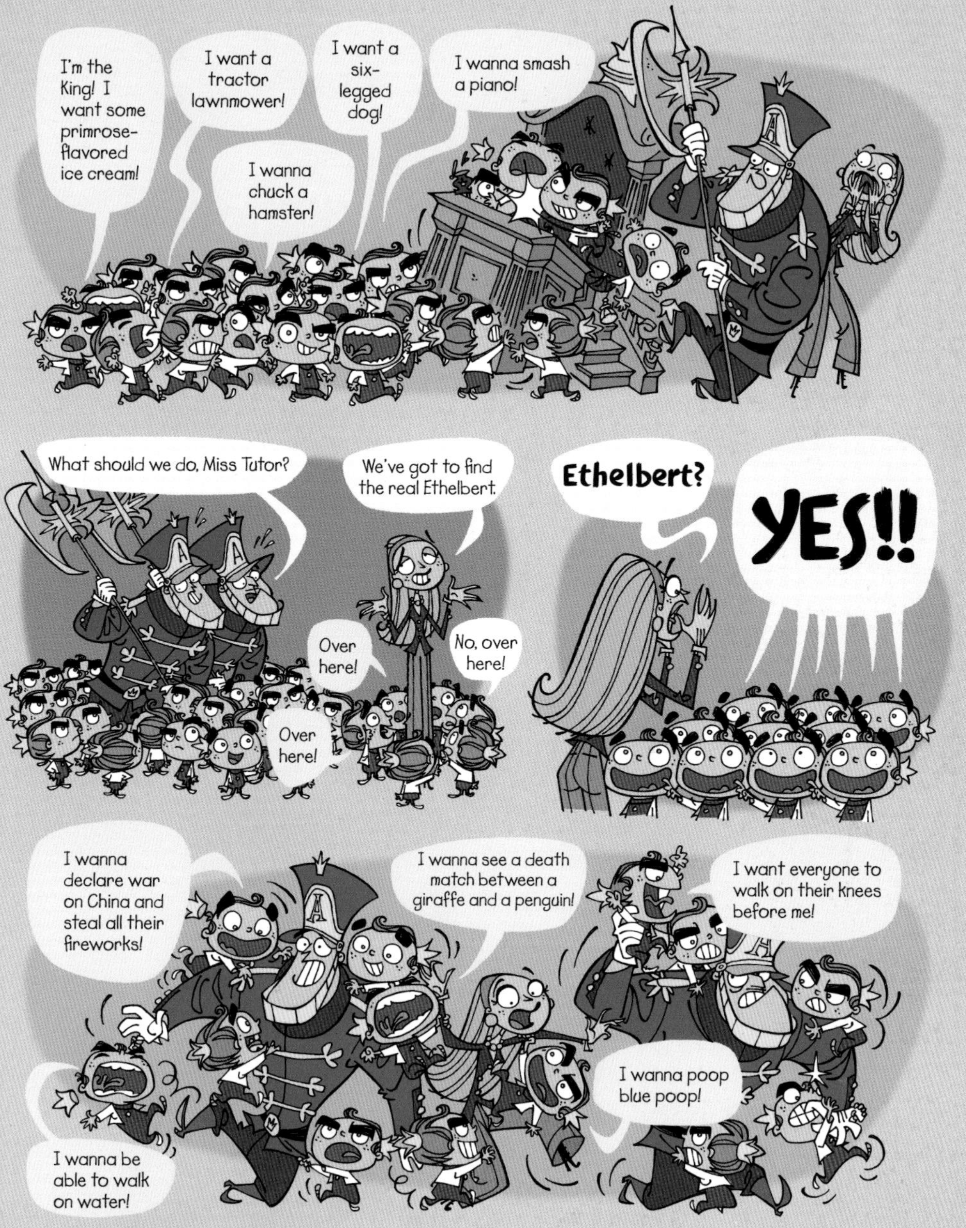

I'm the King! I want some primrose-flavored ice cream!
I want a tractor lawnmower!
I wanna chuck a hamster!
I want a six-legged dog!
I wanna smash a piano!
What should we do, Miss Tutor?
We've got to find the real Ethelbert.
Over here!
No, over here!
Over here!
Ethelbert?
YES!!
I wanna declare war on China and steal all their fireworks!
I wanna see a death match between a giraffe and a penguin!
I want everyone to walk on their knees before me!
I wanna poop blue poop!
I wanna be able to walk on water!

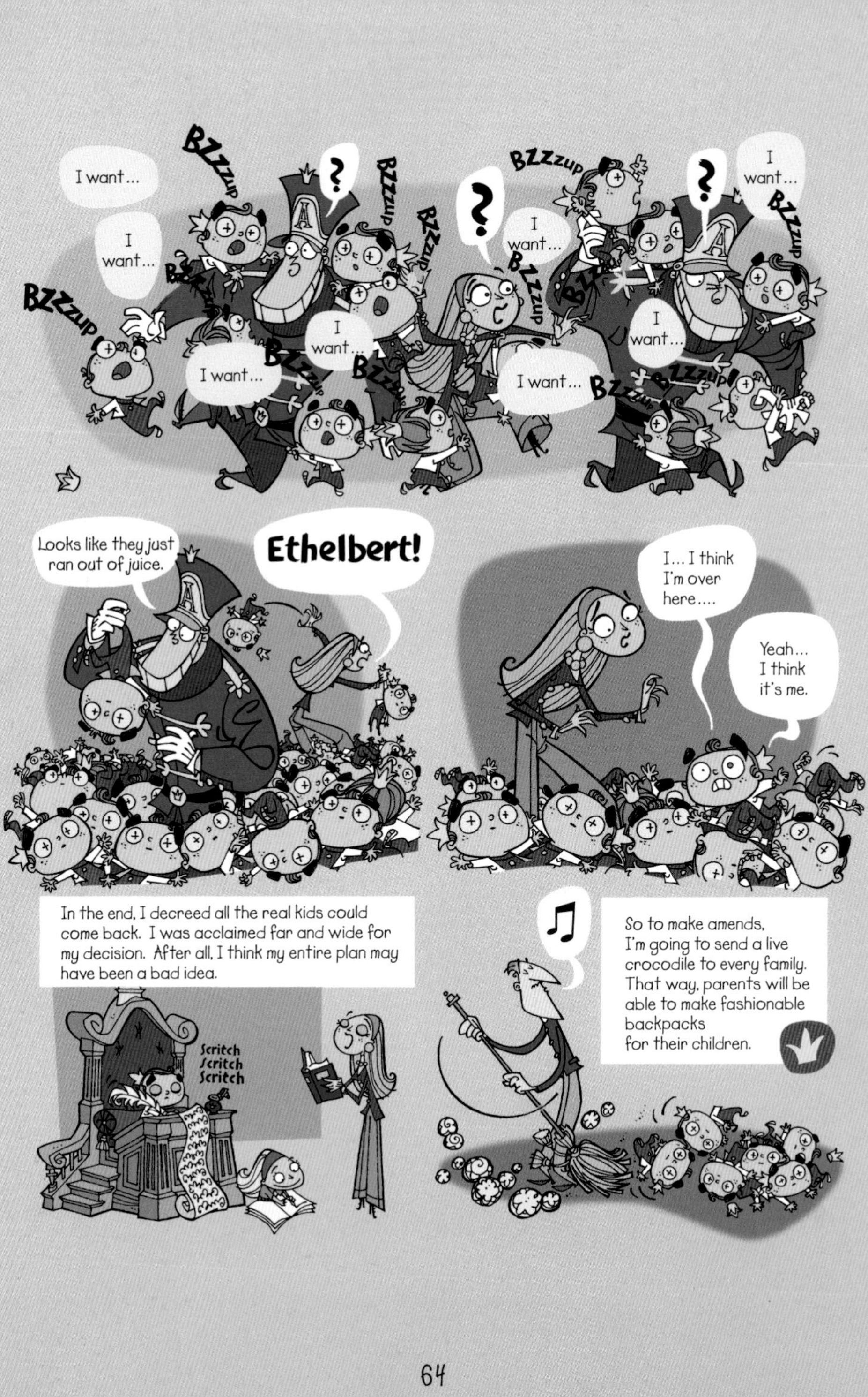
I want...
I want...
BZZzup
BZZzup
?
BZZzup
BZZzup
I want...
I want...
BZZzup
?
I want...
BZZzup
BZZzup
?
I want...
BZZzup
I want...
I want...
BZZzup
BZZzup
Looks like they just ran out of juice.
Ethelbert!
I... I think I'm over here....
Yeah... I think it's me.
In the end, I decreed all the real kids could come back. I was acclaimed far and wide for my decision. After all, I think my entire plan may have been a bad idea.
Scritch Scritch Scritch
♫
So to make amends, I'm going to send a live crocodile to every family. That way, parents will be able to make fashionable backpacks for their children.

A Surprise Visit

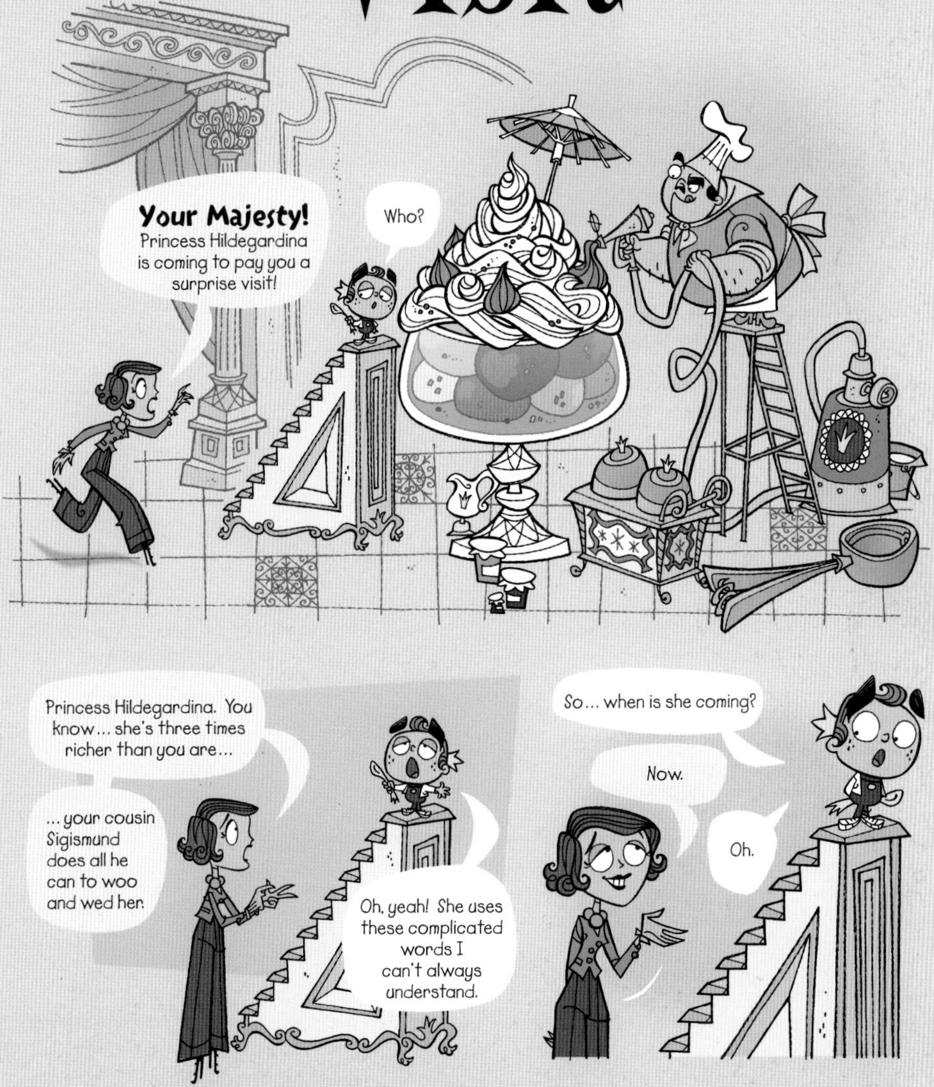
Your Majesty!
Princess Hildegardina is coming to pay you a surprise visit!
Who?
Princess Hildegardina. You know... she's three times richer than you are...
... your cousin Sigismund does all he can to woo and wed her.
Oh, yeah! She uses these complicated words I can't always understand.
So... when is she coming?
Now.
Oh.

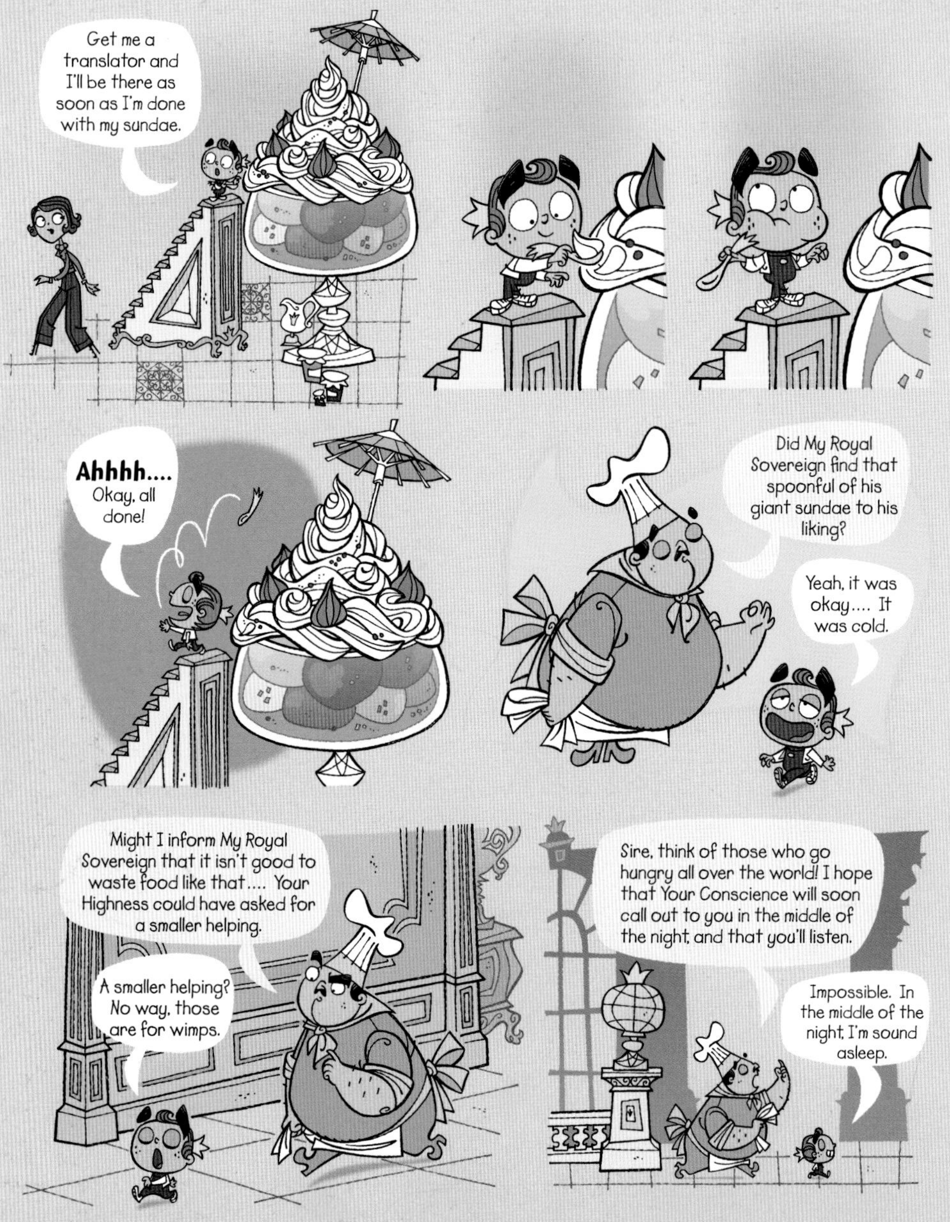

Get me a translator and I'll be there as soon as I'm done with my sundae.
Ahhhh.... Okay, all done!
Did My Royal Sovereign find that spoonful of his giant sundae to his liking?
Yeah, it was okay.... It was cold.
Might I inform My Royal Sovereign that it isn't good to waste food like that.... Your Highness could have asked for a smaller helping.
A smaller helping? No way, those are for wimps.
Sire, think of those who go hungry all over the world! I hope that Your Conscience will soon call out to you in the middle of the night, and that you'll listen.
Impossible. In the middle of the night, I'm sound asleep.

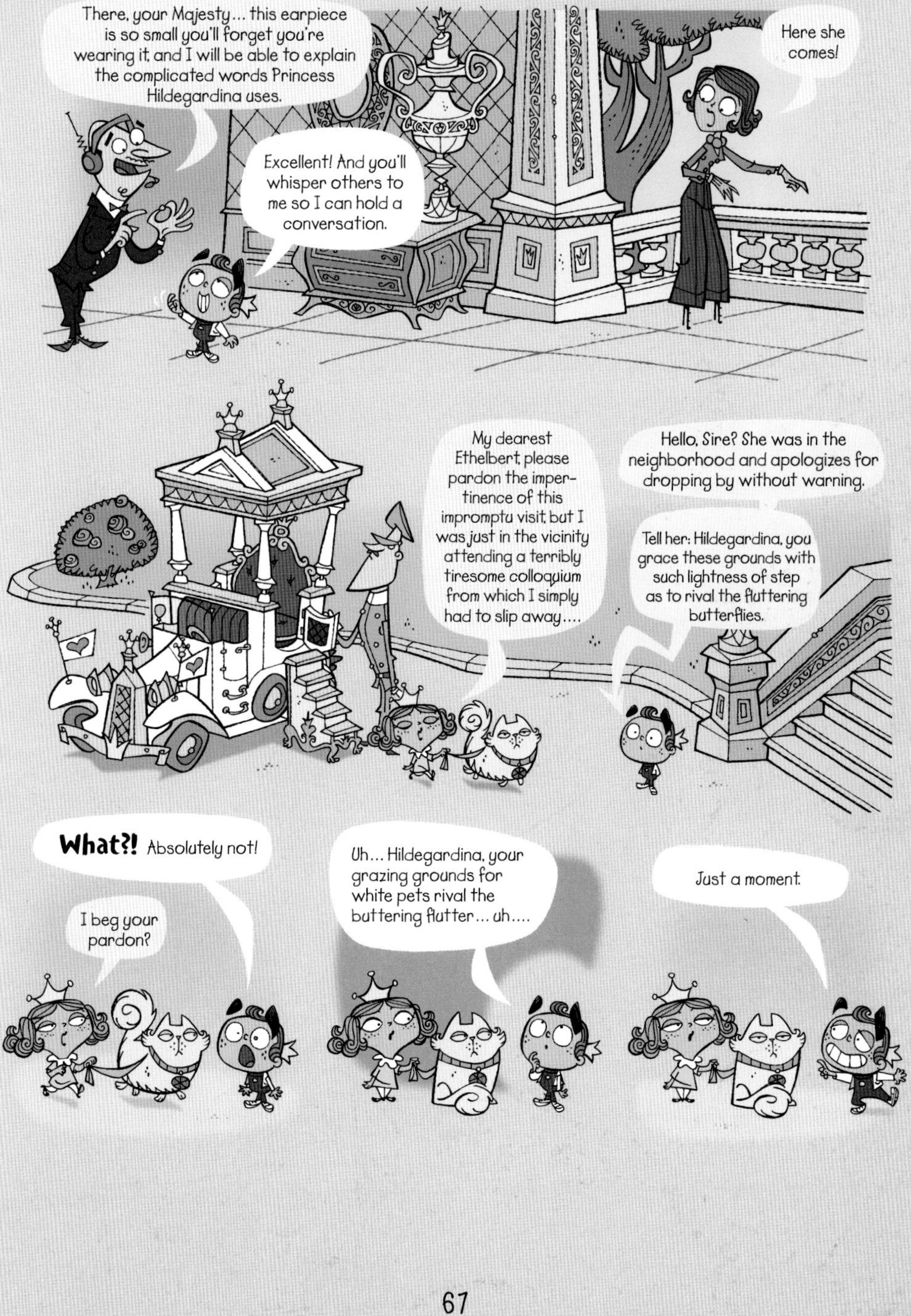

There, your Majesty… this earpiece is so small you'll forget you're wearing it, and I will be able to explain the complicated words Princess Hildegardina uses.
Excellent! And you'll whisper others to me so I can hold a conversation.
Here she comes!
My dearest Ethelbert, please pardon the impertinence of this impromptu visit, but I was just in the vicinity attending a terribly tiresome colloquium from which I simply had to slip away….
Hello, Sire? She was in the neighborhood and apologizes for dropping by without warning.
Tell her: Hildegardina, you grace these grounds with such lightness of step as to rival the fluttering butterflies.
What?! Absolutely not!
I beg your pardon?
Uh… Hildegardina, your grazing grounds for white pets rival the buttering flutter… uh….
Just a moment.

Listen up, you two! Don't be putting any girly words in my mouth, got it?!
Understood, Your Majesty.
Well... uh... I'm back! If you'd like to come inside...
...maybe we could play some video games?
Or have fun wrecking pricey objects?
Dear friend, surely you jest? I've hardly come to engage in obscure and puerile diversions but rather to behold the hidden wonders of your palace. Would you consent to be my guide?
Uh... um... of course.
Hello, Sire! Pray, my dear, follow me, that I might show you my ancestral abode.
Pray, my dear, follow me, that I might show you my ancestral abode.
I shall accompany you gladly.
Your predecessors, I surmise?
Your preeda scissors, eyesore mize?
Are these your ancestors?
Uh... yes, of course... but I'll spare you the list of names. We have enough history lessons as it is.
Tee hee hee! You are so congenial and unaffected!

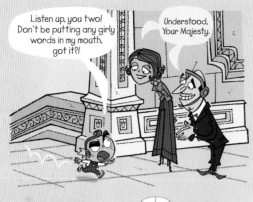

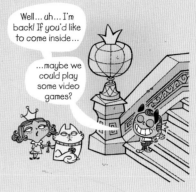

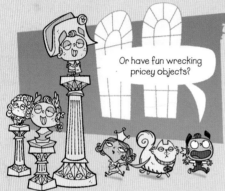

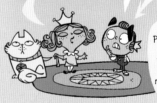

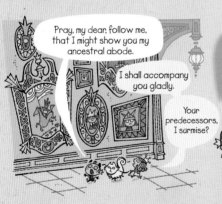

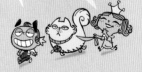

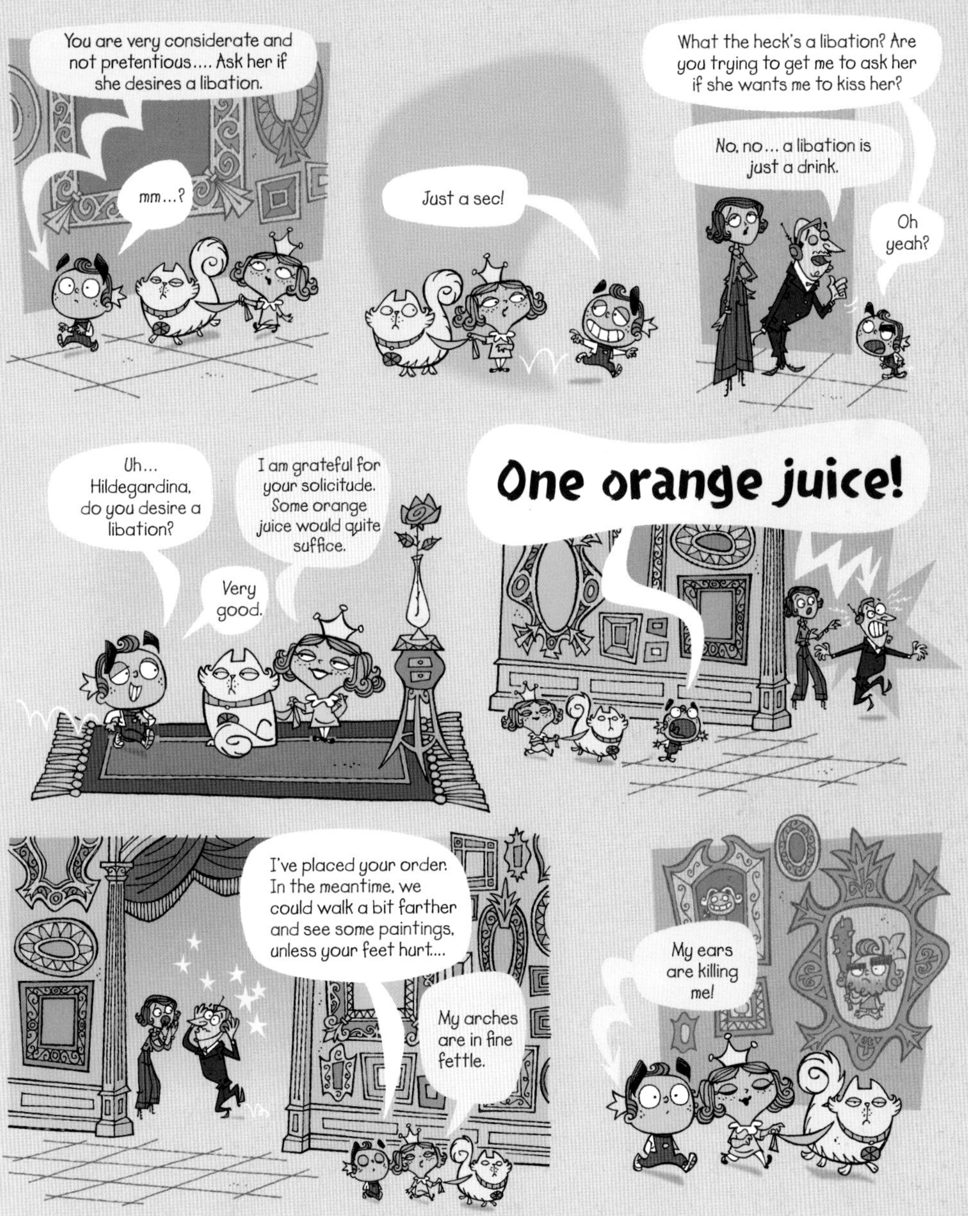
You are very considerate and not pretentious.... Ask her if she desires a libation.
mm...?
Just a sec!
What the heck's a libation? Are you trying to get me to ask her if she wants me to kiss her?
No, no... a libation is just a drink.
Oh yeah?
Uh... Hildegardina, do you desire a libation?
Very good.
I am grateful for your solicitude. Some orange juice would quite suffice.
One orange juice!
I've placed your order. In the meantime, we could walk a bit farther and see some paintings, unless your feet hurt....
My arches are in fine fettle.
My ears are killing me!

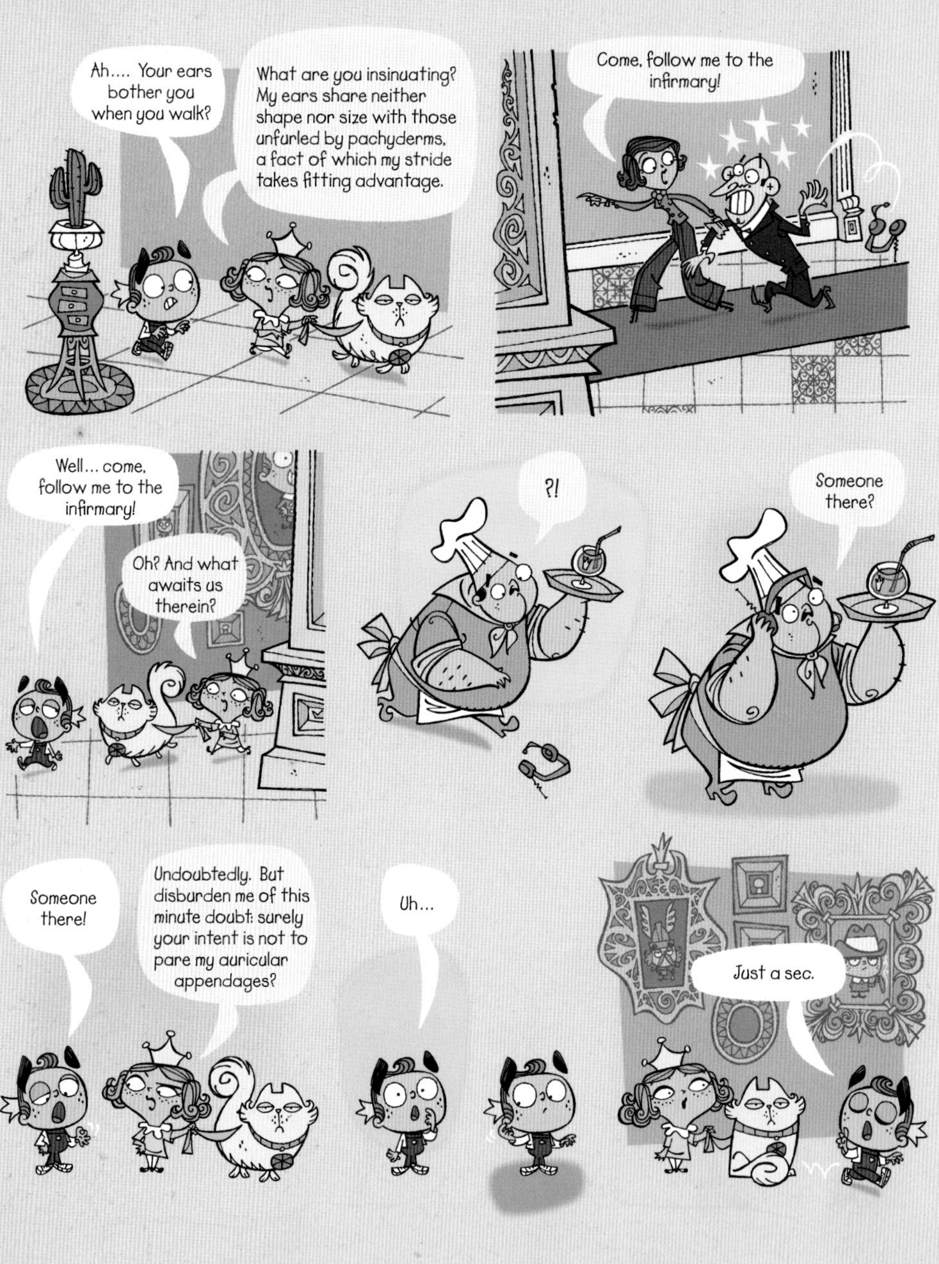
Ah.... Your ears bother you when you walk?
What are you insinuating? My ears share neither shape nor size with those unfurled by pachyderms, a fact of which my stride takes fitting advantage.
Come, follow me to the infirmary!
Well... come, follow me to the infirmary!
Oh? And what awaits us therein?
?!
Someone there?
Someone there!
Undoubtedly. But disburden me of this minute doubt: surely your intent is not to pare my auricular appendages?
Uh...
Just a sec.

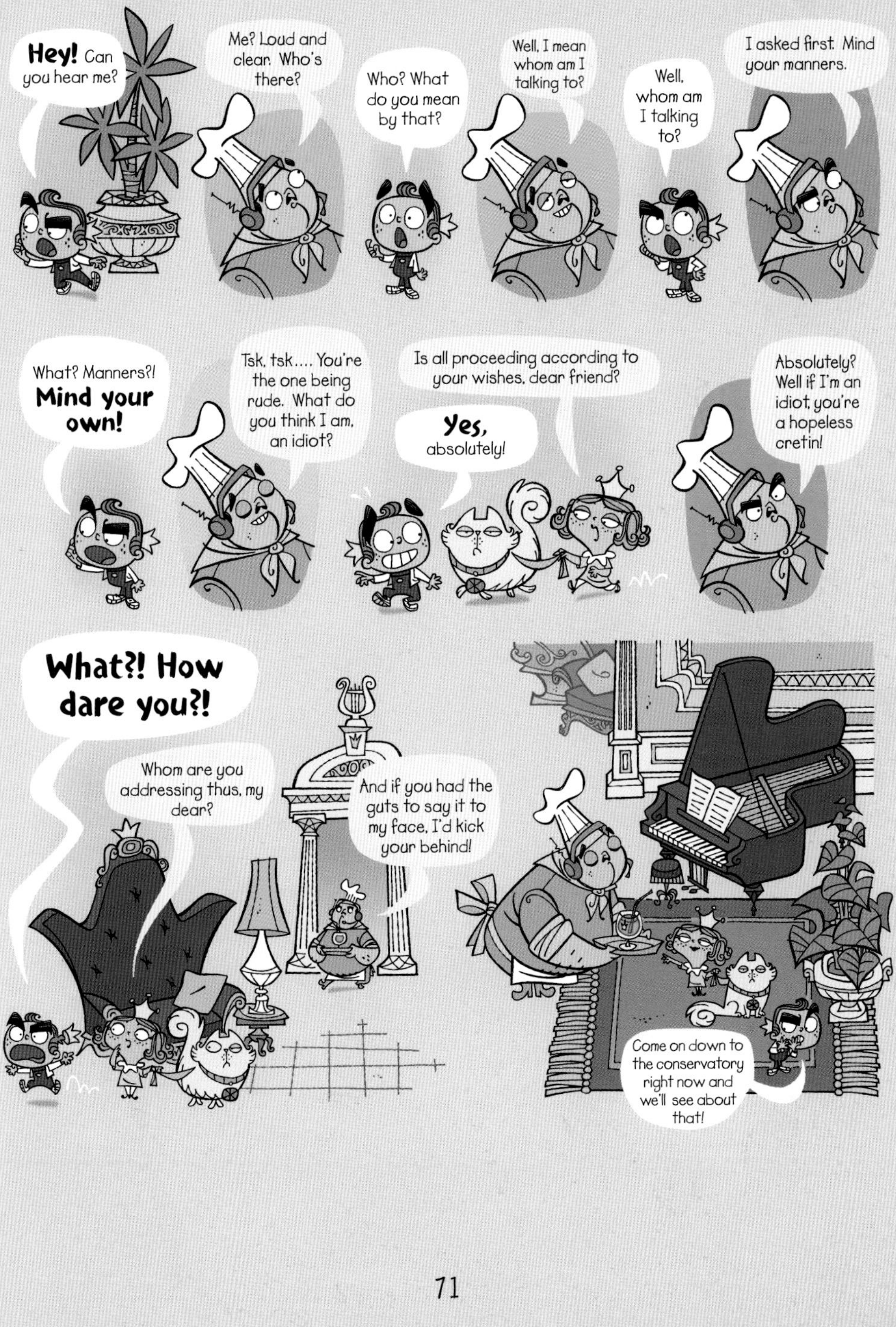
Hey! Can you hear me?
Me? Loud and clear. Who's there?
Who? What do you mean by that?
Well, I mean whom am I talking to?
Well, whom am I talking to?
I asked first. Mind your manners.
What? Manners?! Mind your own!
Tsk, tsk.... You're the one being rude. What do you think I am, an idiot?
Is all proceeding according to your wishes, dear friend?
Yes, absolutely!
Absolutely? Well if I'm an idiot, you're a hopeless cretin!
What?! How dare you?!
Whom are you addressing thus, my dear?
And if you had the guts to say it to my face, I'd kick your behind!
Come on down to the conservatory right now and we'll see about that!

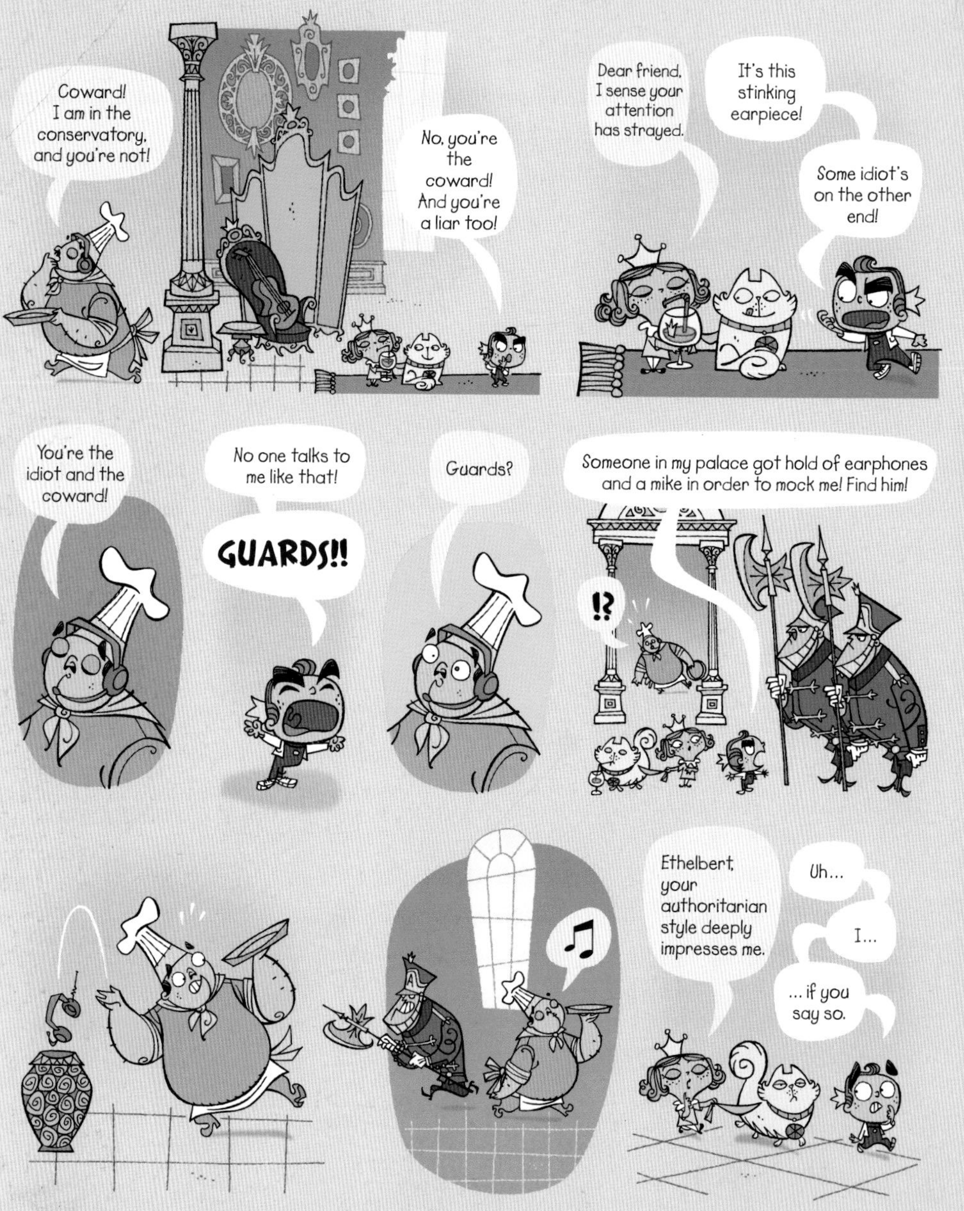
Coward! I am in the conservatory, and you're not!
No, you're the coward! And you're a liar too!
Dear friend, I sense your attention has strayed.
It's this stinking earpiece!
Some idiot's on the other end!
You're the idiot and the coward!
No one talks to me like that!
GUARDS!!
Guards?
Someone in my palace got hold of earphones and a mike in order to mock me! Find him!
!?
Ethelbert, your authoritarian style deeply impresses me.
Uh...
I...
... if you say so.

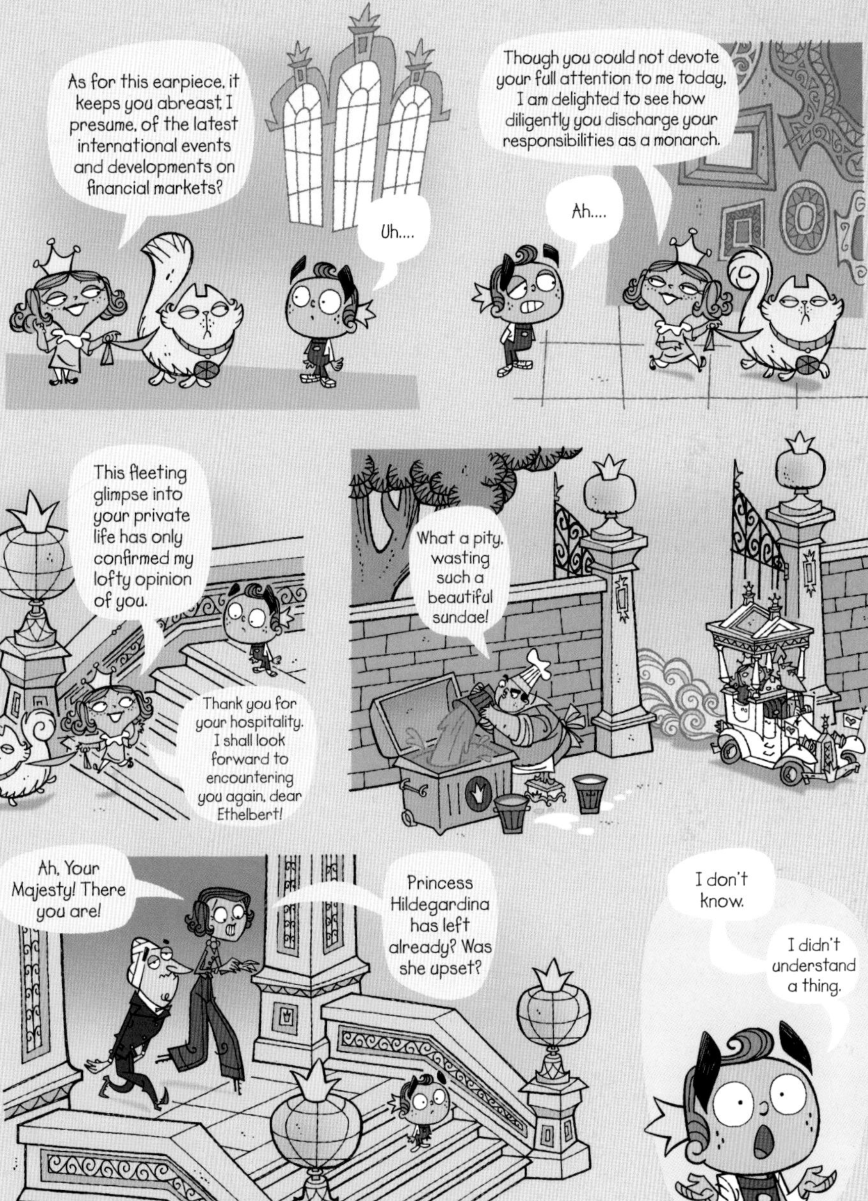
As for this earpiece, it keeps you abreast, I presume, of the latest international events and developments on financial markets?
Uh....
Though you could not devote your full attention to me today, I am delighted to see how diligently you discharge your responsibilities as a monarch.
Ah....
This fleeting glimpse into your private life has only confirmed my lofty opinion of you.
Thank you for your hospitality. I shall look forward to encountering you again, dear Ethelbert!
What a pity, wasting such a beautiful sundae!
Ah, Your Majesty! There you are!
Princess Hildegardina has left already? Was she upset?
I don't know.
I didn't understand a thing.

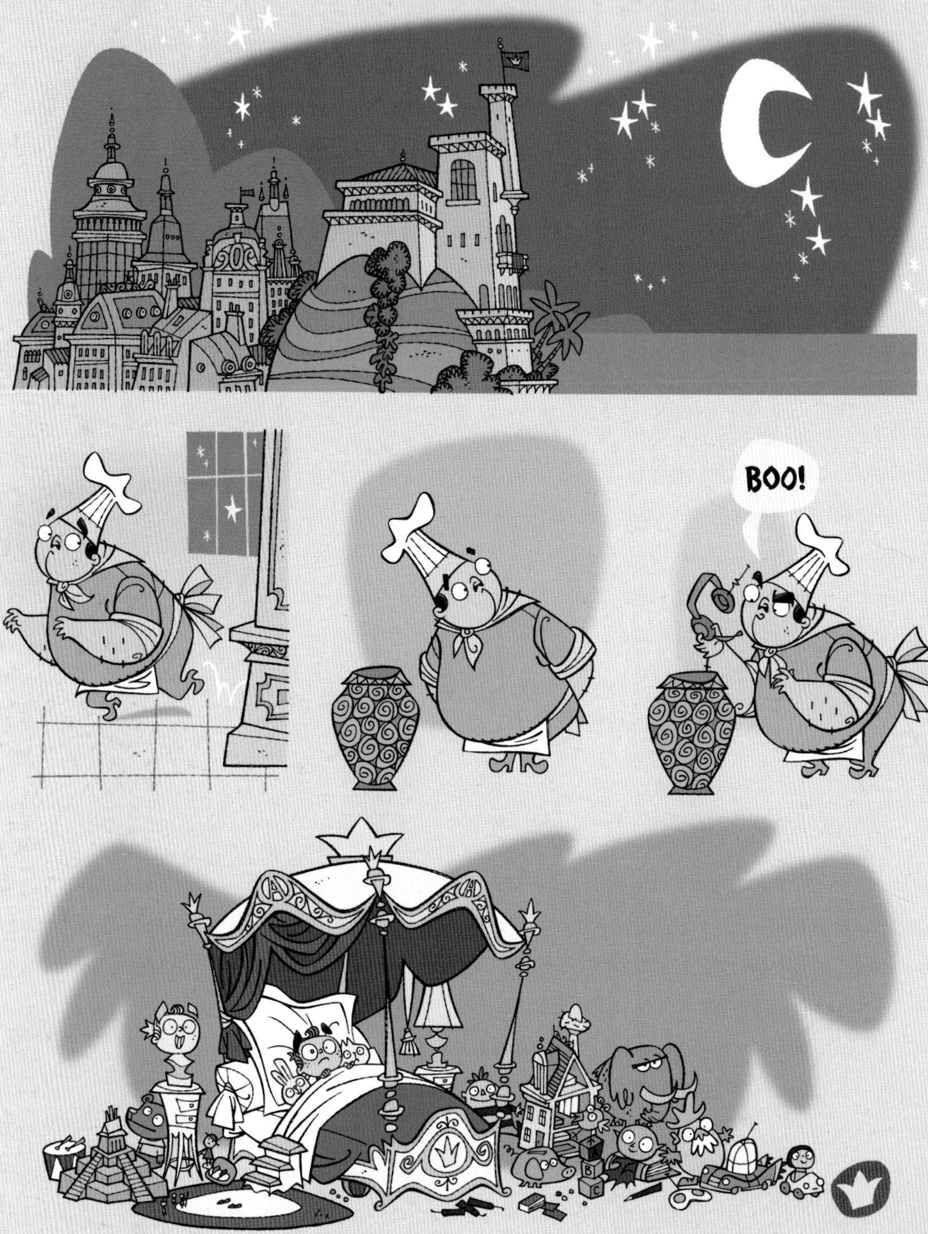
BOO!

The Lucky Winner

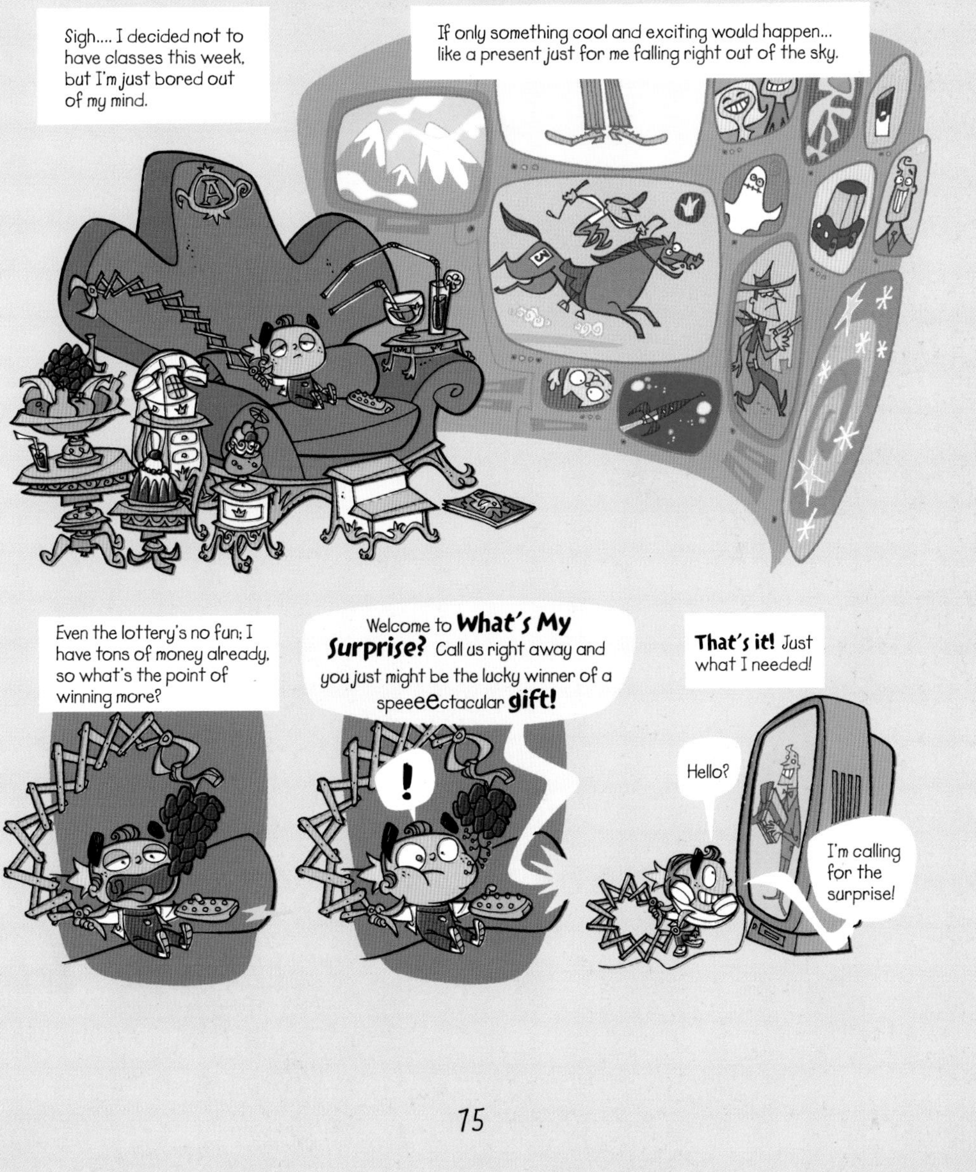

Sigh.... I decided not to have classes this week, but I'm just bored out of my mind.
If only something cool and exciting would happen... like a present just for me falling right out of the sky.
Even the lottery's no fun; I have tons of money already, so what's the point of winning more?
Welcome to **What's My Surprise?** Call us right away and you just might be the lucky winner of a speeeeectacular **gift!**
!
That's it! Just what I needed!
Hello?
I'm calling for the surprise!

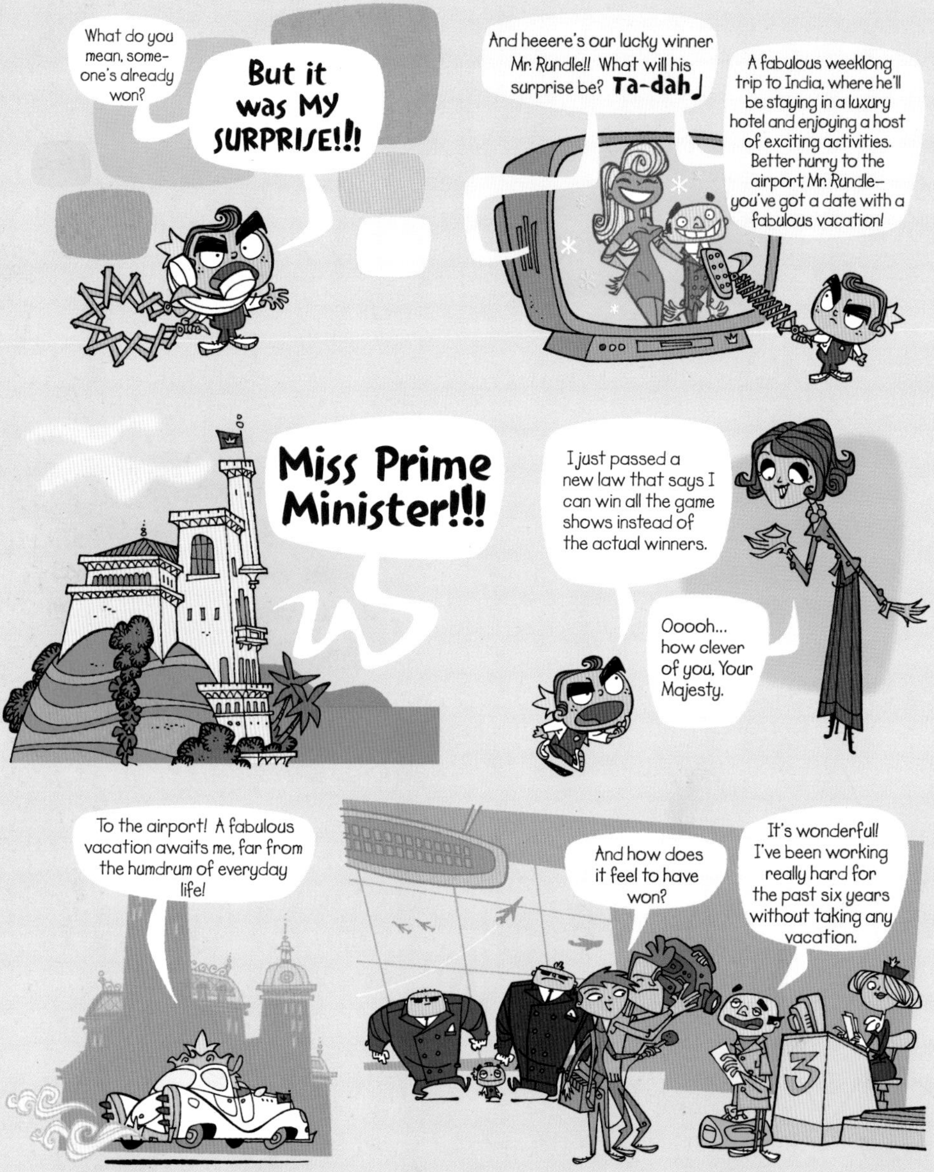
What do you mean, some-one's already won?
But it was MY SURPRISE!!!
And heeere's our lucky winner Mr. Rundle!! What will his surprise be? Ta-dah!
A fabulous weeklong trip to India, where he'll be staying in a luxury hotel and enjoying a host of exciting activities. Better hurry to the airport, Mr. Rundle— you've got a date with a fabulous vacation!
Miss Prime Minister!!!
I just passed a new law that says I can win all the game shows instead of the actual winners.
Ooooh... how clever of you, Your Majesty.
To the airport! A fabulous vacation awaits me, far from the humdrum of everyday life!
And how does it feel to have won?
It's wonderful! I've been working really hard for the past six years without taking any vacation.
3

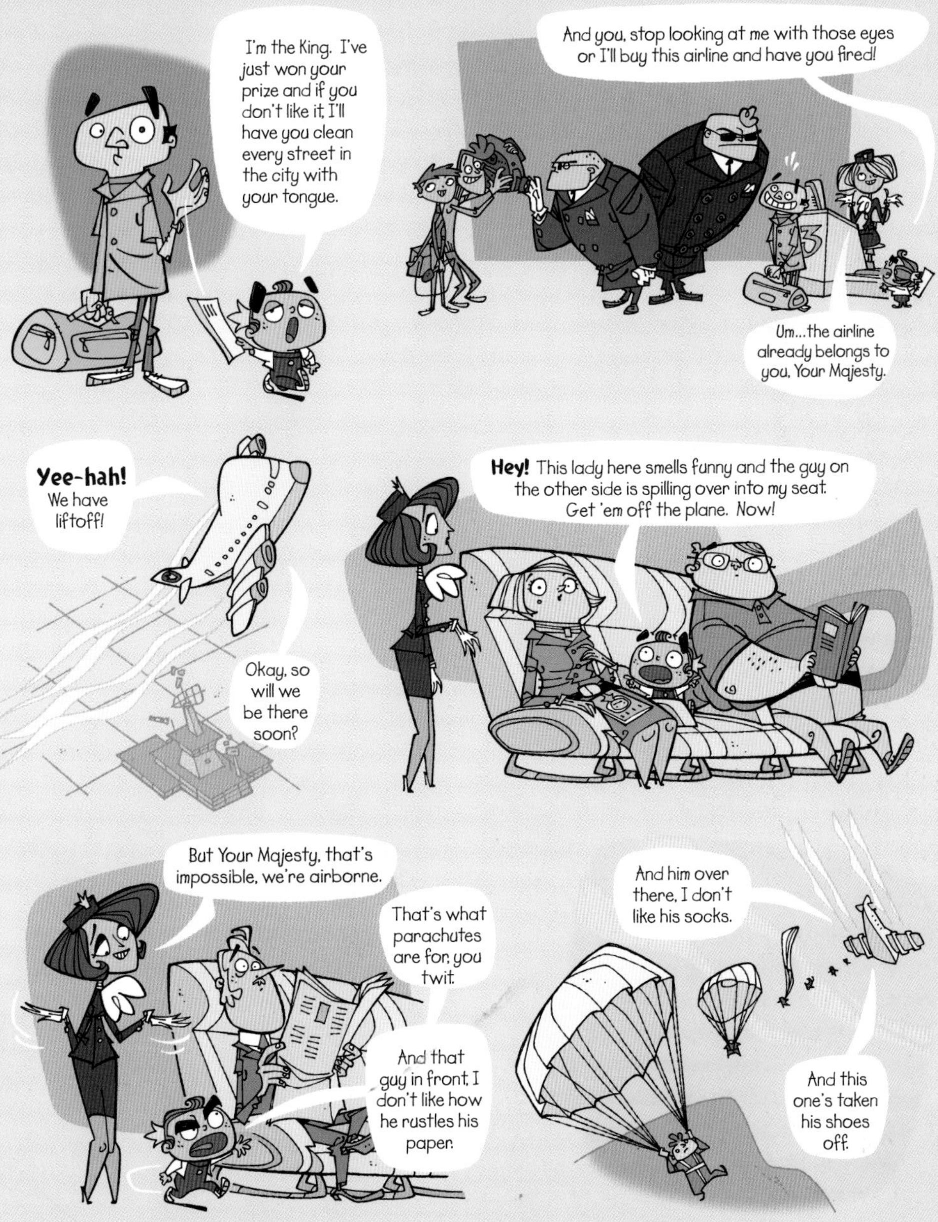
I'm the King. I've just won your prize and if you don't like it, I'll have you clean every street in the city with your tongue.
And you, stop looking at me with those eyes or I'll buy this airline and have you fired!
Um...the airline already belongs to you, Your Majesty.
Yee-hah! We have liftoff!
Okay, so will we be there soon?
Hey! This lady here smells funny and the guy on the other side is spilling over into my seat. Get 'em off the plane. Now!
But Your Majesty, that's impossible, we're airborne.
That's what parachutes are for, you twit.
And that guy in front, I don't like how he rustles his paper.
And him over there, I don't like his socks.
And this one's taken his shoes off.

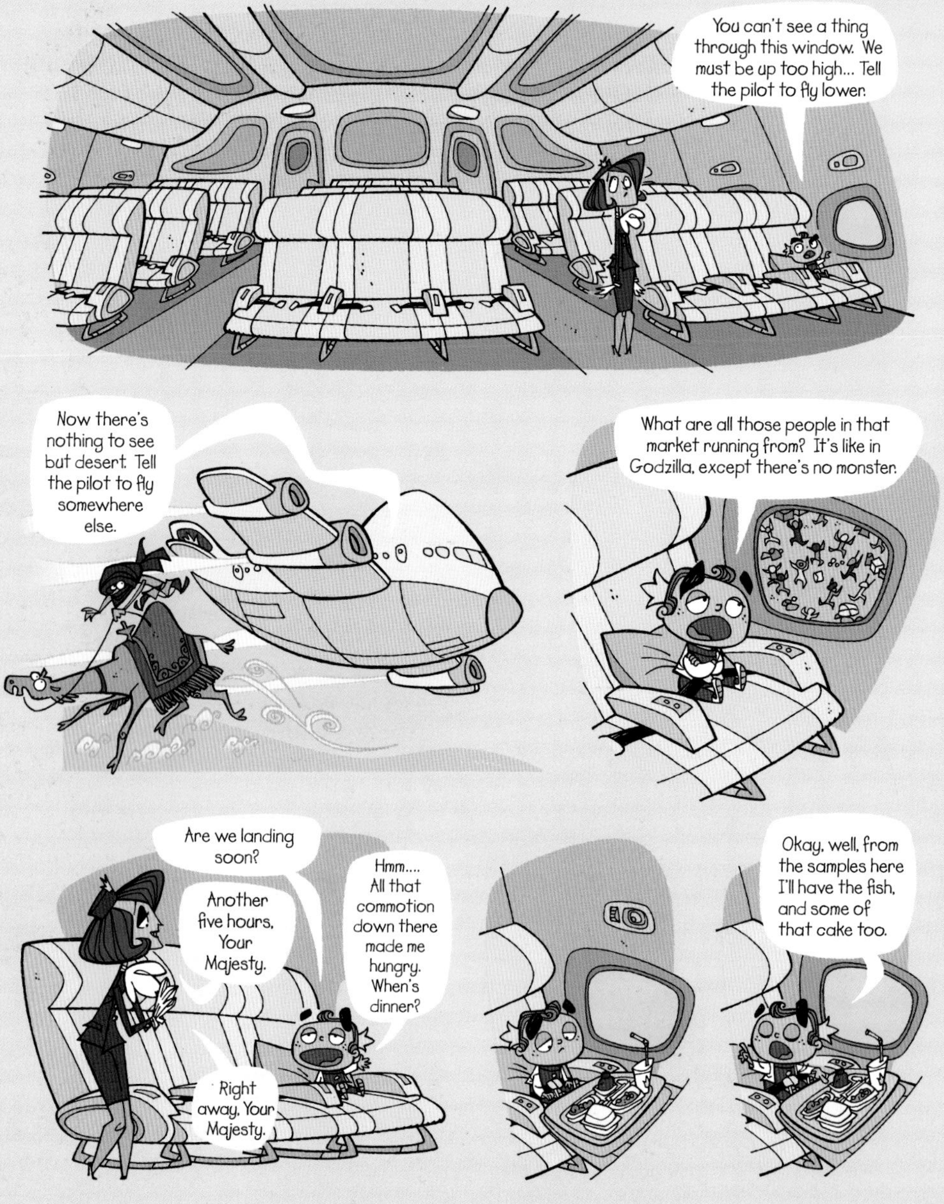

You can't see a thing through this window. We must be up too high... Tell the pilot to fly lower.
Now there's nothing to see but desert. Tell the pilot to fly somewhere else.
What are all those people in that market running from? It's like in Godzilla, except there's no monster.
Are we landing soon?
Another five hours, Your Majesty.
Hmm.... All that commotion down there made me hungry. When's dinner?
Right away, Your Majesty.
Okay, well, from the samples here I'll have the fish, and some of that cake too.

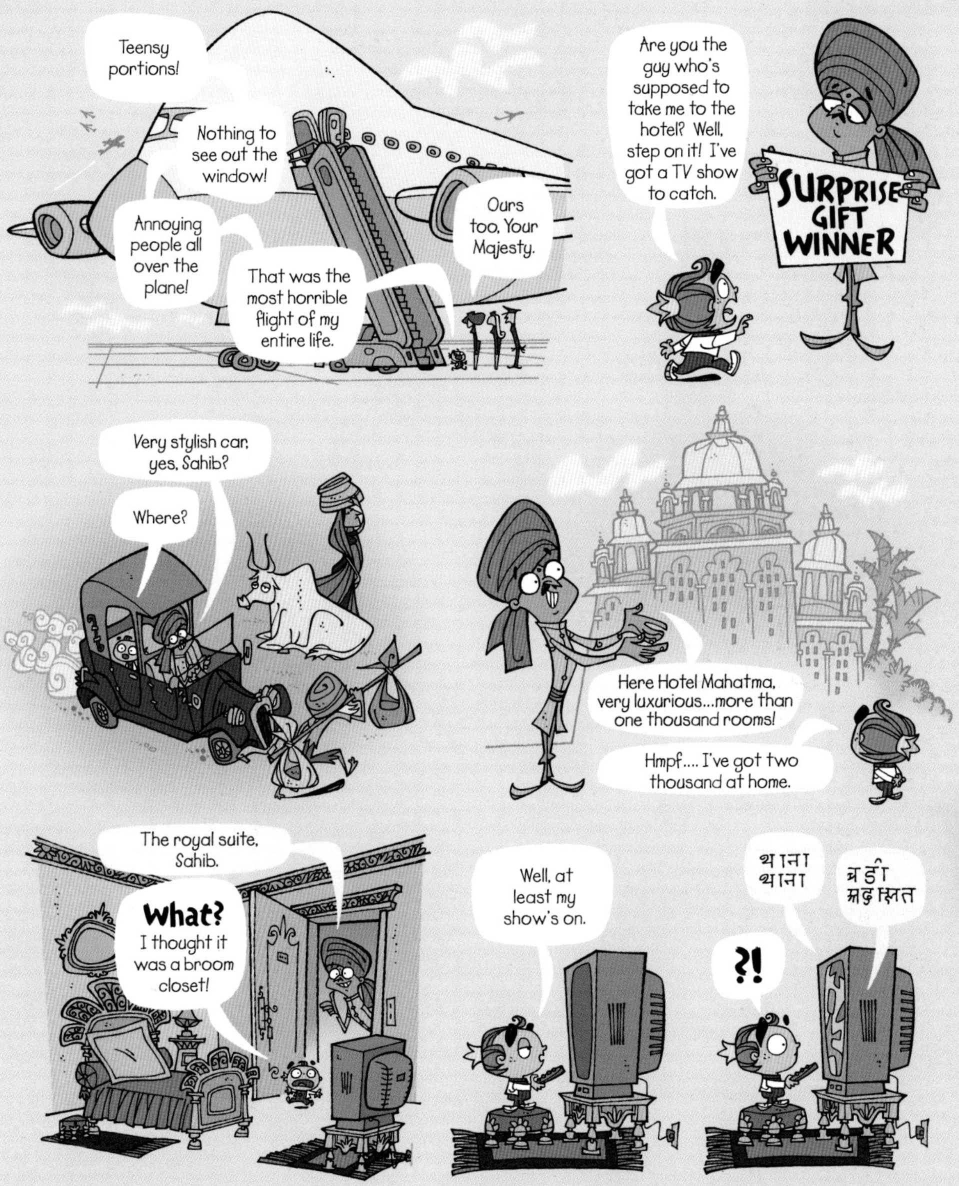
Teensy portions!
Nothing to see out the window!
Annoying people all over the plane!
That was the most horrible flight of my entire life.
Ours too, Your Majesty.
Are you the guy who's supposed to take me to the hotel? Well, step on it! I've got a TV show to catch.
SURPRISE GIFT WINNER
Very stylish car, yes, Sahib?
Where?
Here Hotel Mahatma, very luxurious...more than one thousand rooms!
Hmpf.... I've got two thousand at home.
The royal suite, Sahib.
What? I thought it was a broom closet!
Well, at least my show's on.
?!

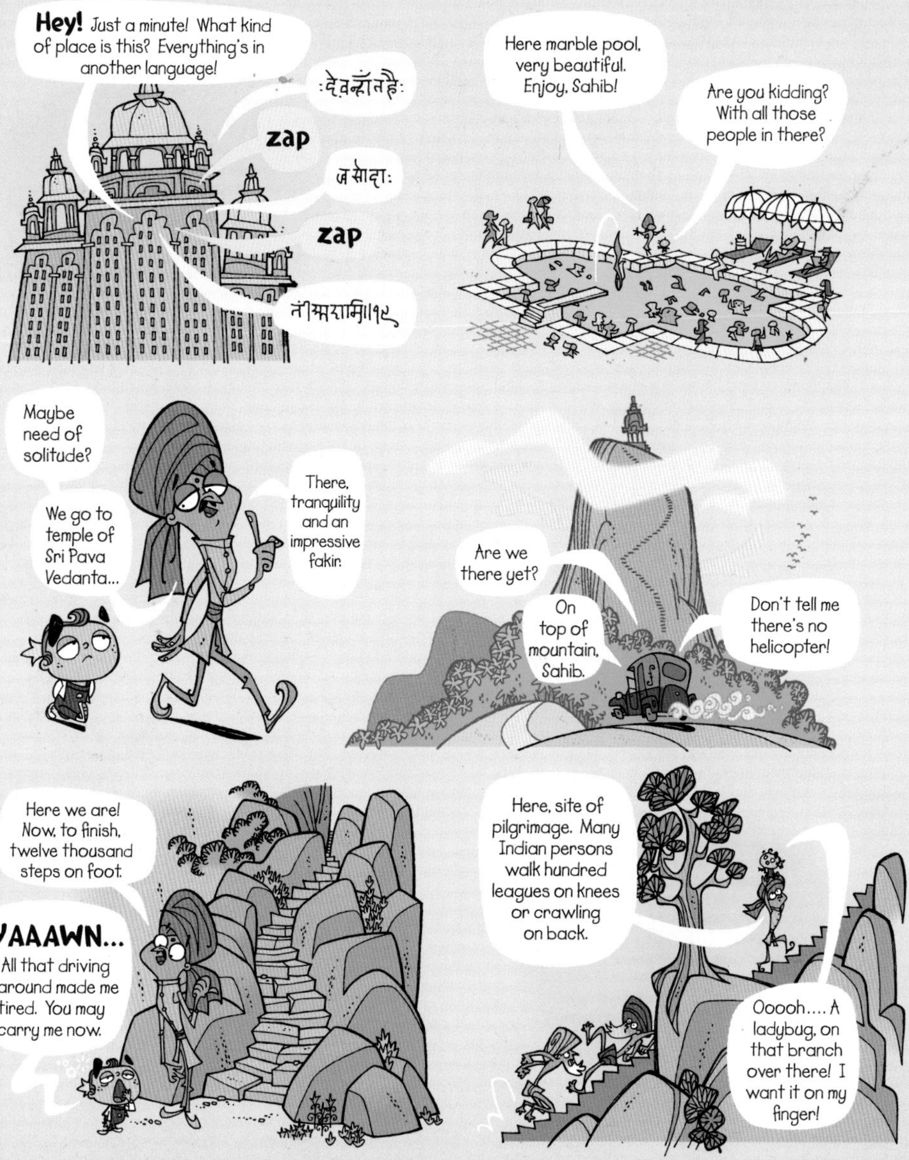
Hey! Just a minute! What kind of place is this? Everything's in another language!
:देवन्हाँतहै:
zap
जसोदा:
zap
तंीश्मरामि॥१९
Here marble pool, very beautiful. Enjoy, Sahib!
Are you kidding? With all those people in there?
Maybe need of solitude?
We go to temple of Sri Pava Vedanta...
There, tranquility and an impressive fakir.
Are we there yet?
On top of mountain, Sahib.
Don't tell me there's no helicopter!
Here we are! Now, to finish, twelve thousand steps on foot.
YAAAWN...
All that driving around made me tired. You may carry me now.
Here, site of pilgrimage. Many Indian persons walk hundred leagues on knees or crawling on back.
Ooooh.... A ladybug, on that branch over there! I want it on my finger!

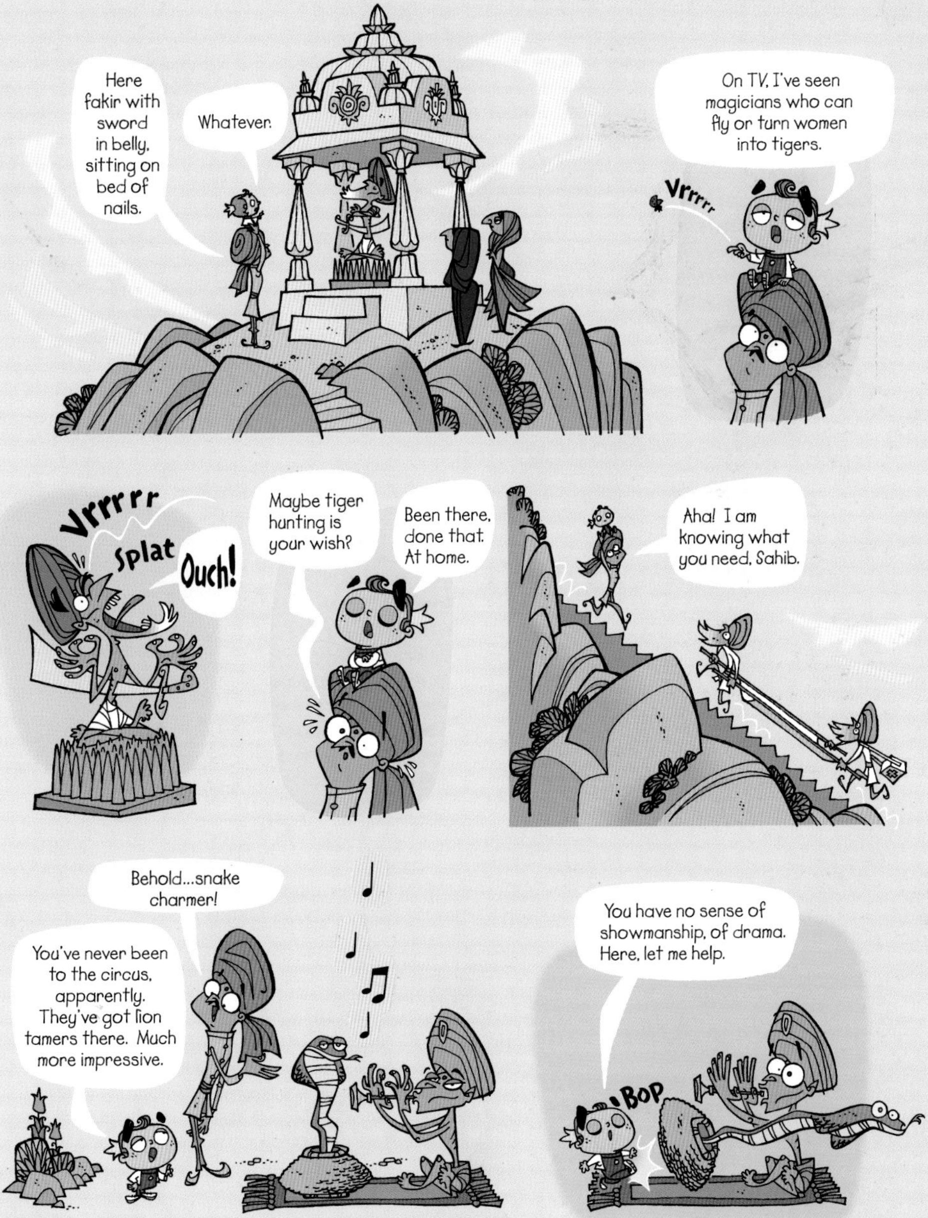
Here fakir with sword in belly, sitting on bed of nails.
Whatever.
On TV, I've seen magicians who can fly or turn women into tigers.
Vrrrrr
Vrrrrr
Splat
Ouch!
Maybe tiger hunting is your wish?
Been there, done that. At home.
Aha! I am knowing what you need, Sahib.
Behold...snake charmer!
You've never been to the circus, apparently. They've got lion tamers there. Much more impressive.
You have no sense of showmanship, of drama. Here, let me help.
BOP

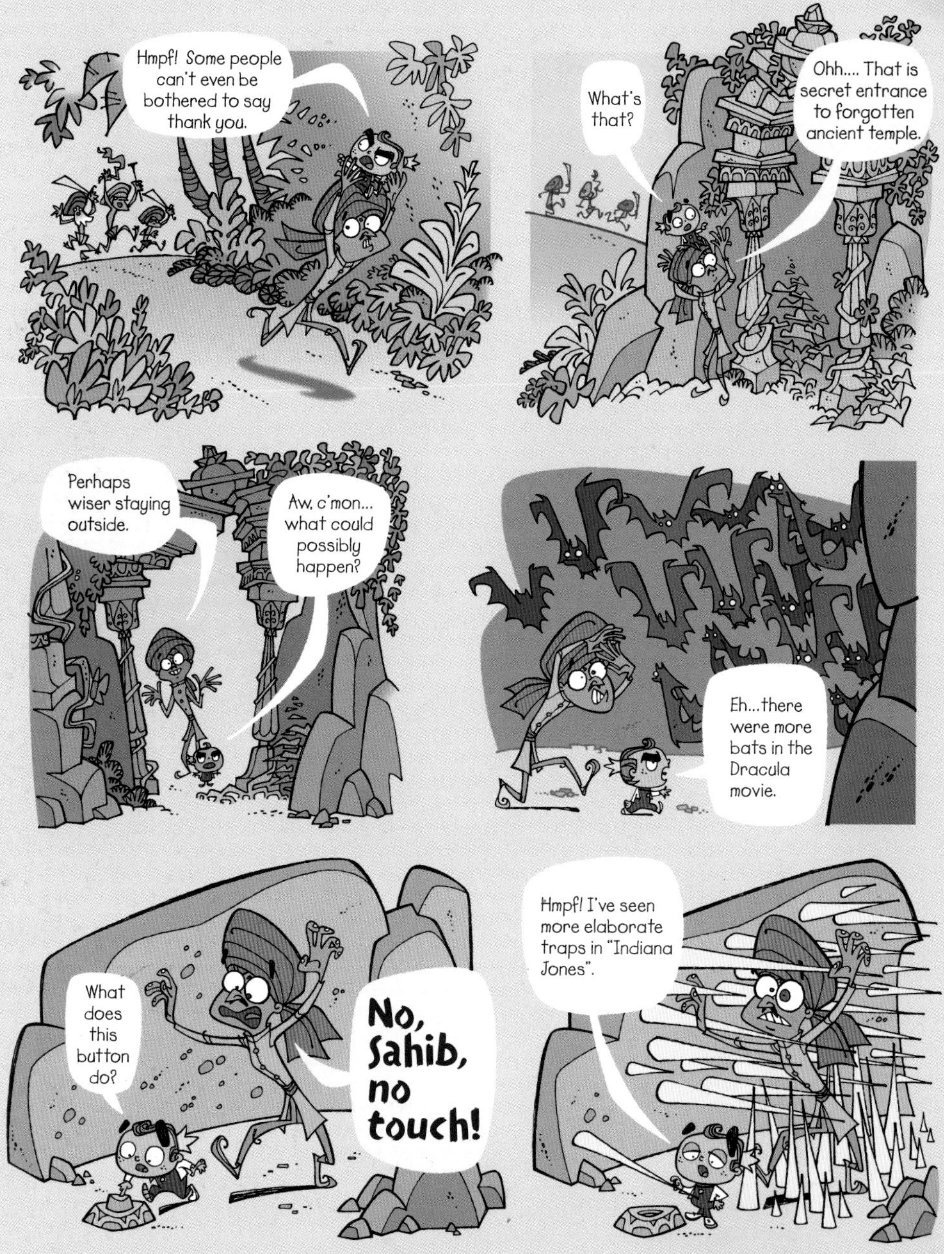
Hmpf! Some people can't even be bothered to say thank you.
What's that?
Ohh.... That is secret entrance to forgotten ancient temple.
Perhaps wiser staying outside.
Aw, c'mon... what could possibly happen?
Eh...there were more bats in the Dracula movie.
What does this button do?
No, Sahib, no touch!
Hmpf! I've seen more elaborate traps in "Indiana Jones".

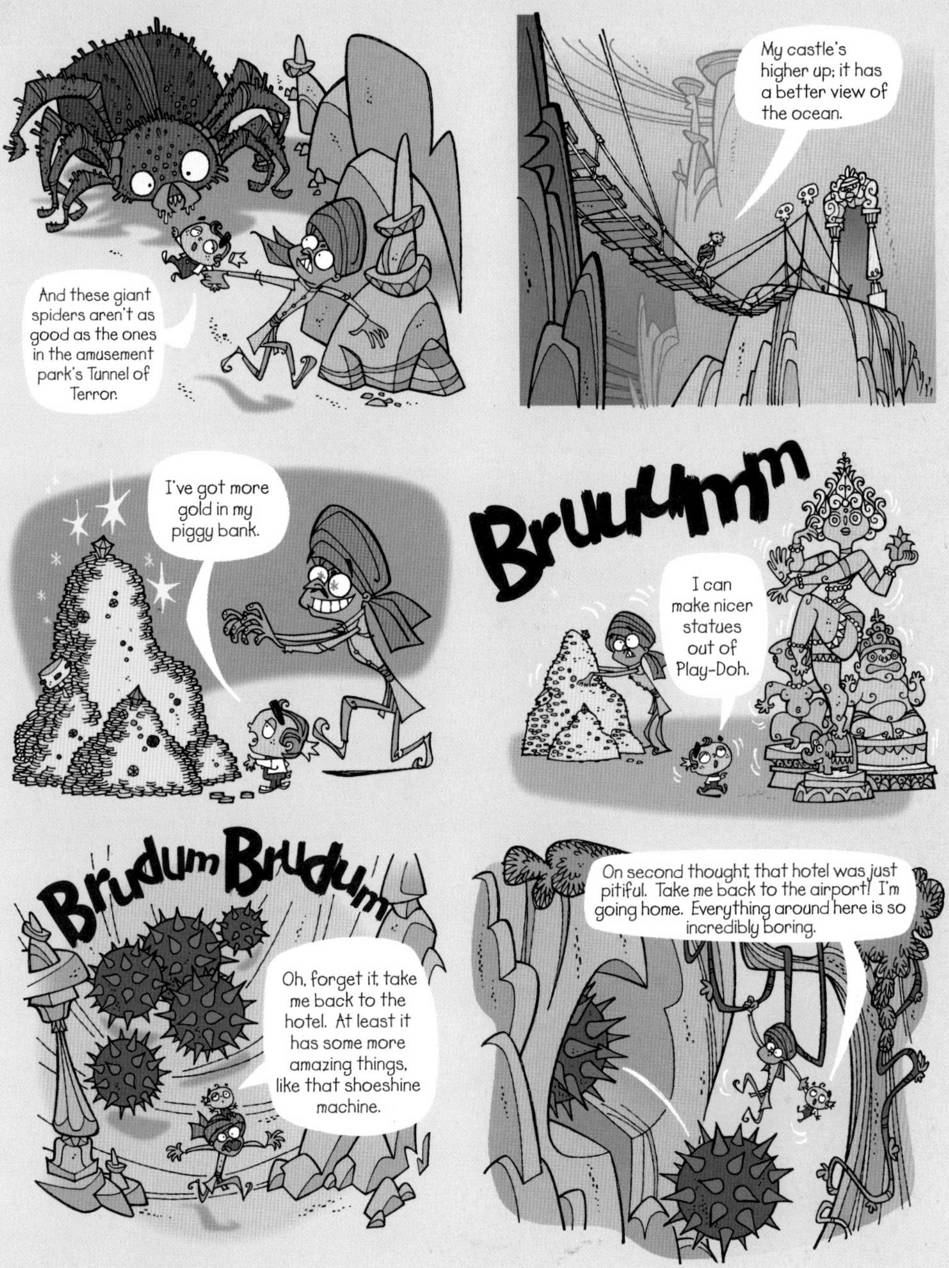
And these giant spiders aren't as good as the ones in the amusement park's Tunnel of Terror.
My castle's higher up; it has a better view of the ocean.
I've got more gold in my piggy bank.
Bruuumm
I can make nicer statues out of Play-Doh.
Brudum Brudum
Oh, forget it, take me back to the hotel. At least it has some more amazing things, like that shoeshine machine.
On second thought, that hotel was just pitiful. Take me back to the airport! I'm going home. Everything around here is so incredibly boring.

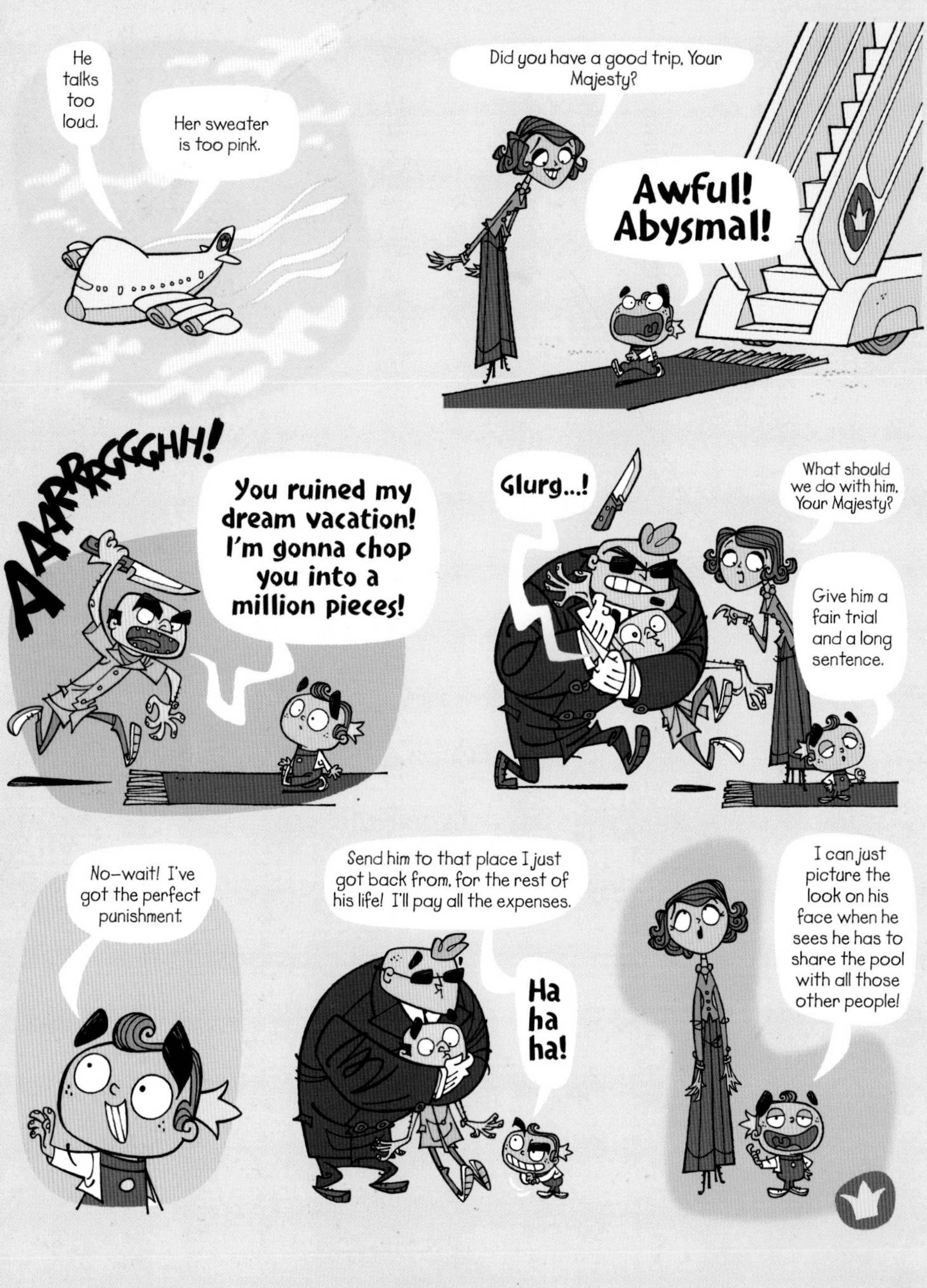
He talks too loud.
Her sweater is too pink.
Did you have a good trip, Your Majesty?
Awful! Abysmal!
AARRRGGHH!
You ruined my dream vacation! I'm gonna chop you into a million pieces!
Glurg...!
What should we do with him, Your Majesty?
Give him a fair trial and a long sentence.
No—wait! I've got the perfect punishment.
Send him to that place I just got back from, for the rest of his life! I'll pay all the expenses.
Ha ha ha!
I can just picture the look on his face when he sees he has to share the pool with all those other people!

A Routine Investigation

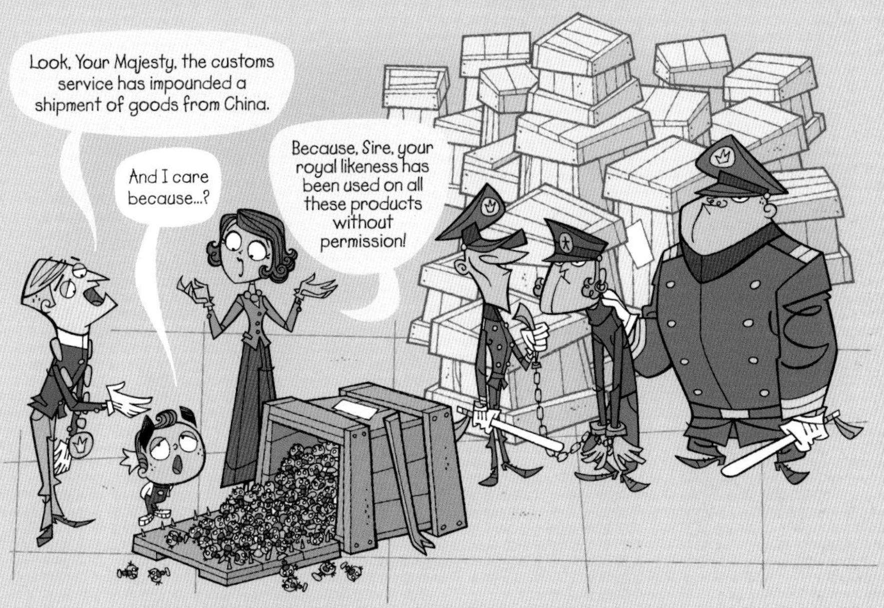

Look, Your Majesty, the customs service has impounded a shipment of goods from China.
And I care because...?
Because, Sire, your royal likeness has been used on all these products without permission!

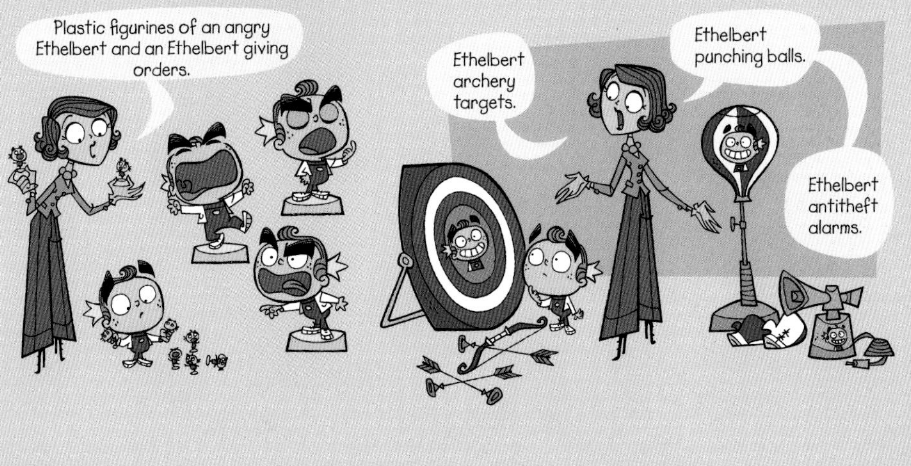

Plastic figurines of an angry Ethelbert and an Ethelbert giving orders.
Ethelbert archery targets.
Ethelbert punching balls.
Ethelbert antitheft alarms.

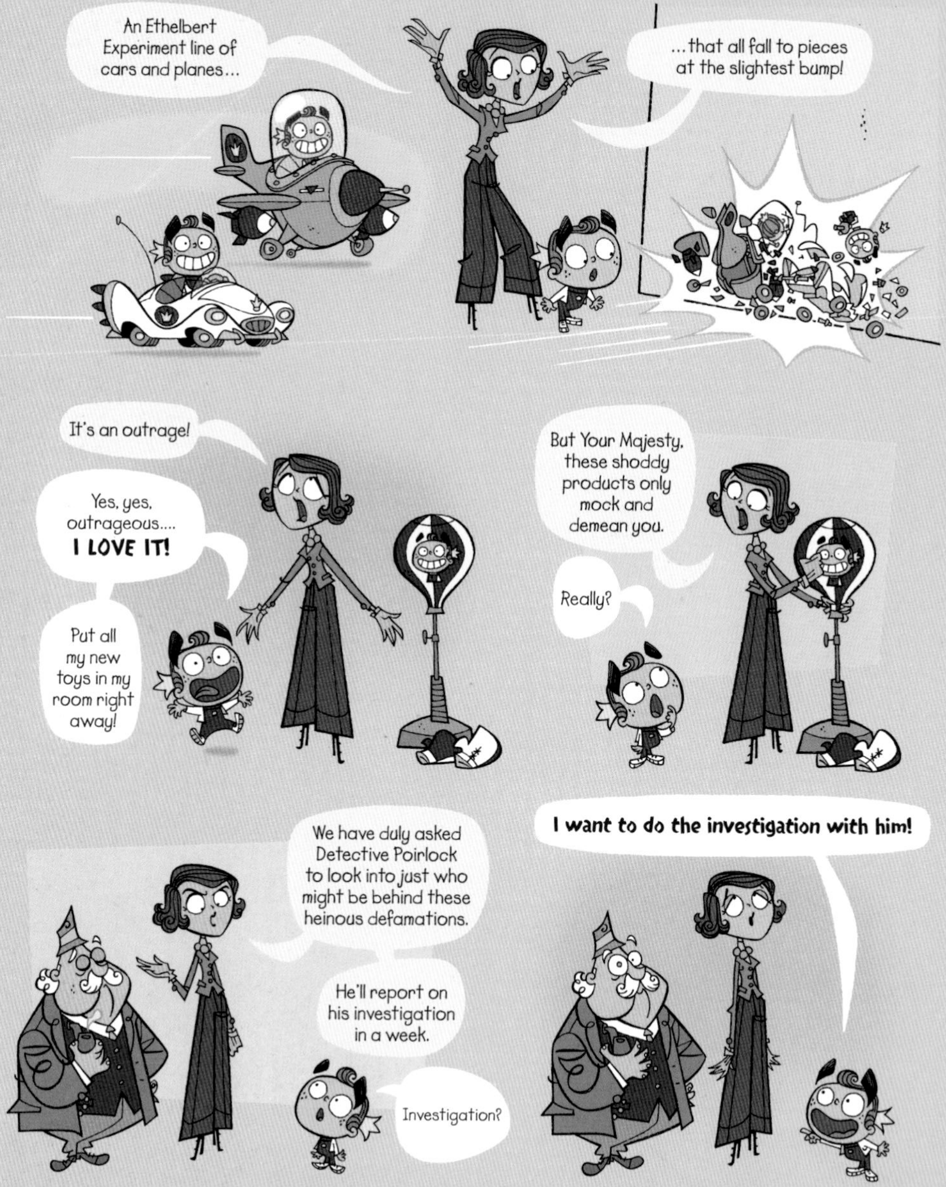
An Ethelbert Experiment line of cars and planes...
...that all fall to pieces at the slightest bump!
It's an outrage!
Yes, yes, outrageous.... I LOVE IT!
Put all my new toys in my room right away!
But Your Majesty, these shoddy products only mock and demean you.
Really?
We have duly asked Detective Poirlock to look into just who might be behind these heinous defamations.
He'll report on his investigation in a week.
Investigation?
I want to do the investigation with him!

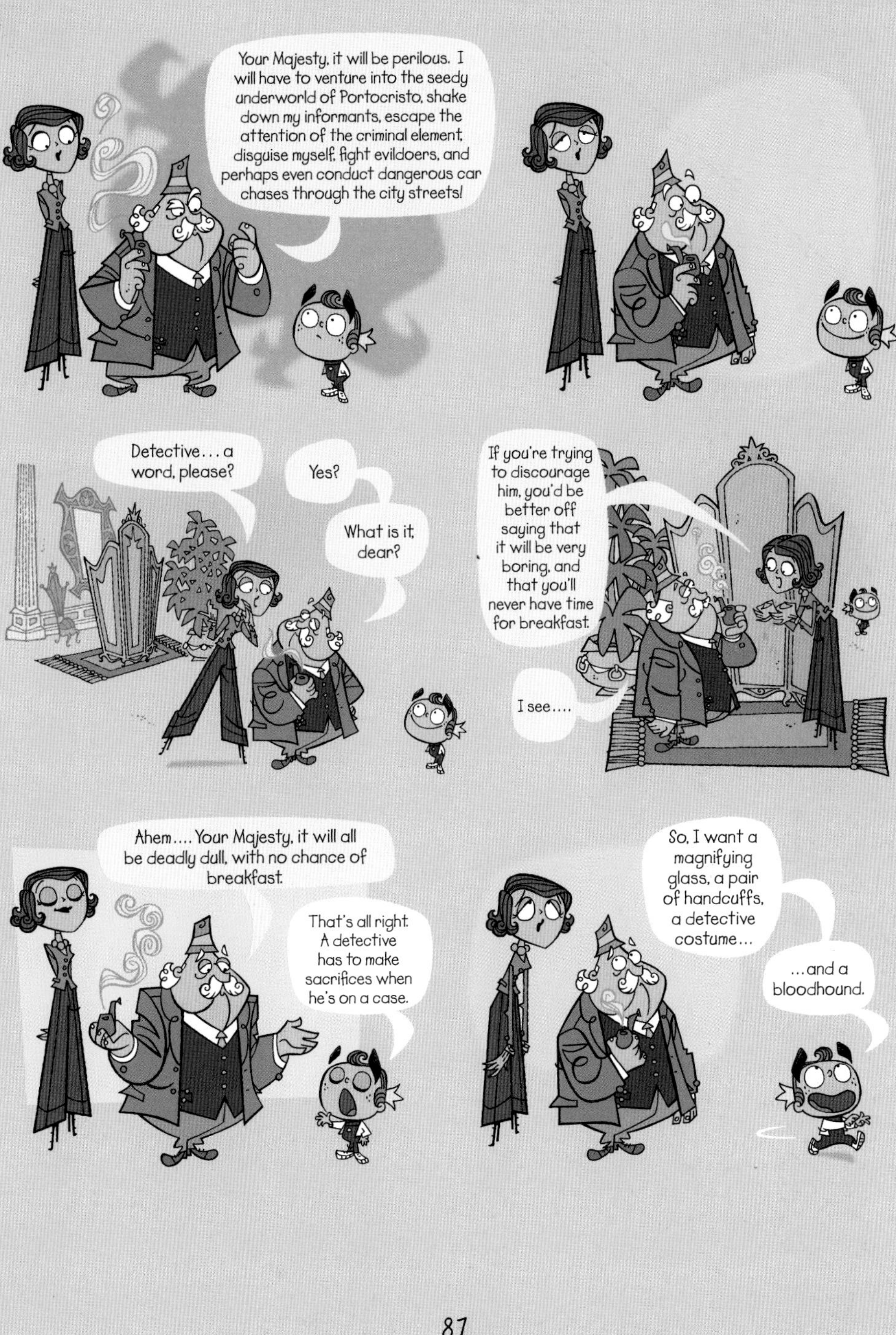

Your Majesty, it will be perilous. I will have to venture into the seedy underworld of Portocristo, shake down my informants, escape the attention of the criminal element, disguise myself, fight evildoers, and perhaps even conduct dangerous car chases through the city streets!
Detective . . . a word, please?
Yes?
What is it, dear?
If you're trying to discourage him, you'd be better off saying that it will be very boring, and that you'll never have time for breakfast.
I see....
Ahem.... Your Majesty, it will all be deadly dull, with no chance of breakfast.
That's all right. A detective has to make sacrifices when he's on a case.
So, I want a magnifying glass, a pair of handcuffs, a detective costume...
...and a bloodhound.

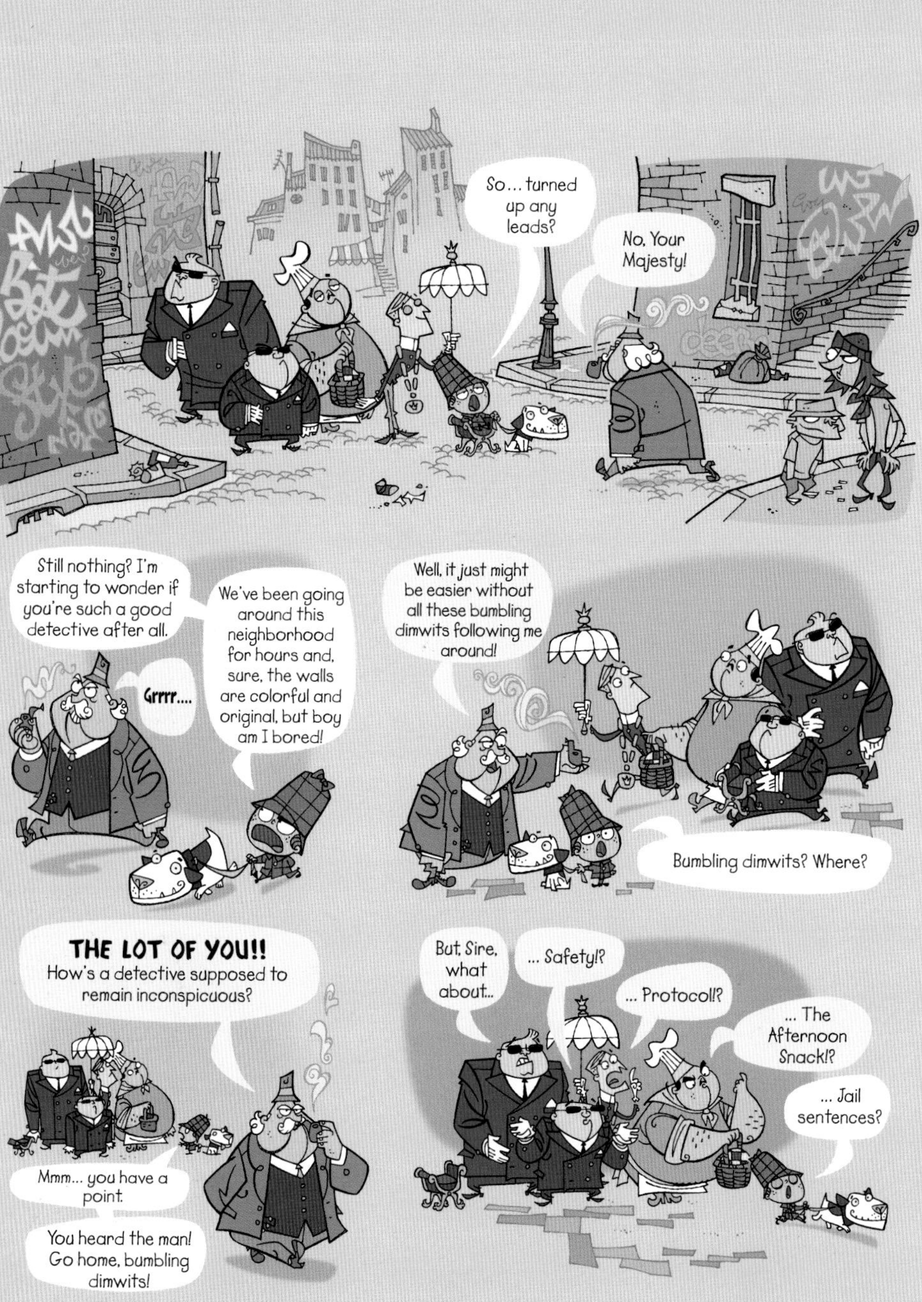

So... turned up any leads?
No, Your Majesty!
Still nothing? I'm starting to wonder if you're such a good detective after all.
Grrrr....
We've been going around this neighborhood for hours and, sure, the walls are colorful and original, but boy am I bored!
Well, it just might be easier without all these bumbling dimwits following me around!
Bumbling dimwits? Where?
THE LOT OF YOU!!
How's a detective supposed to remain inconspicuous?
Mmm... you have a point.
You heard the man! Go home, bumbling dimwits!
But, Sire, what about...
... Safety!?
... Protocol!?
... The Afternoon Snack!?
... Jail sentences?

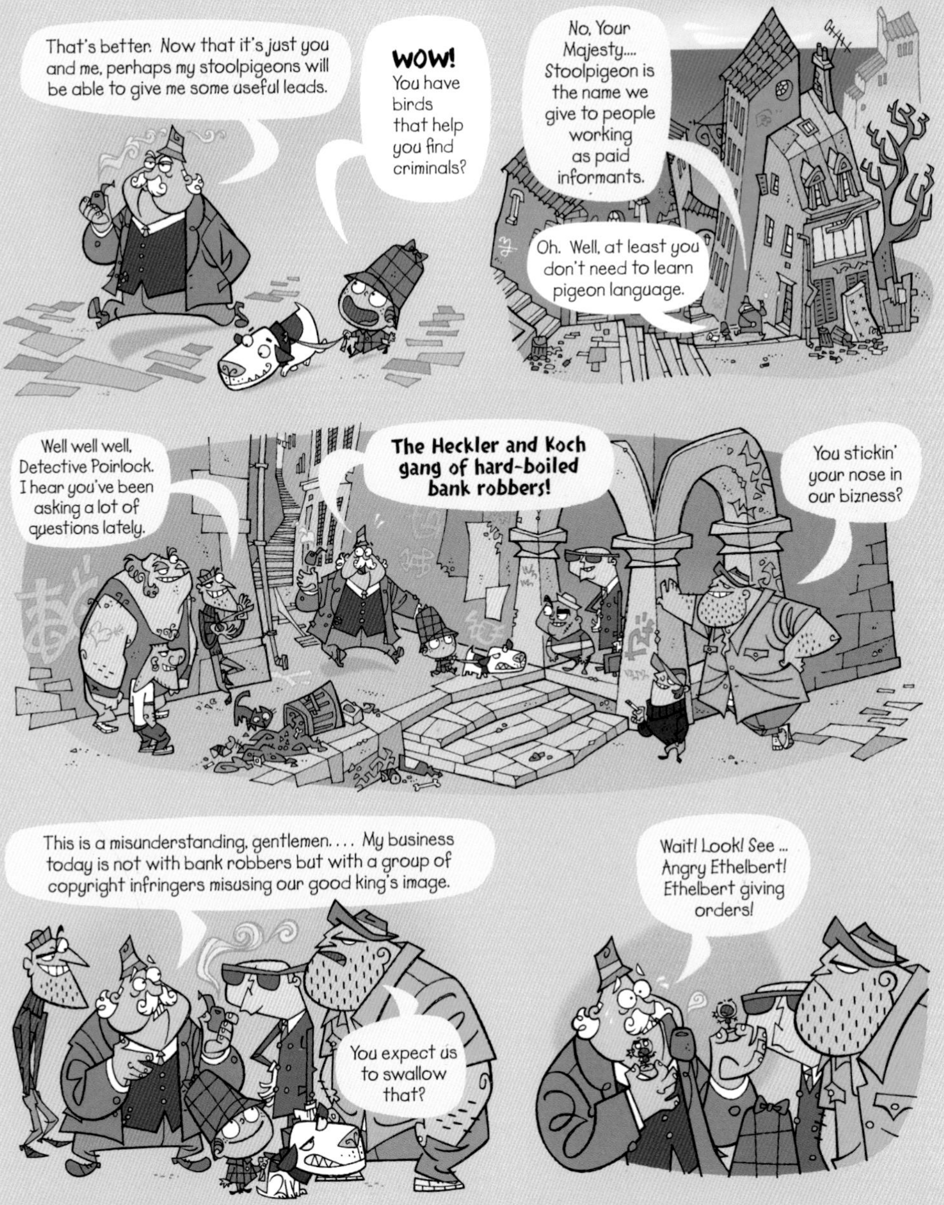
That's better. Now that it's just you and me, perhaps my stoolpigeons will be able to give me some useful leads.
WOW! You have birds that help you find criminals?
No, Your Majesty.... Stoolpigeon is the name we give to people working as paid informants.
Oh. Well, at least you don't need to learn pigeon language.
Well well well, Detective Poirlock. I hear you've been asking a lot of questions lately.
The Heckler and Koch gang of hard-boiled bank robbers!
You stickin' your nose in our bizness?
This is a misunderstanding, gentlemen.... My business today is not with bank robbers but with a group of copyright infringers misusing our good king's image.
You expect us to swallow that?
Wait! Look! See ... Angry Ethelbert! Ethelbert giving orders!

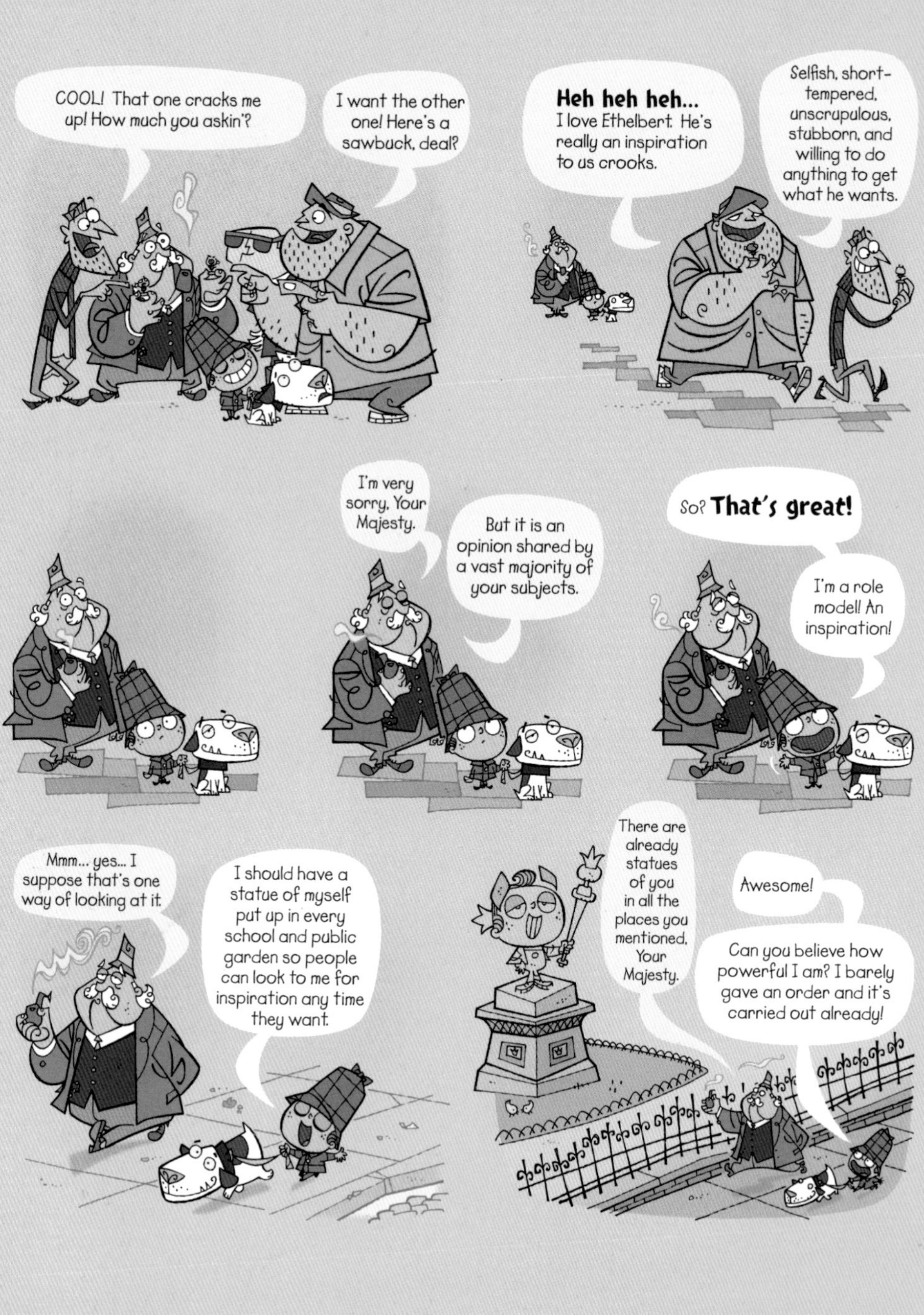
COOL! That one cracks me up! How much you askin'?
I want the other one! Here's a sawbuck, deal?
Heh heh heh... I love Ethelbert. He's really an inspiration to us crooks.
Selfish, short-tempered, unscrupulous, stubborn, and willing to do anything to get what he wants.
I'm very sorry, Your Majesty.
But it is an opinion shared by a vast majority of your subjects.
So? **That's great!**
I'm a role model! An inspiration!
Mmm... yes... I suppose that's one way of looking at it.
I should have a statue of myself put up in every school and public garden so people can look to me for inspiration any time they want.
There are already statues of you in all the places you mentioned, Your Majesty.
Awesome!
Can you believe how powerful I am? I barely gave an order and it's carried out already!

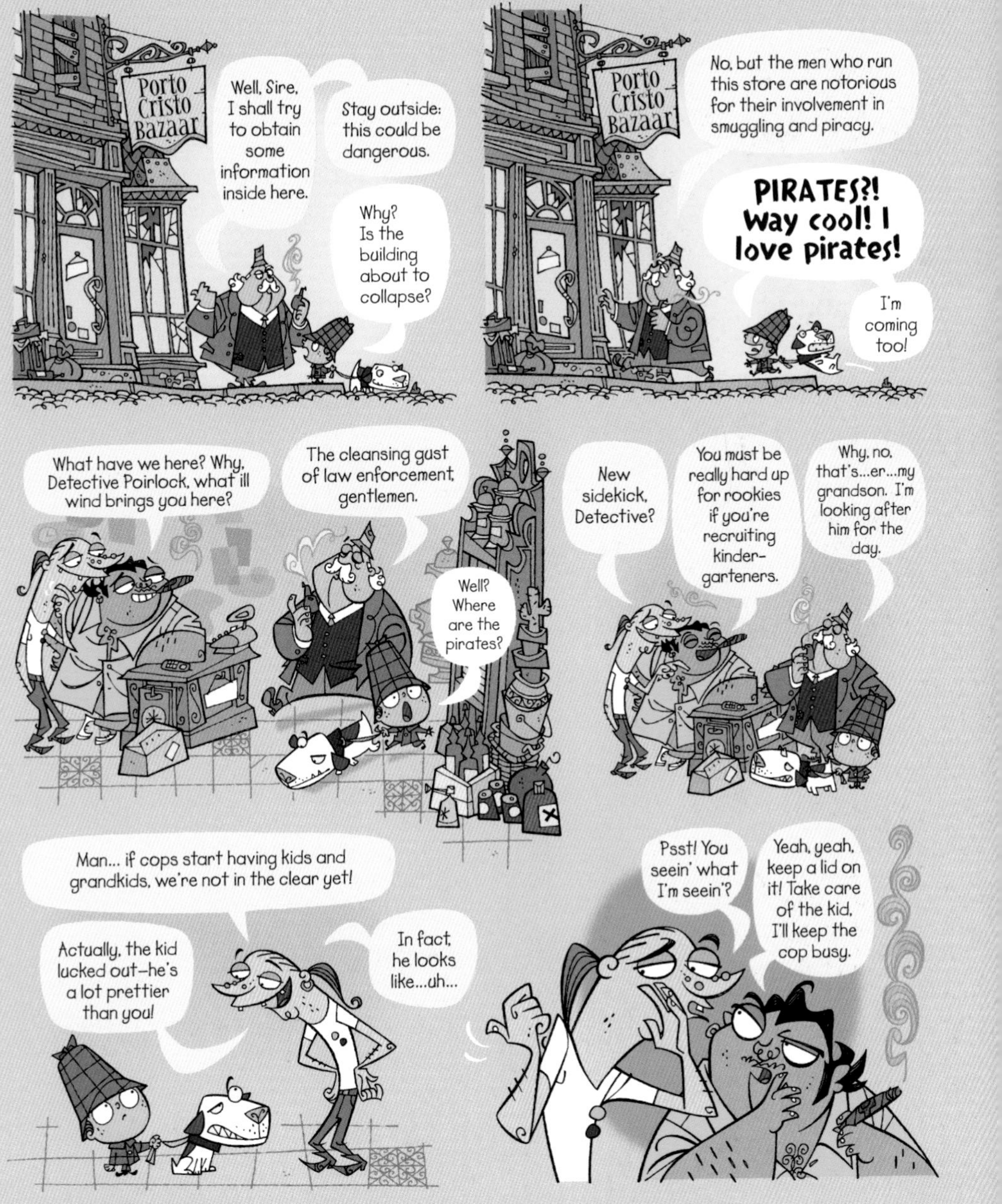
Porto Cristo Bazaar
Well, Sire, I shall try to obtain some information inside here.
Stay outside: this could be dangerous.
Why? Is the building about to collapse?
Porto Cristo Bazaar
No, but the men who run this store are notorious for their involvement in smuggling and piracy.
PIRATES?! Way cool! I love pirates!
I'm coming too!
What have we here? Why, Detective Poirlock, what ill wind brings you here?
The cleansing gust of law enforcement, gentlemen.
Well? Where are the pirates?
New sidekick, Detective?
You must be really hard up for rookies if you're recruiting kinder-garteners.
Why, no, that's...er...my grandson. I'm looking after him for the day.
Man... if cops start having kids and grandkids, we're not in the clear yet!
In fact, he looks like...uh...
Actually, the kid lucked out—he's a lot prettier than you!
Psst! You seein' what I'm seein'?
Yeah, yeah, keep a lid on it! Take care of the kid, I'll keep the cop busy.

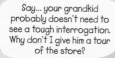

Say... your grandkid probably doesn't need to see a tough interrogation. Why don't I give him a tour of the store?

Hmmm ... the one time that you're a bit considerate, I'm not going to say no.

So how's it hanging, kiddo?

What do you wanna be when you grow up?

Bigger and richer than *my* cousin!

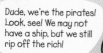

Ha ha ha... kids, man! Gotta love 'em!

And what do you think of our good king Ethelbert?

The same as everyone. He's selfish, short-tempered, unscrupulous, stubborn, and willing to do anything to get what he wants.

Excellent! So how'd you like to pull a prank on him?

You look a lot like him and we could have a little fun.

Okay, but only if you show me where the pirates are.

Dude, we're the pirates! Look, see! We may not have a ship, but we still rip off the rich!

But what would you want with a little boy like me?

I want you to step right this way, into my secret passage.

Oh boy, I love secret passages!

92

Here, put on this Ethelbert costume!

I'm gonna snap a few pictures.

Wow! This place is great!

Are you the guys who make all the Ethelbert toys?

Yeah.... We had a little trouble with our shipment this morning, but we'll make up for it with this rockin' line of posters.

There ... push the crown back on your head a little. ... Perfect!

Just like the real McCoy!

What'll it say on the rockin' posters?

I dunno, we'll figure something out.

Why not make it a game? Like 'Can you spot the pig?' or 'Can you find the mule?'

Hey, that's great! Let me write that down ....

You got any other ideas that would go with Ethelbert?

Uh....

If you're getting toys made, you could add some exploding candy cigars!

O-kayyy... what else?

I don't know. What would I want to play with? An Ethelbert dart set.

A video game where he bosses around the entire world...

Ethelbert drums, Ethelbert whoopee cushions, an Ethelbert trumpet, Ethelbert itching powder....

93

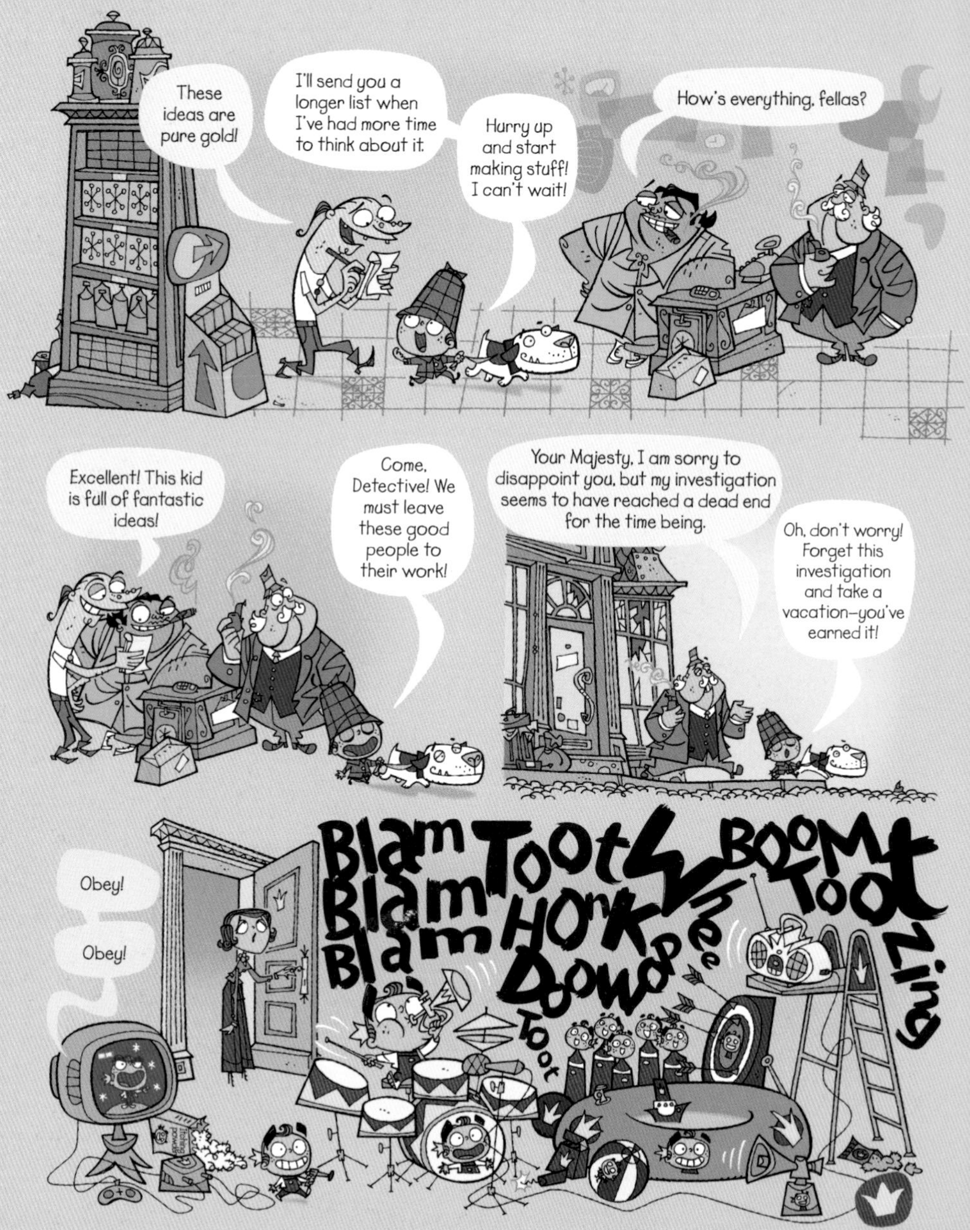
These ideas are pure gold!
I'll send you a longer list when I've had more time to think about it.
Hurry up and start making stuff! I can't wait!
How's everything, fellas?
Excellent! This kid is full of fantastic ideas!
Come, Detective! We must leave these good people to their work!
Your Majesty, I am sorry to disappoint you, but my investigation seems to have reached a dead end for the time being.
Oh, don't worry! Forget this investigation and take a vacation—you've earned it!
Obey!
Obey!
Blam Blam Blam
Toot
HONK
Doowop
Toot
Whee
BOOM
Toot
Zing

A Mountaintop Inheritance

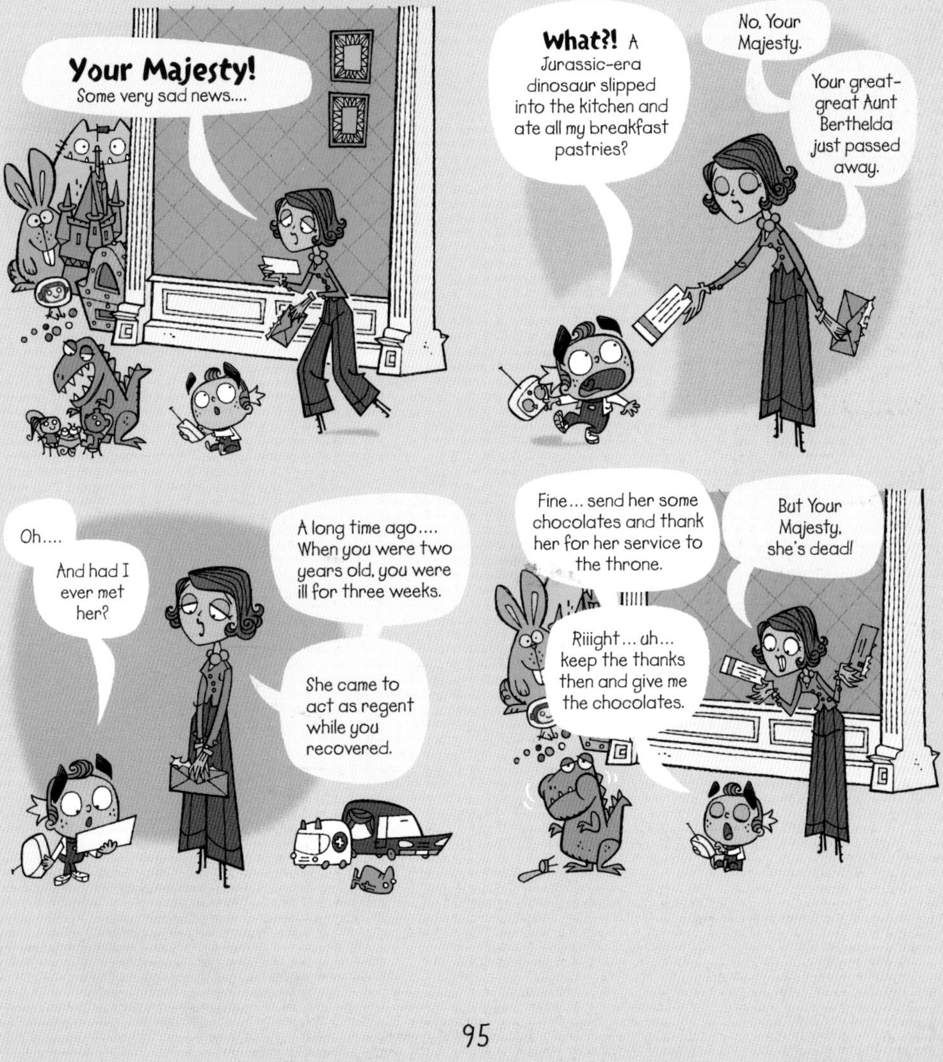

Your Majesty! Some very sad news....
What?! A Jurassic-era dinosaur slipped into the kitchen and ate all my breakfast pastries?
No, Your Majesty.
Your great-great Aunt Berthelda just passed away.
Oh....
And had I ever met her?
A long time ago.... When you were two years old, you were ill for three weeks.
She came to act as regent while you recovered.
Fine... send her some chocolates and thank her for her service to the throne.
But Your Majesty, she's dead!
Riiight... uh... keep the thanks then and give me the chocolates.

There's also the issue of her inheritance, Sire.

Who cares, let her keep her old black-and-white photos.

Her lawyer is to read her will this afternoon in her Swiss chalet.

She was fairly well off. If she's left you her wealth, you could be richer than your cousin Sigismund.

TO THE AIRPORT!! NO, TELEPORT ME THERE!!

Too long! It's taking too long!

It's this plane that's poorly designed! And there's a window missing here. Back to the hangar!

It was Your Majesty who delayed us by insisting on fitting the elephant into the plane.

Here at last! What shall we do with your elephant, Sire?

I don't need it anymore! Can we buy yetis here?

Your Majesty! Isn't that your cousin Sigismund's plane arriving?

The blackguard! I bet he's come to steal my inheritance!

96

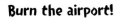

Burn the airport!

Tear down the control tower!

Rip up the tarmac!

Your Majesty, we're in Switzerland, not Portocristo.

Hurry! Quickly, to my aunt's chalet! We'll find a way to keep that idiot Sigismund away!

No! That way, Sire!

What are these car seats without cars around 'em?

They're called ski lifts, Sire. They'll take us straight up the mountain to Aunt Berthelda's.

If we cut this cable... Sigismund could never follow us then!

Unless he decided to cut it to make us fall.

Arrgghh! The thief! He's always stealing my best ideas!

Welcome to the chalet, Your Highness.

Do you have any sulfuric acid?

Only tea, Sire.

97

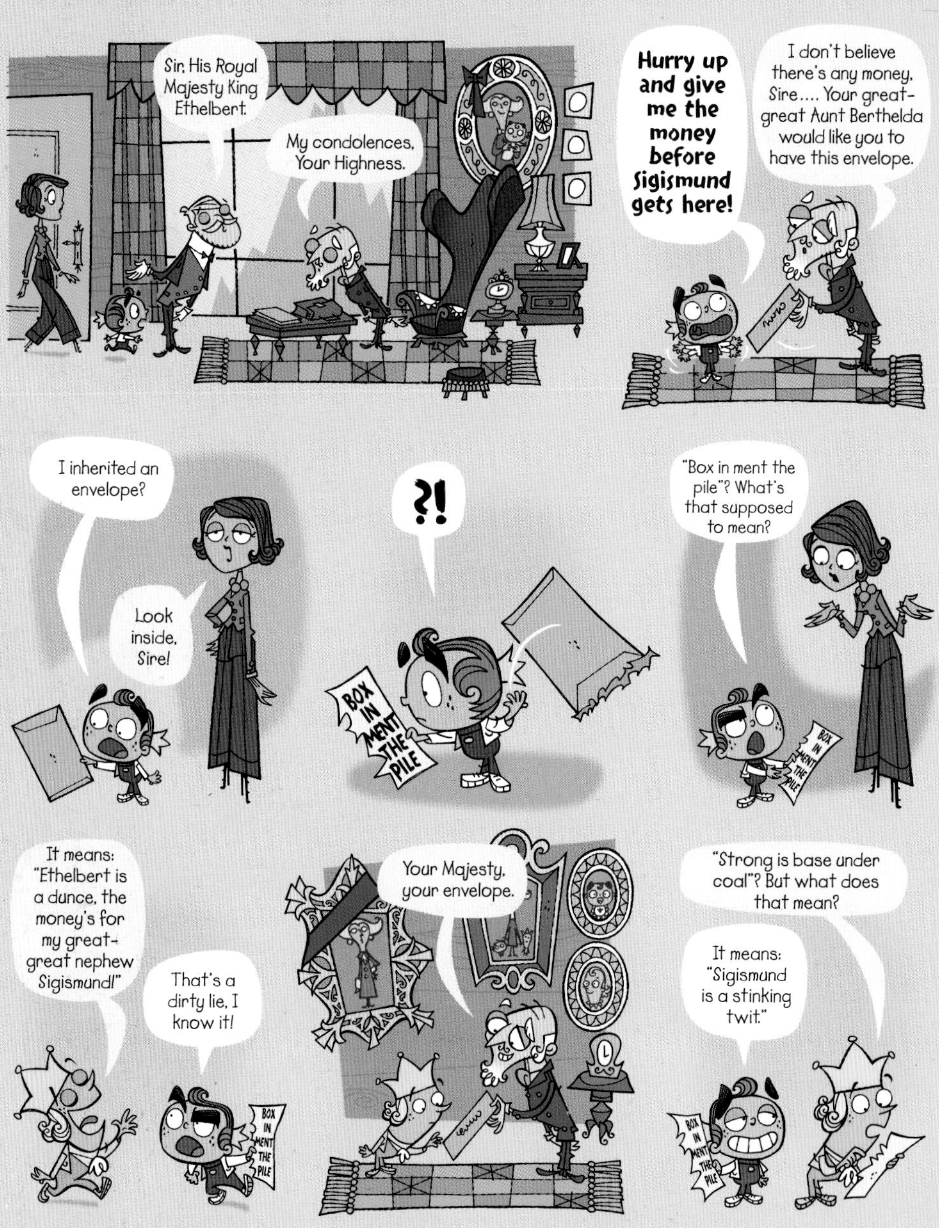
Sir, His Royal Majesty King Ethelbert.
My condolences, Your Highness.
Hurry up and give me the money before Sigismund gets here!
I don't believe there's any money, Sire.... Your great-great Aunt Berthelda would like you to have this envelope.
I inherited an envelope?
Look inside, Sire!
?!
BOX IN MENT THE PILE
"Box in ment the pile"? What's that supposed to mean?
BOX IN MENT THE PILE
It means: "Ethelbert is a dunce, the money's for my great-great nephew Sigismund!"
That's a dirty lie, I know it!
BOX IN MENT THE PILE
Your Majesty, your envelope.
"Strong is base under coal"? But what does that mean?
It means: "Sigismund is a stinking twit."
BOX IN MENT THE PILE

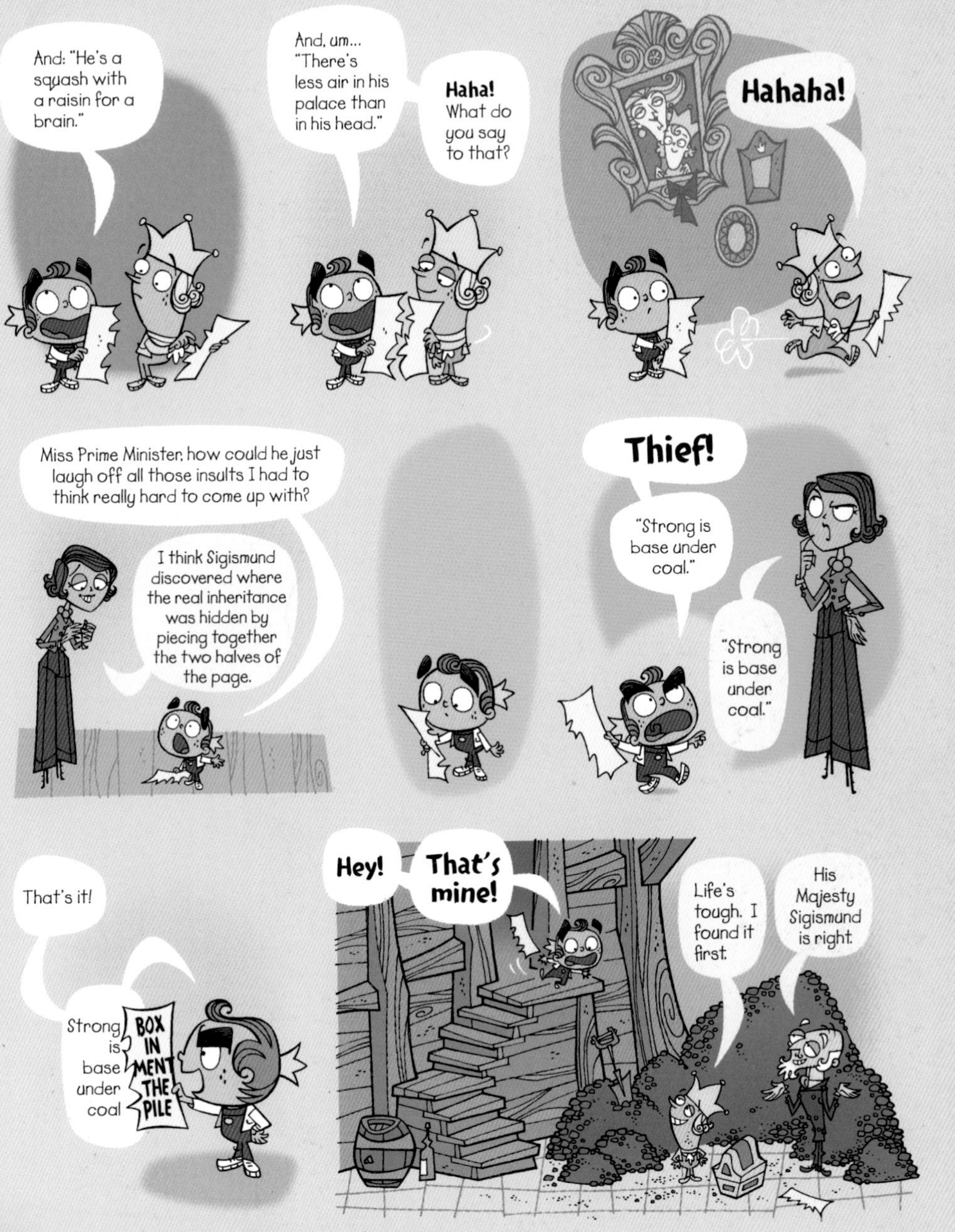

And: "He's a squash with a raisin for a brain."
And, um... "There's less air in his palace than in his head."
Haha! What do you say to that?
Hahaha!
Miss Prime Minister, how could he just laugh off all those insults I had to think really hard to come up with?
I think Sigismund discovered where the real inheritance was hidden by piecing together the two halves of the page.
Thief!
"Strong is base under coal."
"Strong is base under coal."
That's it!
Strong is base under coal
BOX IN MENT THE PILE
Hey!
That's mine!
Life's tough. I found it first.
His Majesty Sigismund is right.

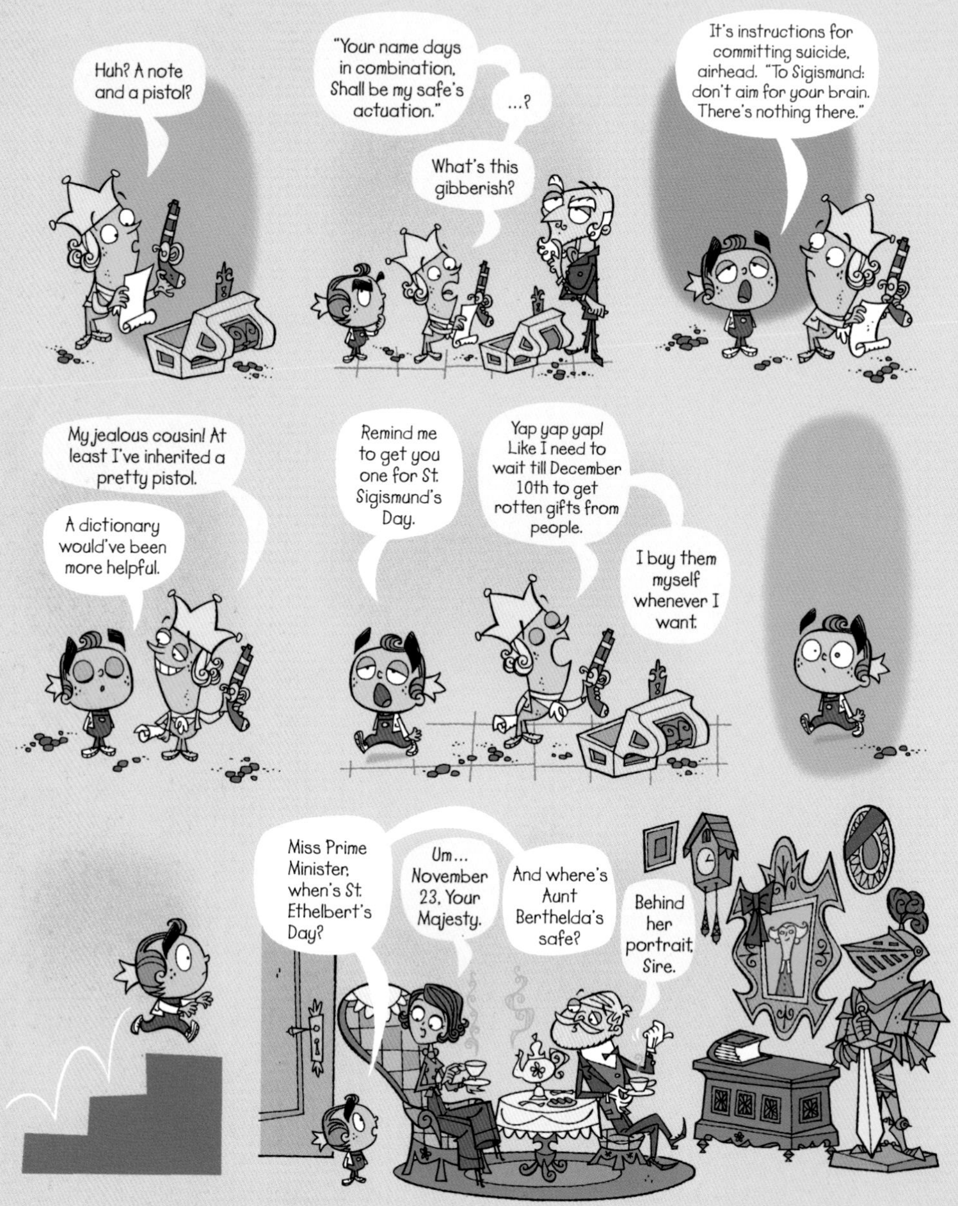
Huh? A note and a pistol?
"Your name days in combination, Shall be my safe's actuation."
...?
What's this gibberish?
It's instructions for committing suicide, airhead. "To Sigismund: don't aim for your brain. There's nothing there."
My jealous cousin! At least I've inherited a pretty pistol.
A dictionary would've been more helpful.
Remind me to get you one for St. Sigismund's Day.
Yap yap yap! Like I need to wait till December 10th to get rotten gifts from people.
I buy them myself whenever I want.
Miss Prime Minister, when's St. Ethelbert's Day?
Um... November 23, Your Majesty.
And where's Aunt Berthelda's safe?
Behind her portrait, Sire.

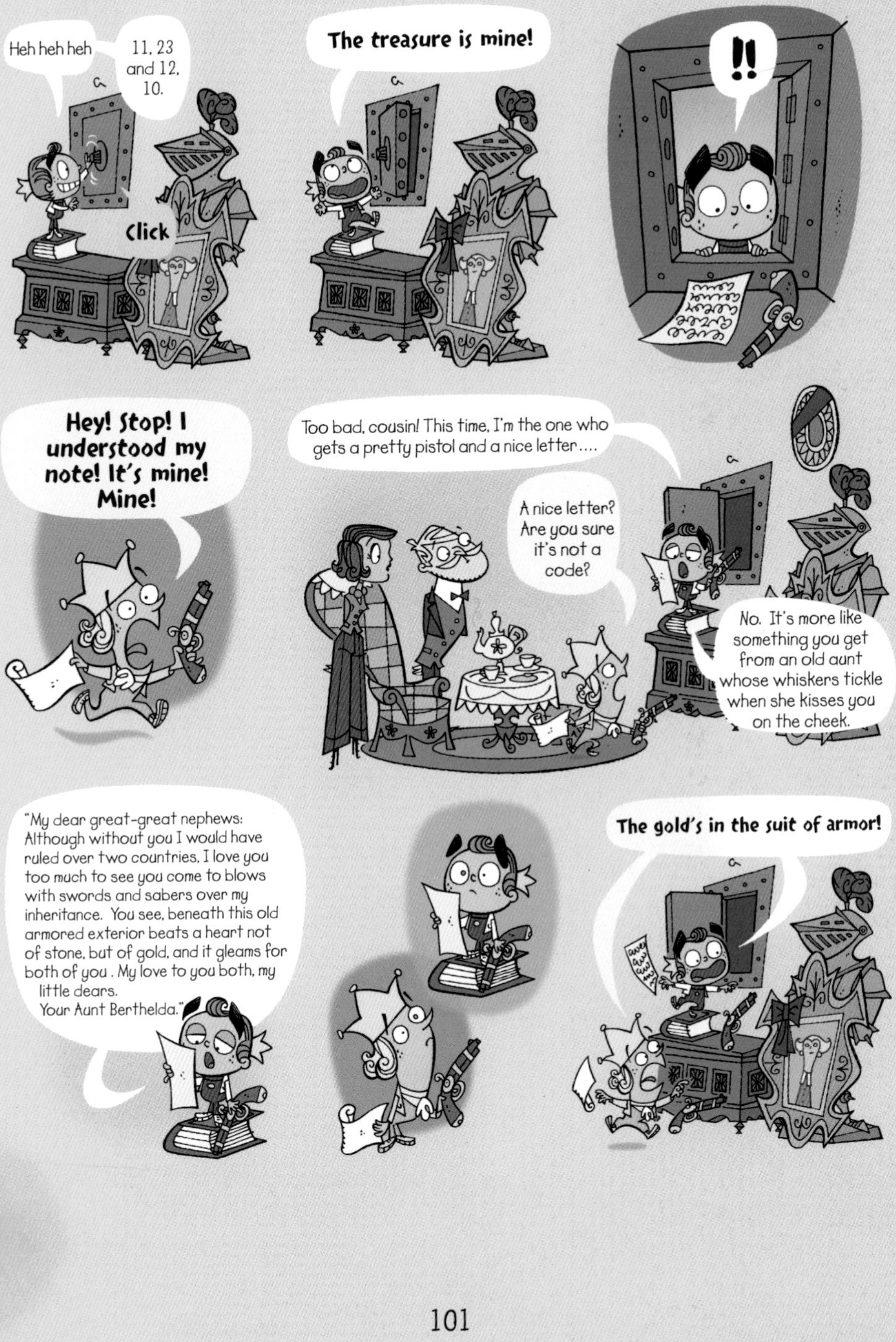

Heh heh heh
11, 23 and 12, 10.
Click
The treasure is mine!
!!
Hey! Stop! I understood my note! It's mine! Mine!
Too bad, cousin! This time, I'm the one who gets a pretty pistol and a nice letter....
A nice letter? Are you sure it's not a code?
No. It's more like something you get from an old aunt whose whiskers tickle when she kisses you on the cheek.
"My dear great-great nephews: Although without you I would have ruled over two countries, I love you too much to see you come to blows with swords and sabers over my inheritance. You see, beneath this old armored exterior beats a heart not of stone, but of gold, and it gleams for both of you . My love to you both, my little dears.
Your Aunt Berthelda."
The gold's in the suit of armor!

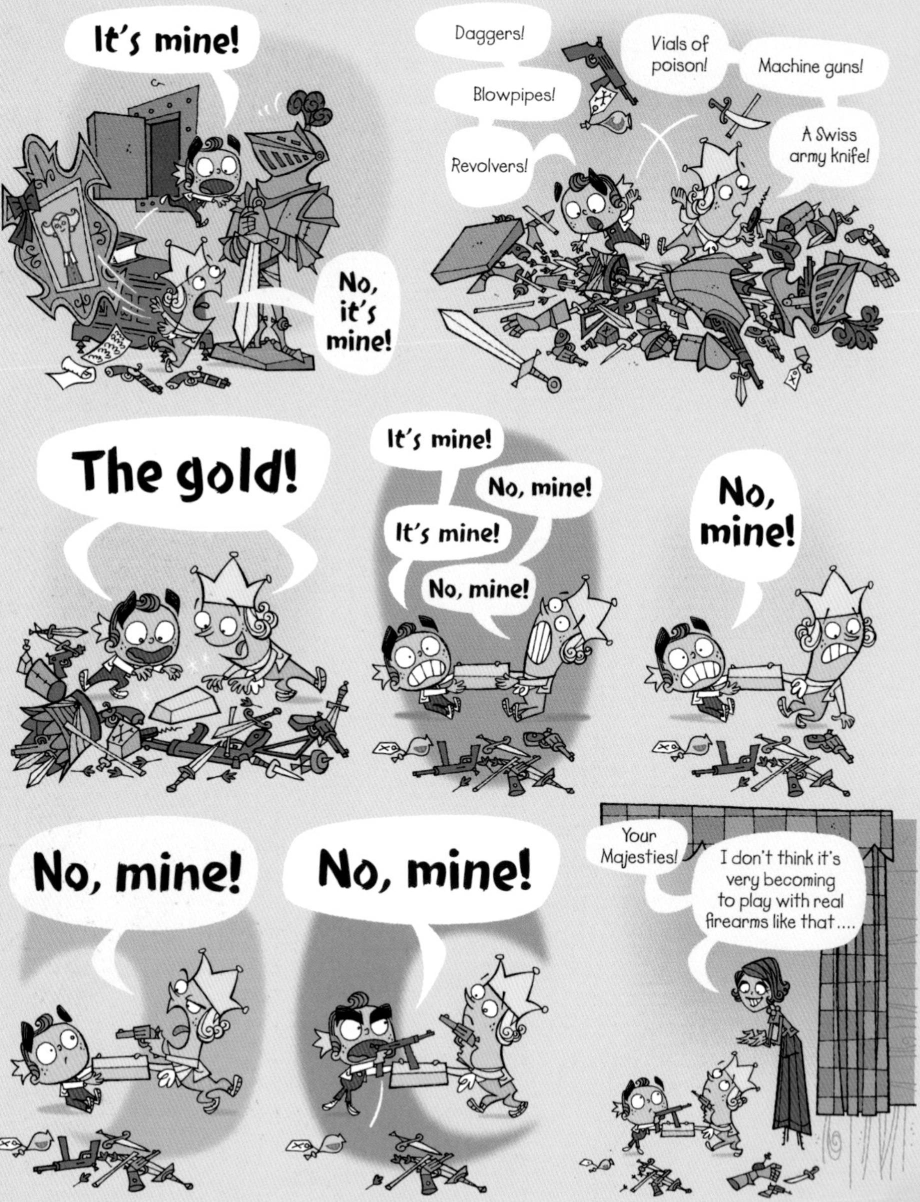
It's mine!
No, it's mine!
Daggers!
Blowpipes!
Revolvers!
Vials of poison!
Machine guns!
A Swiss army knife!
The gold!
It's mine!
No, mine!
It's mine!
No, mine!
No, mine!
No, mine!
No, mine!
Your Majesties!
I don't think it's very becoming to play with real firearms like that....

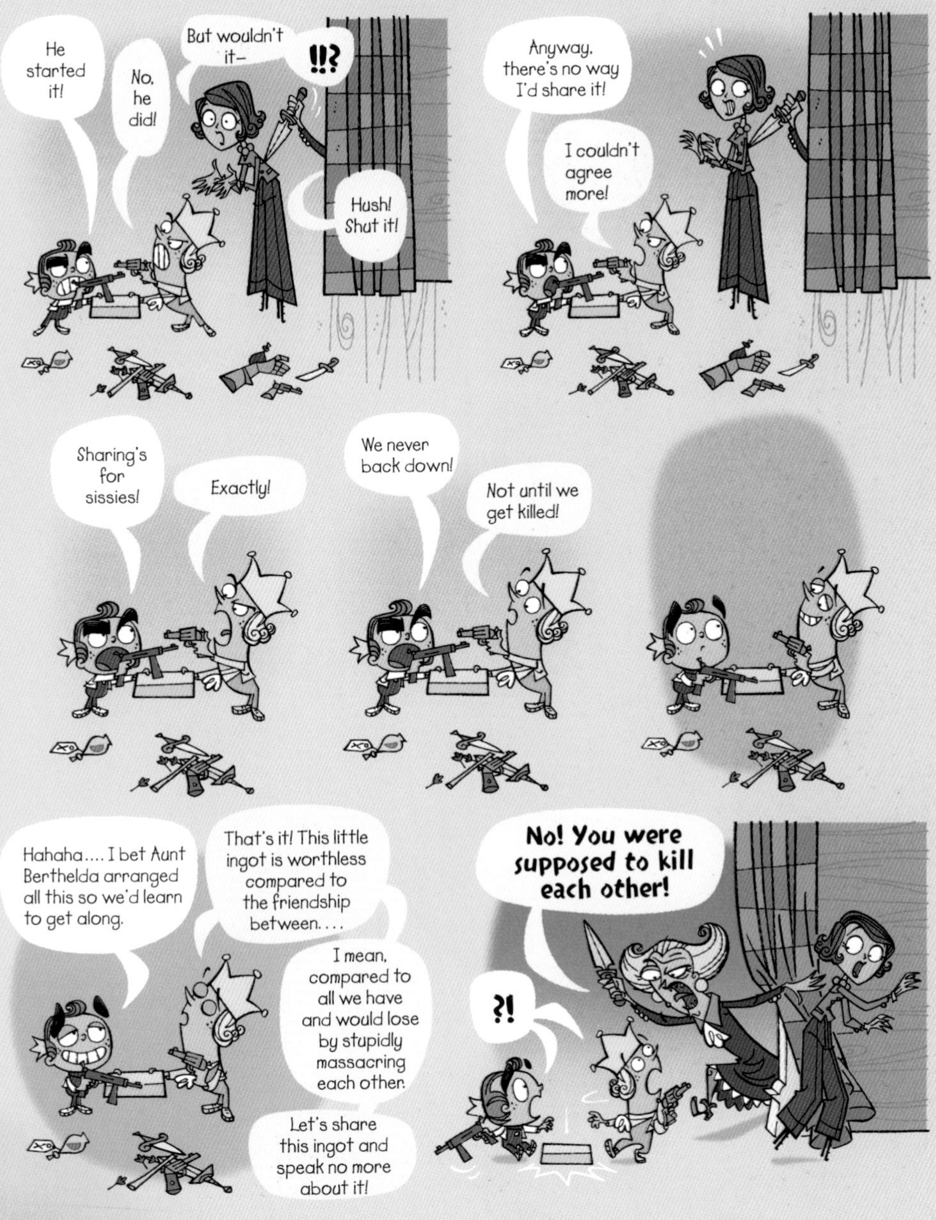

He started it!
No, he did!
But wouldn't it–
!!?
Hush! Shut it!
Anyway, there's no way I'd share it!
I couldn't agree more!
Sharing's for sissies!
Exactly!
We never back down!
Not until we get killed!
Hahaha.... I bet Aunt Berthelda arranged all this so we'd learn to get along.
That's it! This little ingot is worthless compared to the friendship between....
I mean, compared to all we have and would lose by stupidly massacring each other.
Let's share this ingot and speak no more about it!
No! You were supposed to kill each other!
?!

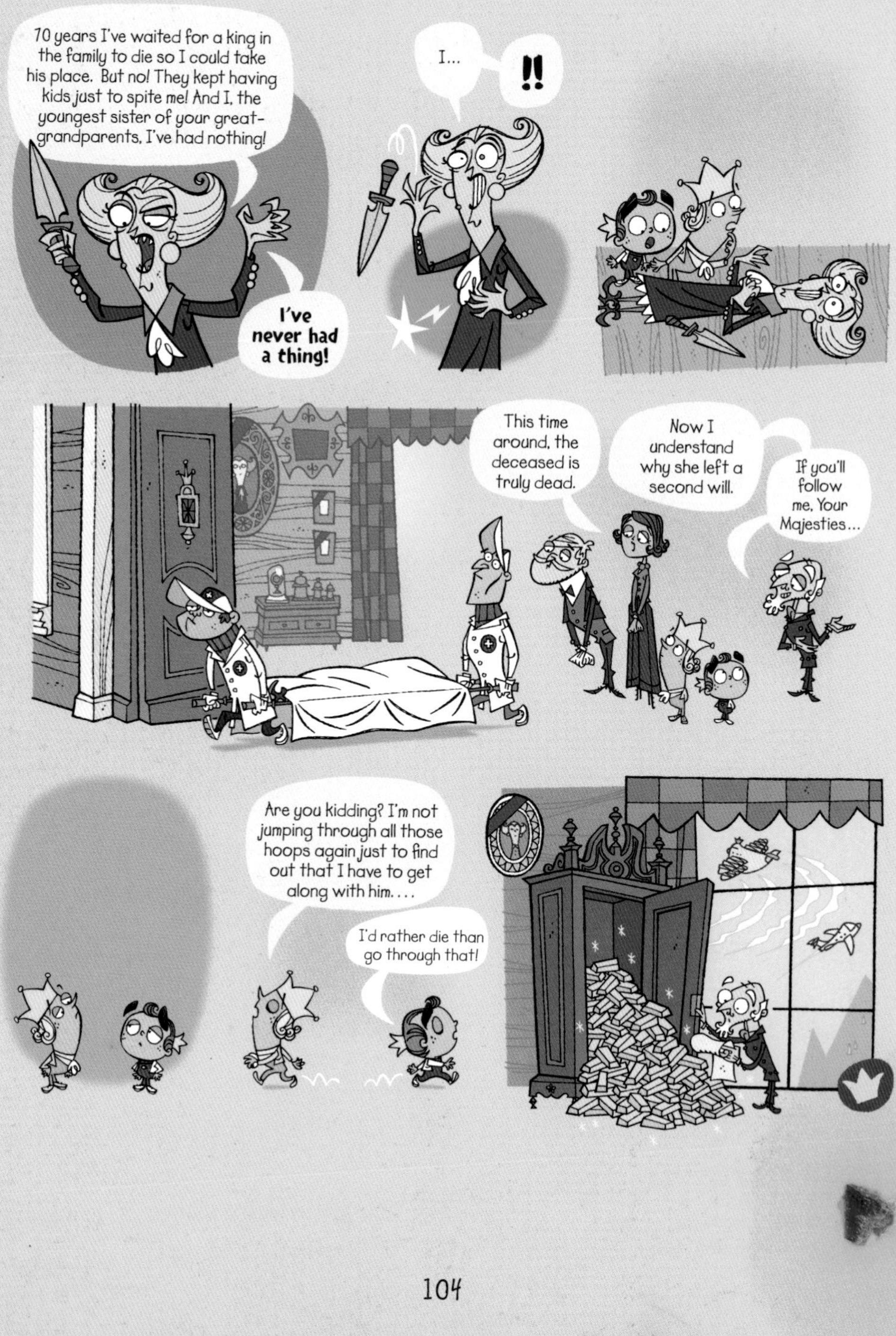
70 years I've waited for a king in the family to die so I could take his place. But no! They kept having kids just to spite me! And I, the youngest sister of your great-grandparents, I've had nothing!
I've never had a thing!
I...
!!
This time around, the deceased is truly dead.
Now I understand why she left a second will.
If you'll follow me, Your Majesties...
Are you kidding? I'm not jumping through all those hoops again just to find out that I have to get along with him....
I'd rather die than go through that!

Rightsizing

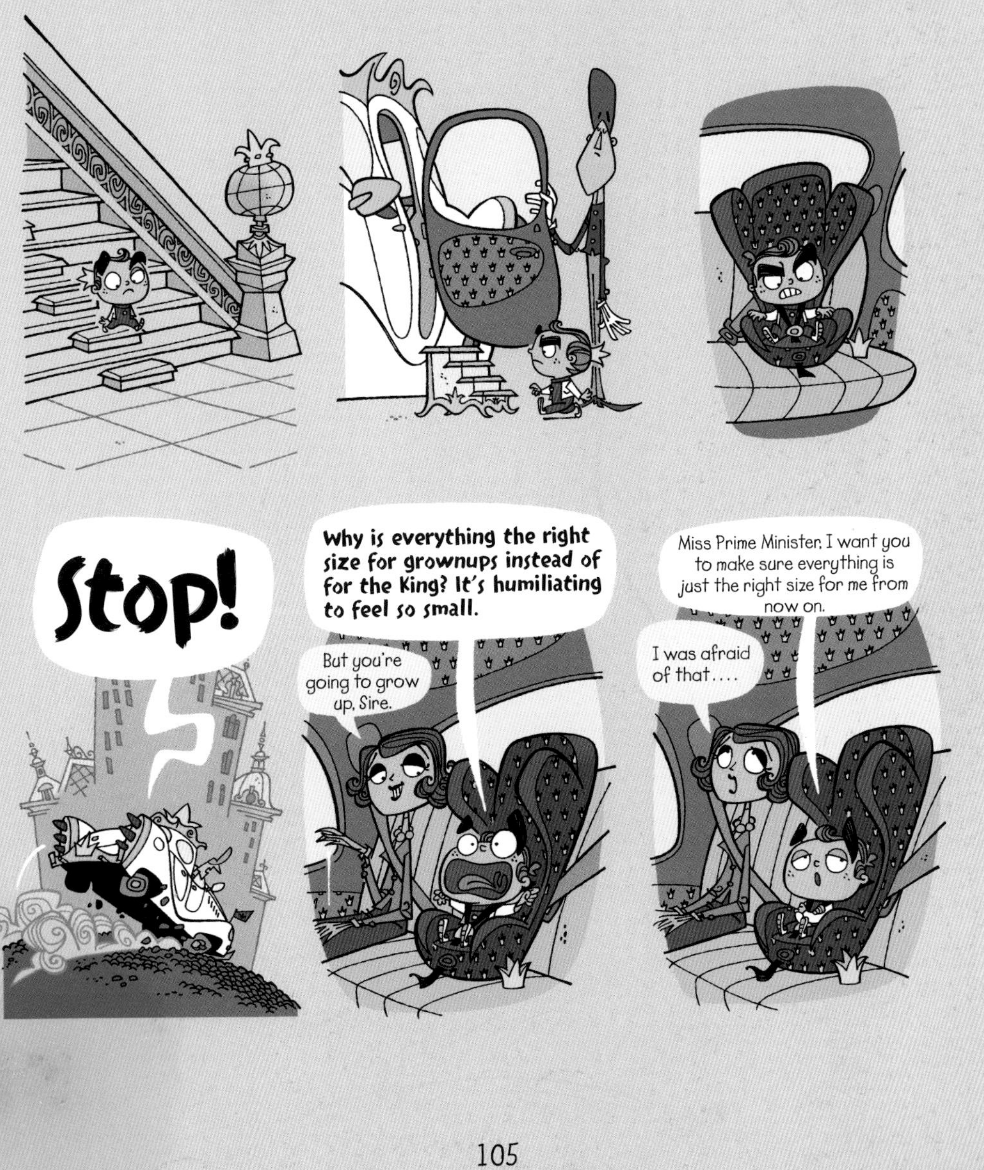
Stop!
Why is everything the right size for grownups instead of for the King? It's humiliating to feel so small.
But you're going to grow up, Sire.
Miss Prime Minister, I want you to make sure everything is just the right size for me from now on.
I was afraid of that....

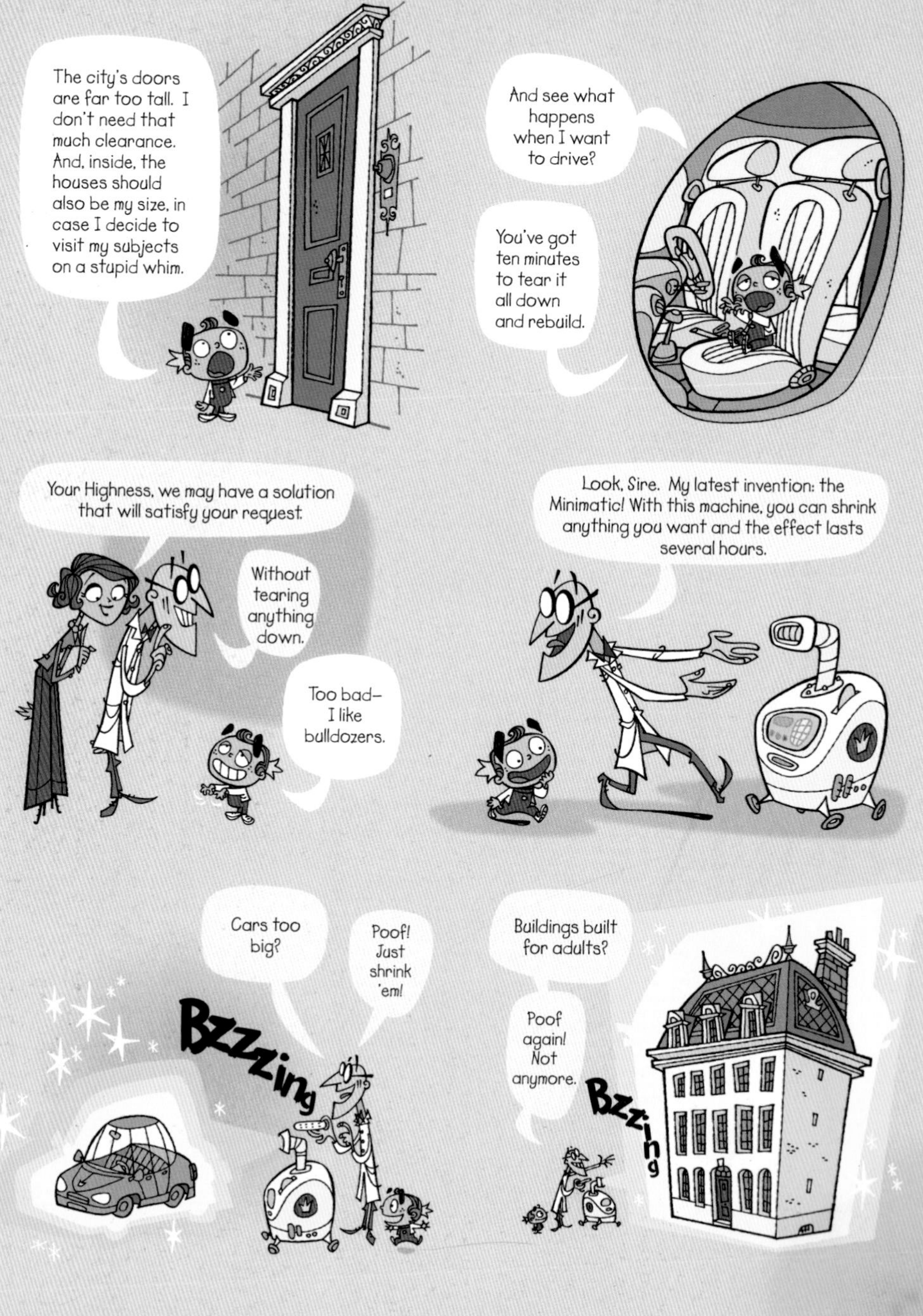

The city's doors are far too tall. I don't need that much clearance. And, inside, the houses should also be my size, in case I decide to visit my subjects on a stupid whim.
And see what happens when I want to drive?
You've got ten minutes to tear it all down and rebuild.
Your Highness, we may have a solution that will satisfy your request.
Without tearing anything down.
Too bad– I like bulldozers.
Look, Sire. My latest invention: the Minimatic! With this machine, you can shrink anything you want and the effect lasts several hours.
Cars too big?
Poof! Just shrink 'em!
Bzzzing
Buildings built for adults?
Poof again! Not anymore.
Bzzing

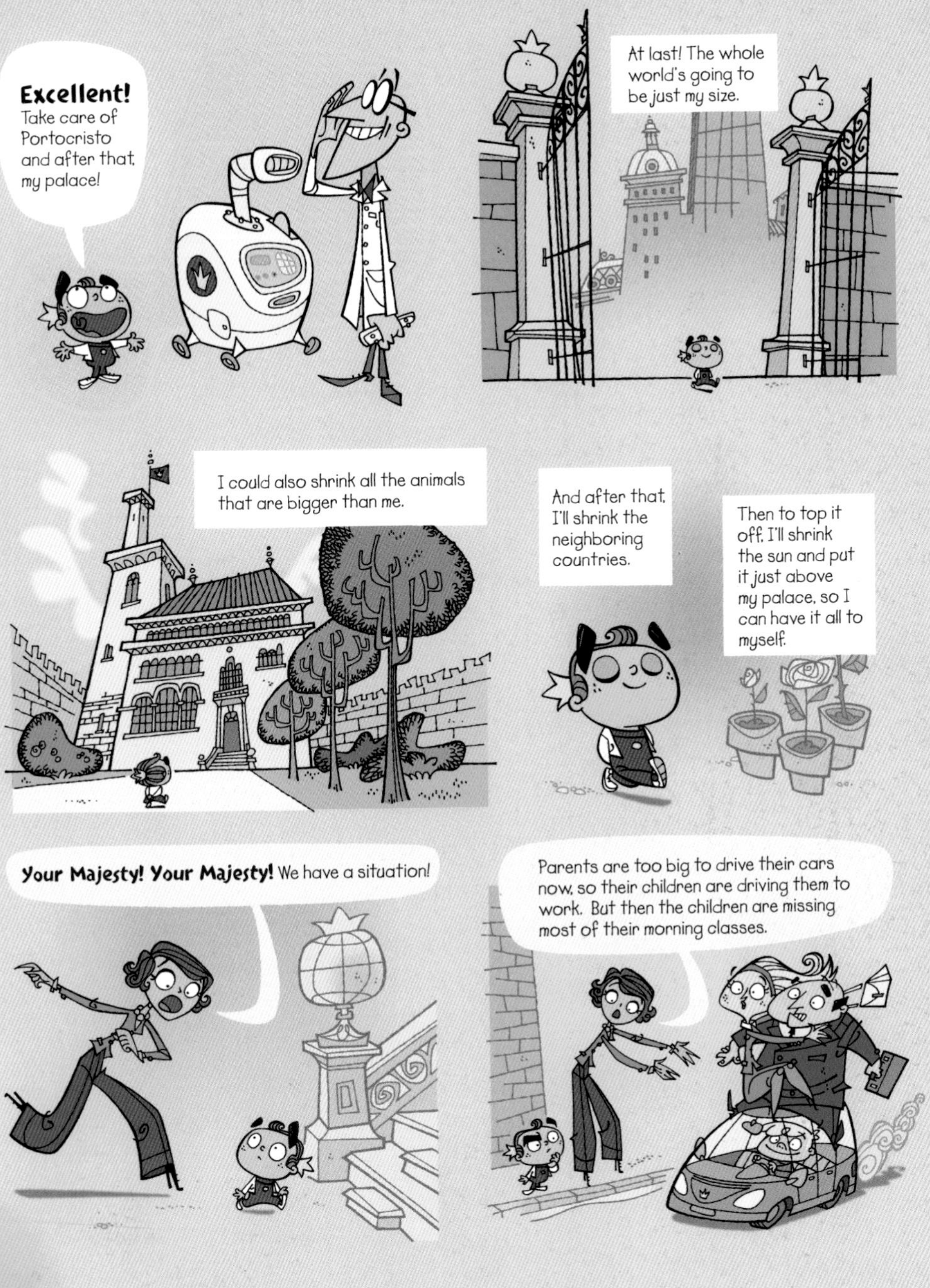
Excellent! Take care of Portocristo and after that, my palace!
At last! The whole world's going to be just my size.
I could also shrink all the animals that are bigger than me.
And after that, I'll shrink the neighboring countries.
Then to top it off, I'll shrink the sun and put it just above my palace, so I can have it all to myself.
Your Majesty! Your Majesty! We have a situation!
Parents are too big to drive their cars now, so their children are driving them to work. But then the children are missing most of their morning classes.

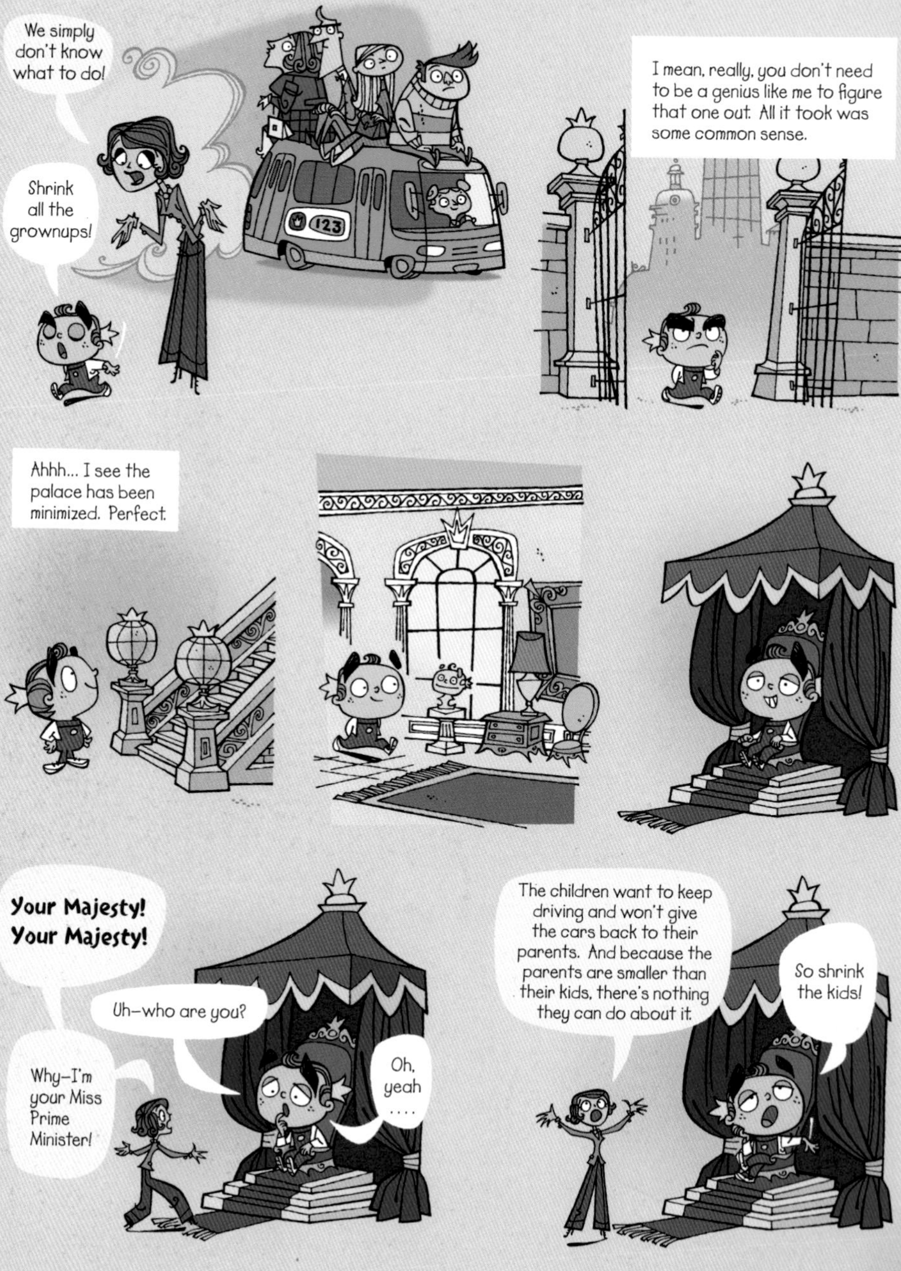

We simply don't know what to do!
Shrink all the grownups!
I mean, really, you don't need to be a genius like me to figure that one out. All it took was some common sense.
Ahhh... I see the palace has been minimized. Perfect.
Your Majesty! Your Majesty!
Uh—who are you?
Why—I'm your Miss Prime Minister!
Oh, yeah . . . .
The children want to keep driving and won't give the cars back to their parents. And because the parents are smaller than their kids, there's nothing they can do about it.
So shrink the kids!

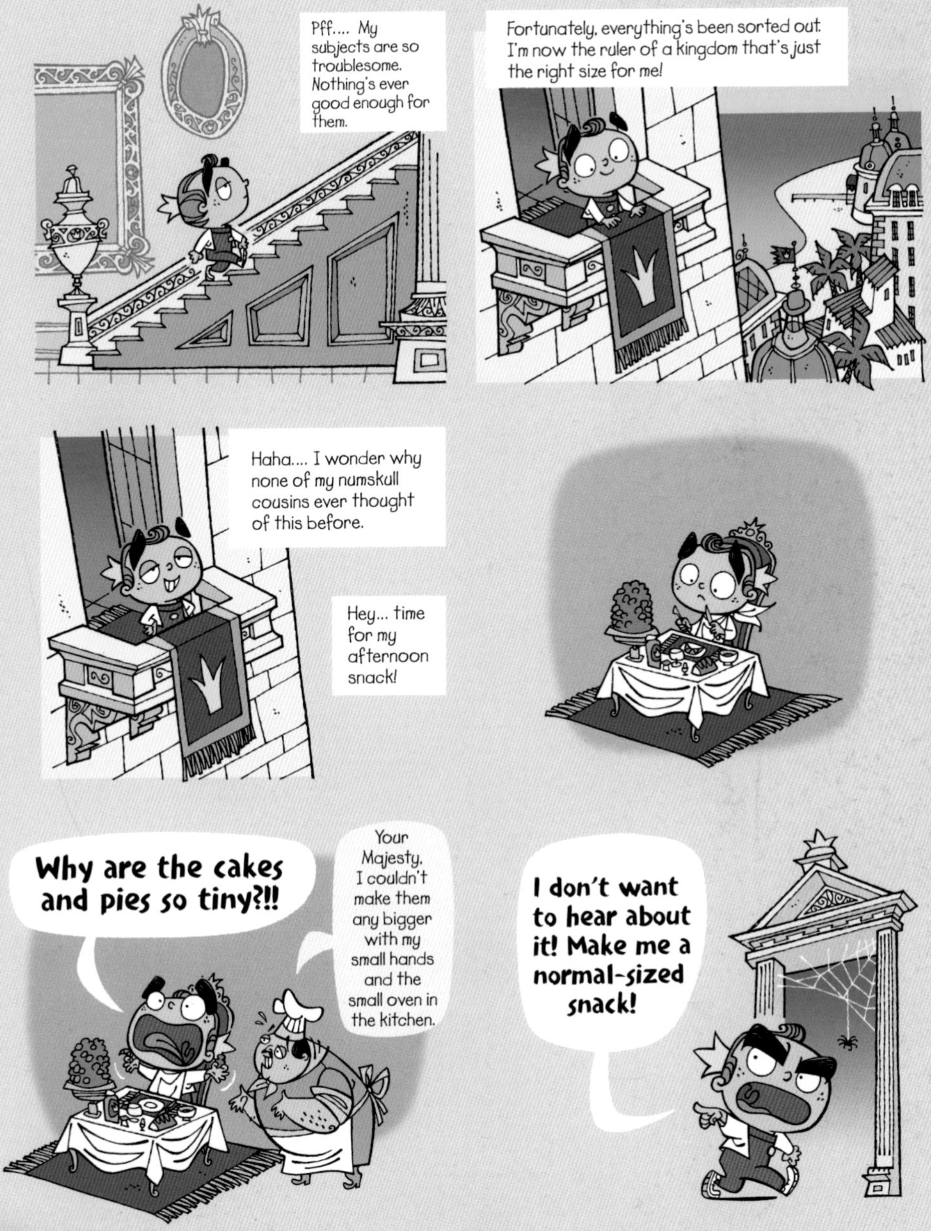

Pff.... My subjects are so troublesome. Nothing's ever good enough for them.
Fortunately, everything's been sorted out. I'm now the ruler of a kingdom that's just the right size for me!
Haha.... I wonder why none of my numskull cousins ever thought of this before.
Hey... time for my afternoon snack!
Why are the cakes and pies so tiny?!!
Your Majesty, I couldn't make them any bigger with my small hands and the small oven in the kitchen.
I don't want to hear about it! Make me a normal-sized snack!

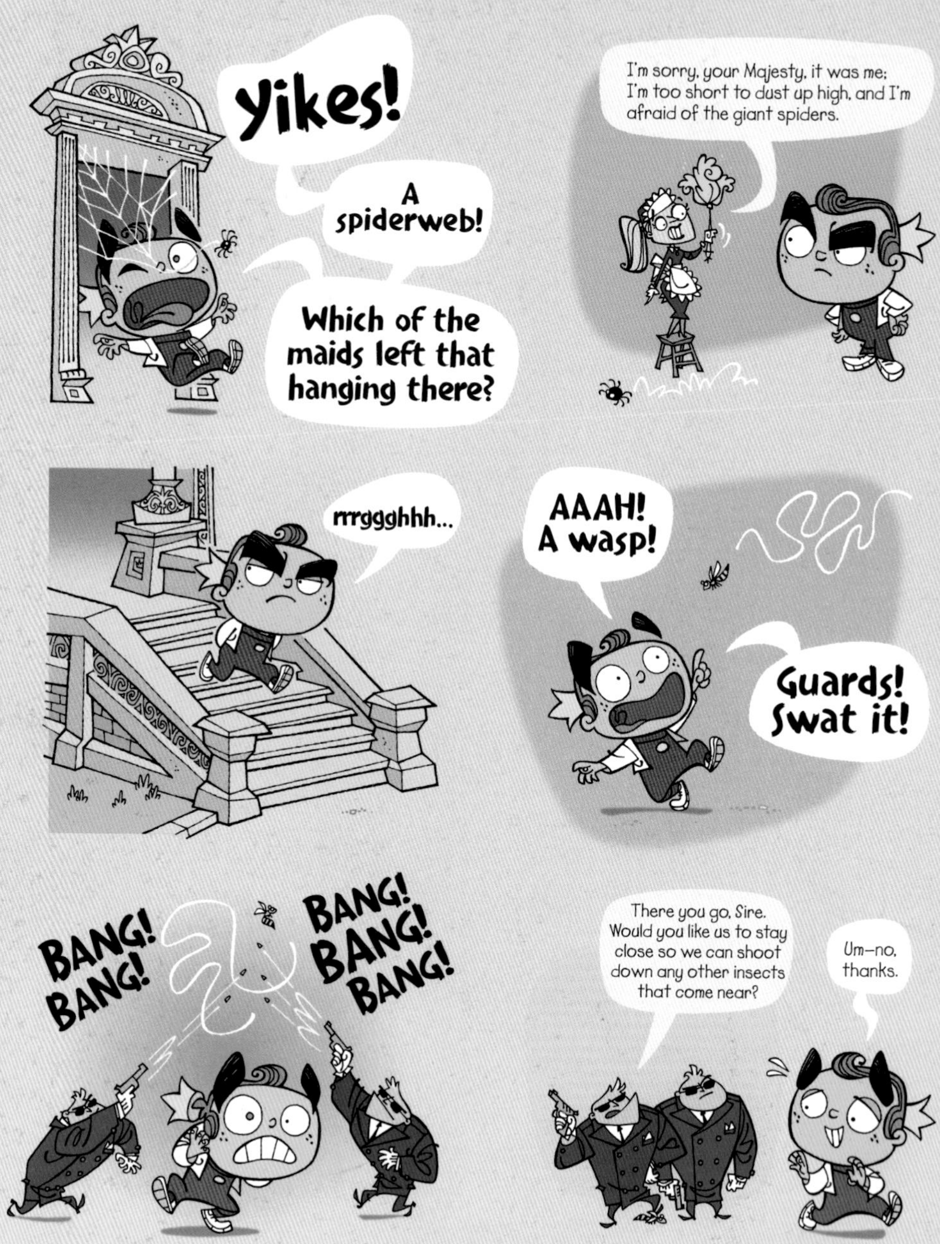
Yikes!
A spiderweb!
Which of the maids left that hanging there?
I'm sorry, your Majesty, it was me; I'm too short to dust up high, and I'm afraid of the giant spiders.
rrrggghhh...
AAAH! A wasp!
Guards! Swat it!
BANG! BANG!
BANG! BANG! BANG!
There you go, Sire. Would you like us to stay close so we can shoot down any other insects that come near?
Um—no, thanks.

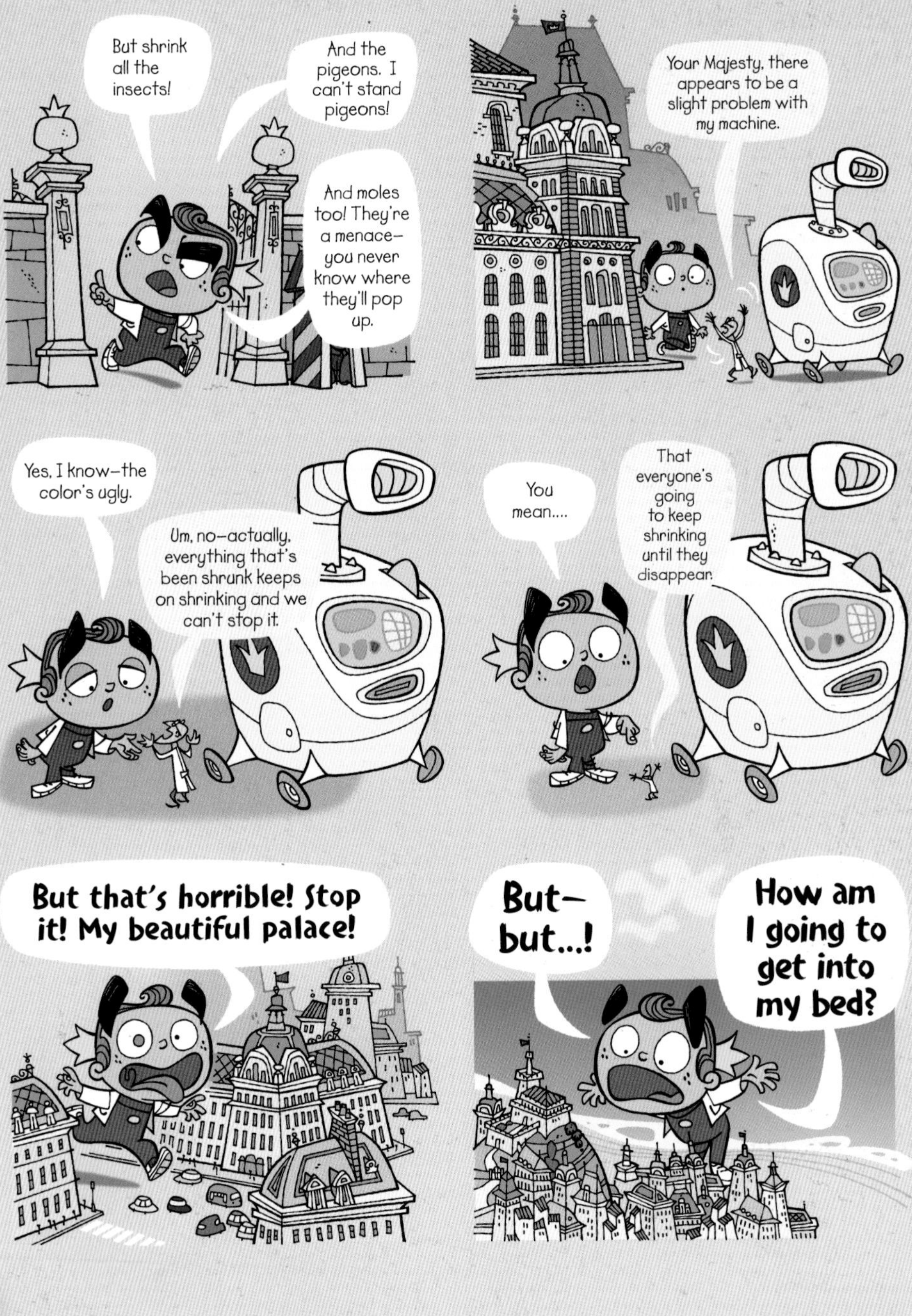

But shrink all the insects!
And the pigeons. I can't stand pigeons!
And moles too! They're a menace–you never know where they'll pop up.
Your Majesty, there appears to be a slight problem with my machine.
Yes, I know–the color's ugly.
Um, no–actually, everything that's been shrunk keeps on shrinking and we can't stop it.
You mean....
That everyone's going to keep shrinking until they disappear.
But that's horrible! Stop it! My beautiful palace!
But–but...!
How am I going to get into my bed?

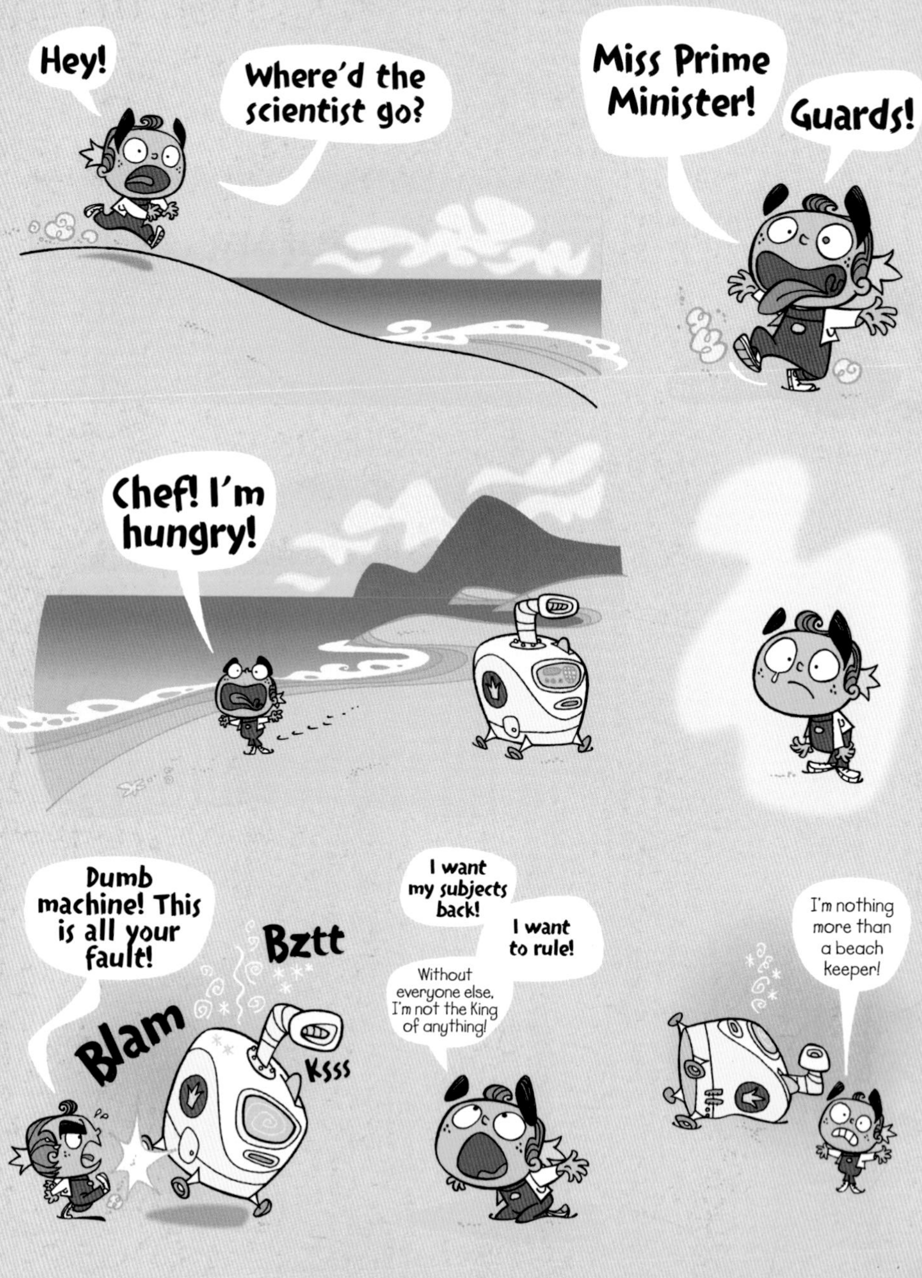
Hey!
Where'd the scientist go?
Miss Prime Minister!
Guards!
Chef! I'm hungry!
Dumb machine! This is all your fault!
Bztt
Blam
Ksss
I want my subjects back!
I want to rule!
Without everyone else, I'm not the King of anything!
I'm nothing more than a beach keeper!

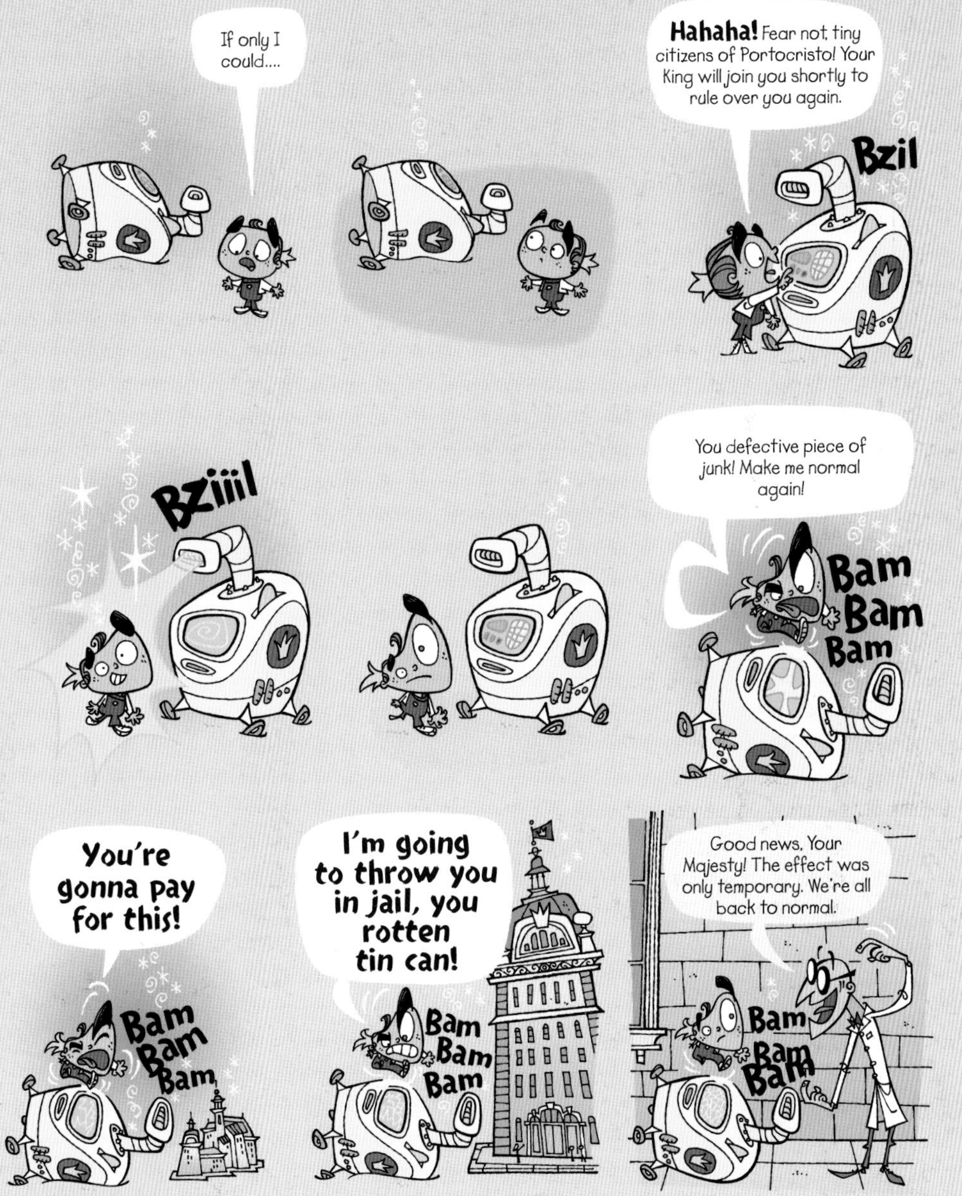
If only I could....
Hahaha! Fear not, tiny citizens of Portocristo! Your King will join you shortly to rule over you again.
Bzil
Bziiil
You defective piece of junk! Make me normal again!
Bam Bam Bam
You're gonna pay for this!
Bam Bam Bam
I'm going to throw you in jail, you rotten tin can!
Bam Bam Bam
Good news, Your Majesty! The effect was only temporary. We're all back to normal.
Bam Bam Bam

What about me, you incompetent creep? You call this normal?
Uh... OW! Haven't you always looked like that, Sire?
Bam Bam Bam
OUCH!!
Guards! Seize him!
Please! Don't worry, Your Majesty. It'll wear off soon.
I'm the King! I can't be uglier than everyone else, even for five minutes!
It's humiliating!
Ahhhh.... It sure is nice to have everything back to normal again.

A Full Life

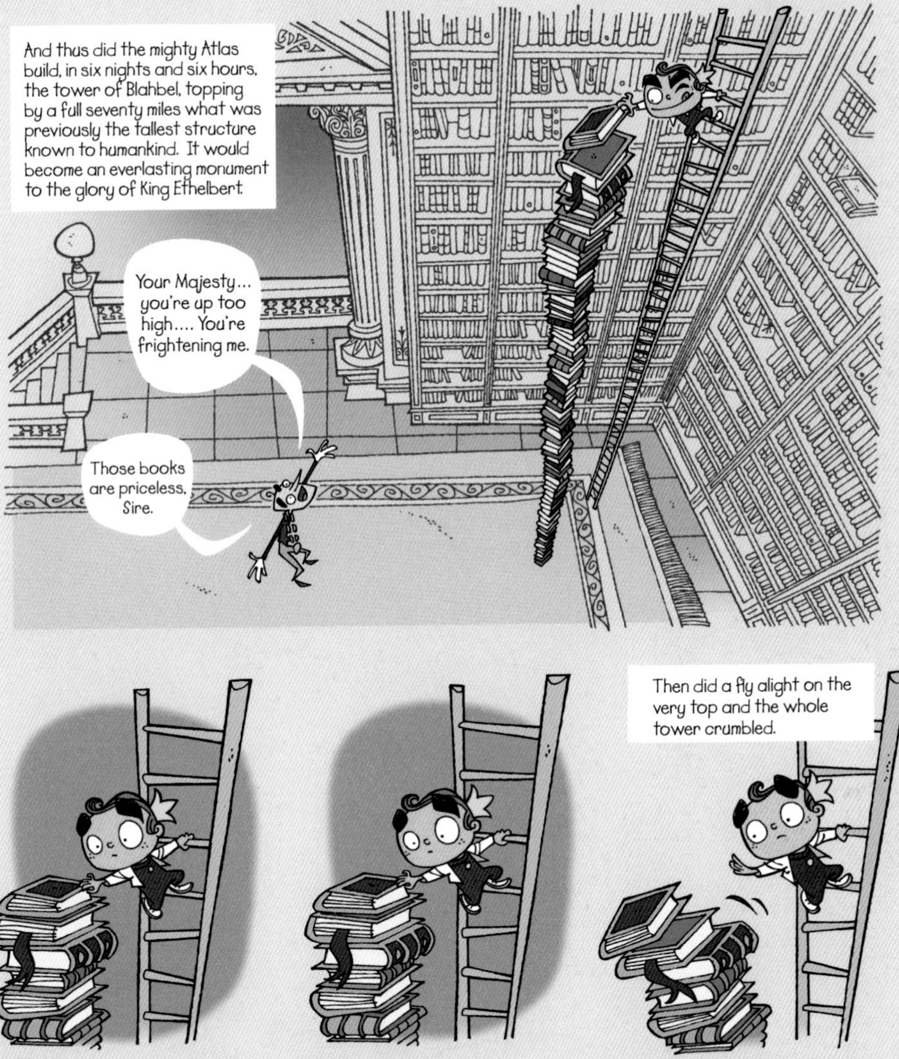
And thus did the mighty Atlas build, in six nights and six hours, the tower of Blahbel, topping by a full seventy miles what was previously the tallest structure known to humankind. It would become an everlasting monument to the glory of King Ethelbert.
Your Majesty... you're up too high.... You're frightening me.
Those books are priceless, Sire.
Then did a fly alight on the very top and the whole tower crumbled.

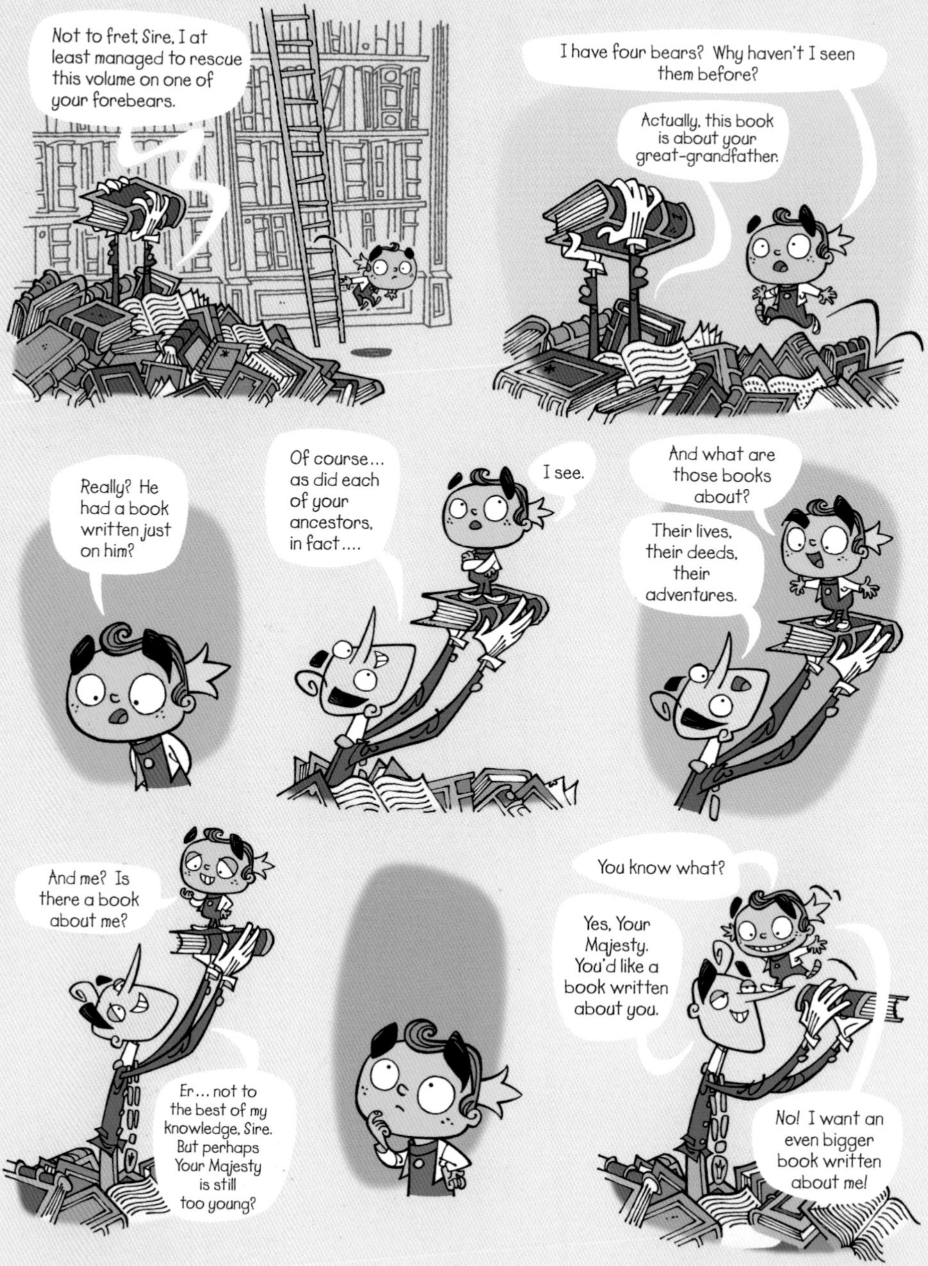

Not to fret, Sire, I at least managed to rescue this volume on one of your forebears.
I have four bears? Why haven't I seen them before?
Actually, this book is about your great-grandfather.
Really? He had a book written just on him?
Of course... as did each of your ancestors, in fact....
I see.
And what are those books about?
Their lives, their deeds, their adventures.
And me? Is there a book about me?
Er... not to the best of my knowledge, Sire. But perhaps Your Majesty is still too young?
You know what?
Yes, Your Majesty. You'd like a book written about you.
No! I want an even bigger book written about me!

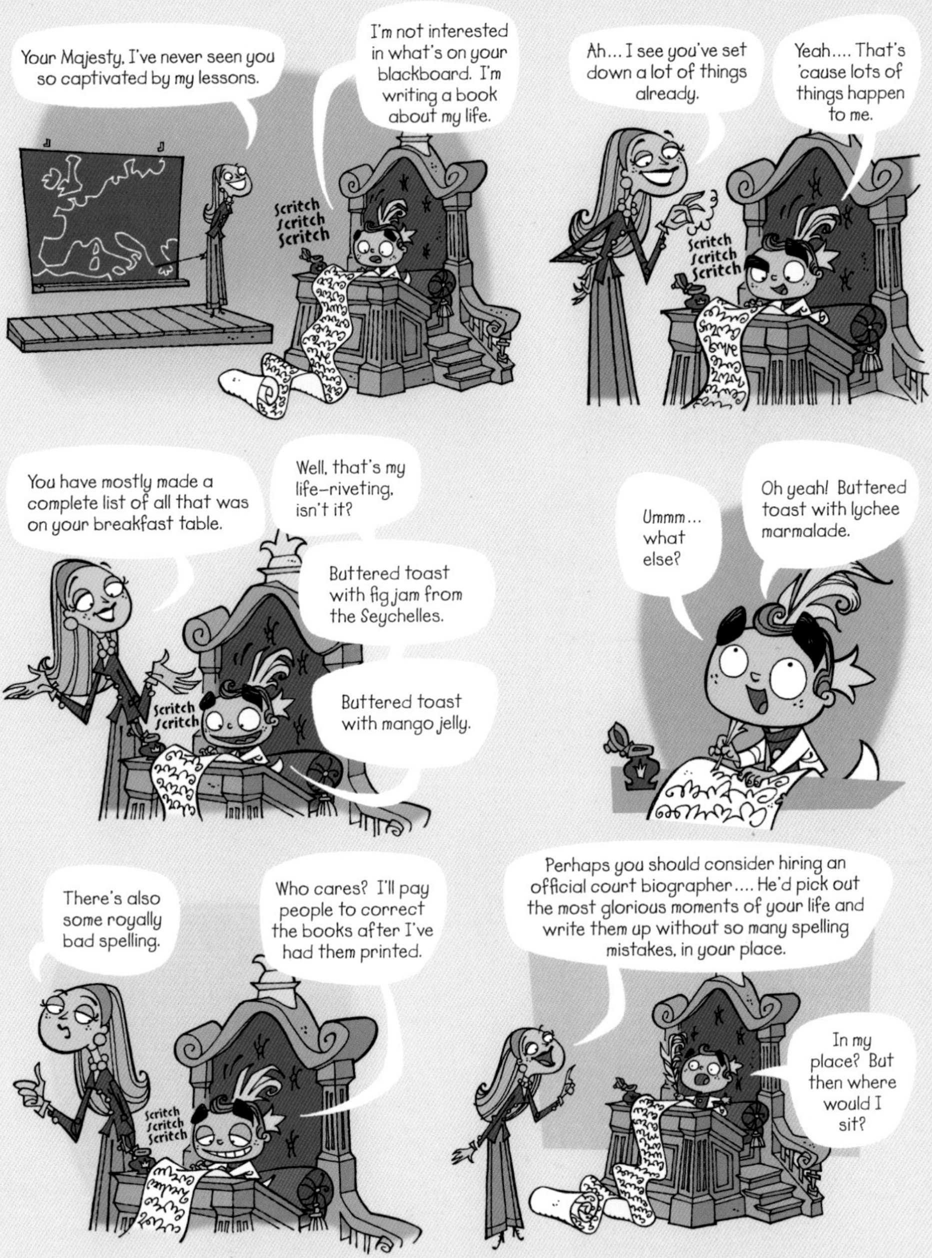
Your Majesty, I've never seen you so captivated by my lessons.
I'm not interested in what's on your blackboard. I'm writing a book about my life.
Scritch Scritch Scritch
Ah... I see you've set down a lot of things already.
Yeah.... That's 'cause lots of things happen to me.
Scritch Scritch Scritch
You have mostly made a complete list of all that was on your breakfast table.
Well, that's my life–riveting, isn't it?
Buttered toast with fig jam from the Seychelles.
Buttered toast with mango jelly.
Scritch Scritch
Ummm... what else?
Oh yeah! Buttered toast with lychee marmalade.
There's also some royally bad spelling.
Who cares? I'll pay people to correct the books after I've had them printed.
Scritch Scritch Scritch
Perhaps you should consider hiring an official court biographer.... He'd pick out the most glorious moments of your life and write them up without so many spelling mistakes, in your place.
In my place? But then where would I sit?

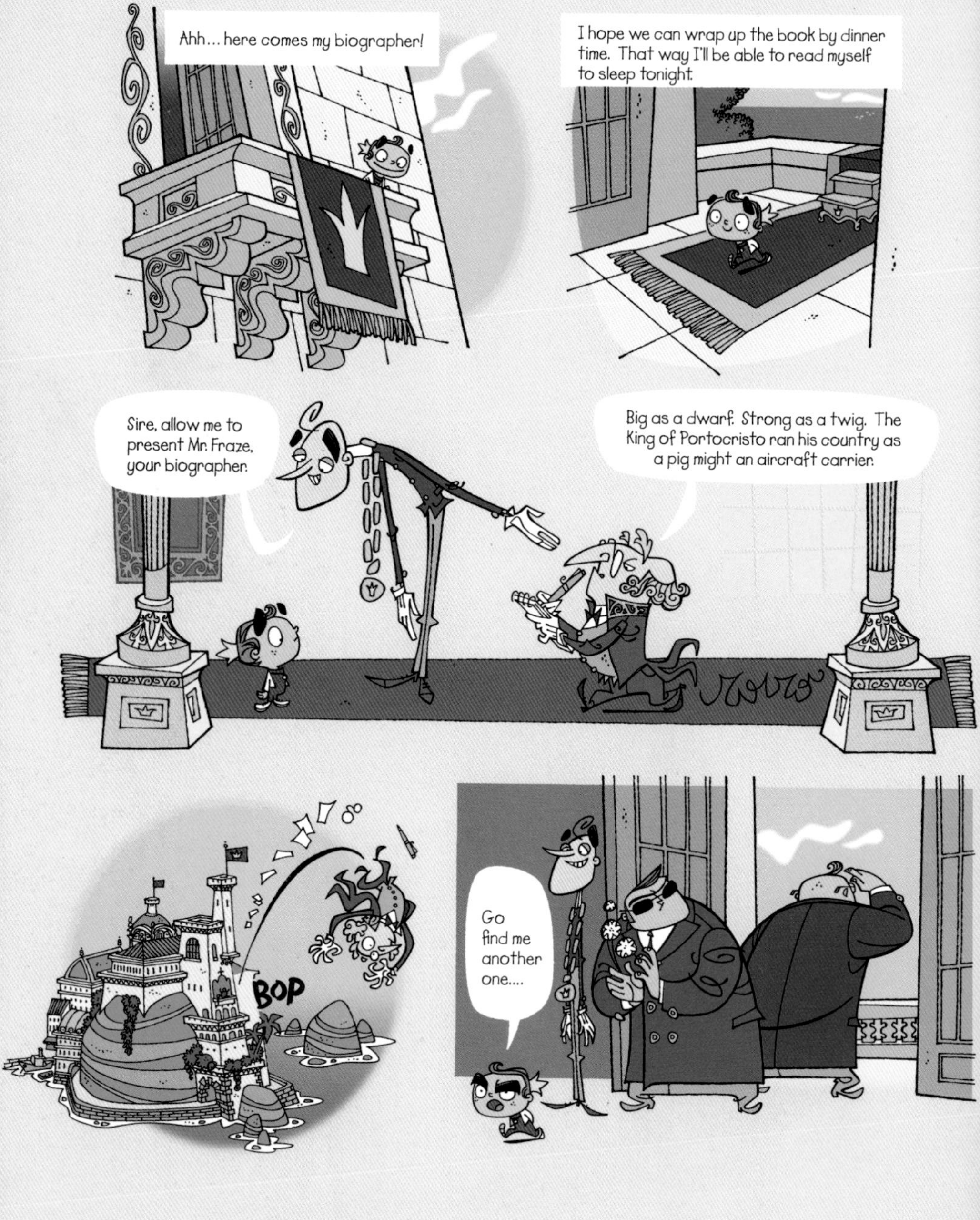

Ahh... here comes my biographer!
I hope we can wrap up the book by dinner time. That way I'll be able to read myself to sleep tonight.
Sire, allow me to present Mr. Fraze, your biographer.
Big as a dwarf. Strong as a twig. The King of Portocristo ran his country as a pig might an aircraft carrier.
BOP
Go find me another one....

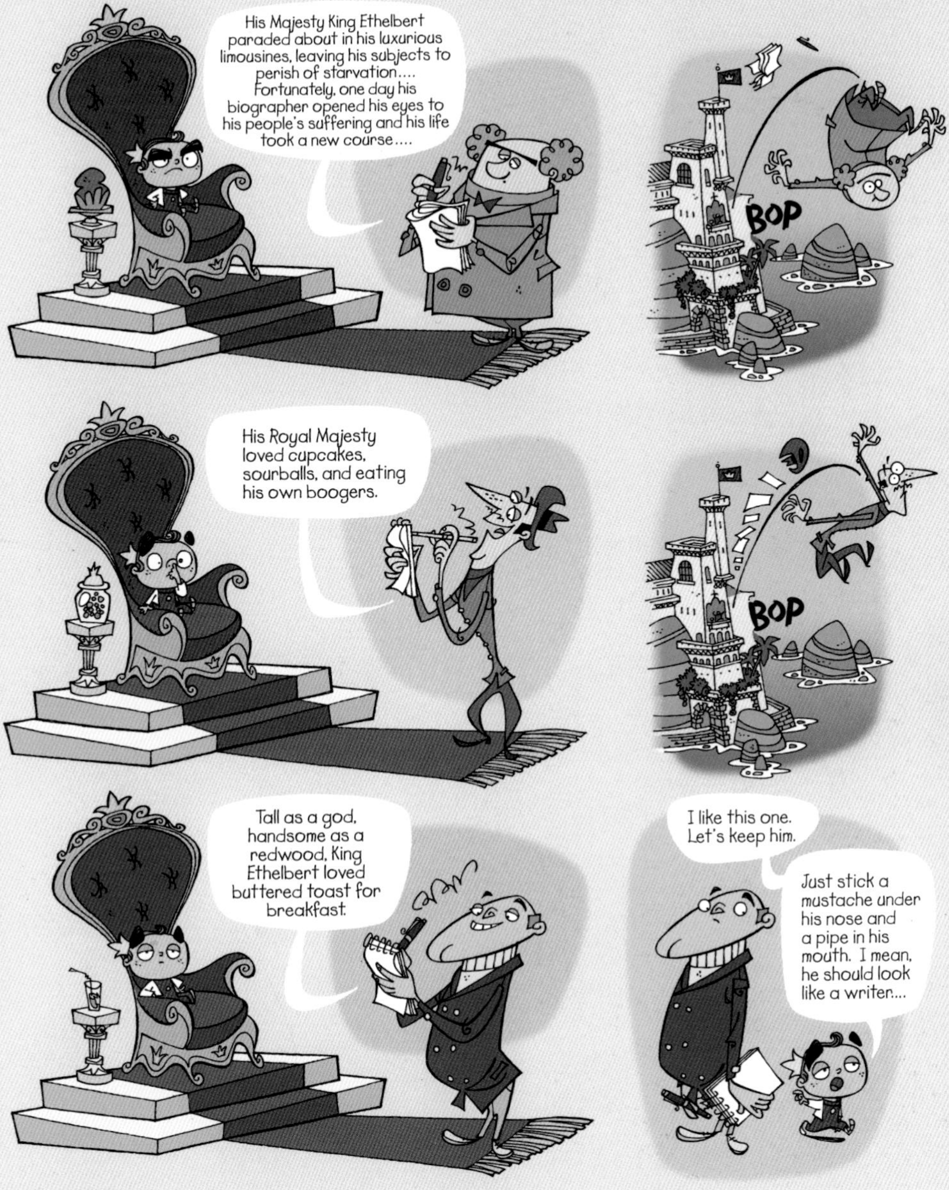
His Majesty King Ethelbert paraded about in his luxurious limousines, leaving his subjects to perish of starvation.... Fortunately, one day his biographer opened his eyes to his people's suffering and his life took a new course....
BOP
His Royal Majesty loved cupcakes, sourballs, and eating his own boogers.
BOP
Tall as a god, handsome as a redwood, King Ethelbert loved buttered toast for breakfast.
I like this one. Let's keep him.
Just stick a mustache under his nose and a pipe in his mouth. I mean, he should look like a writer...

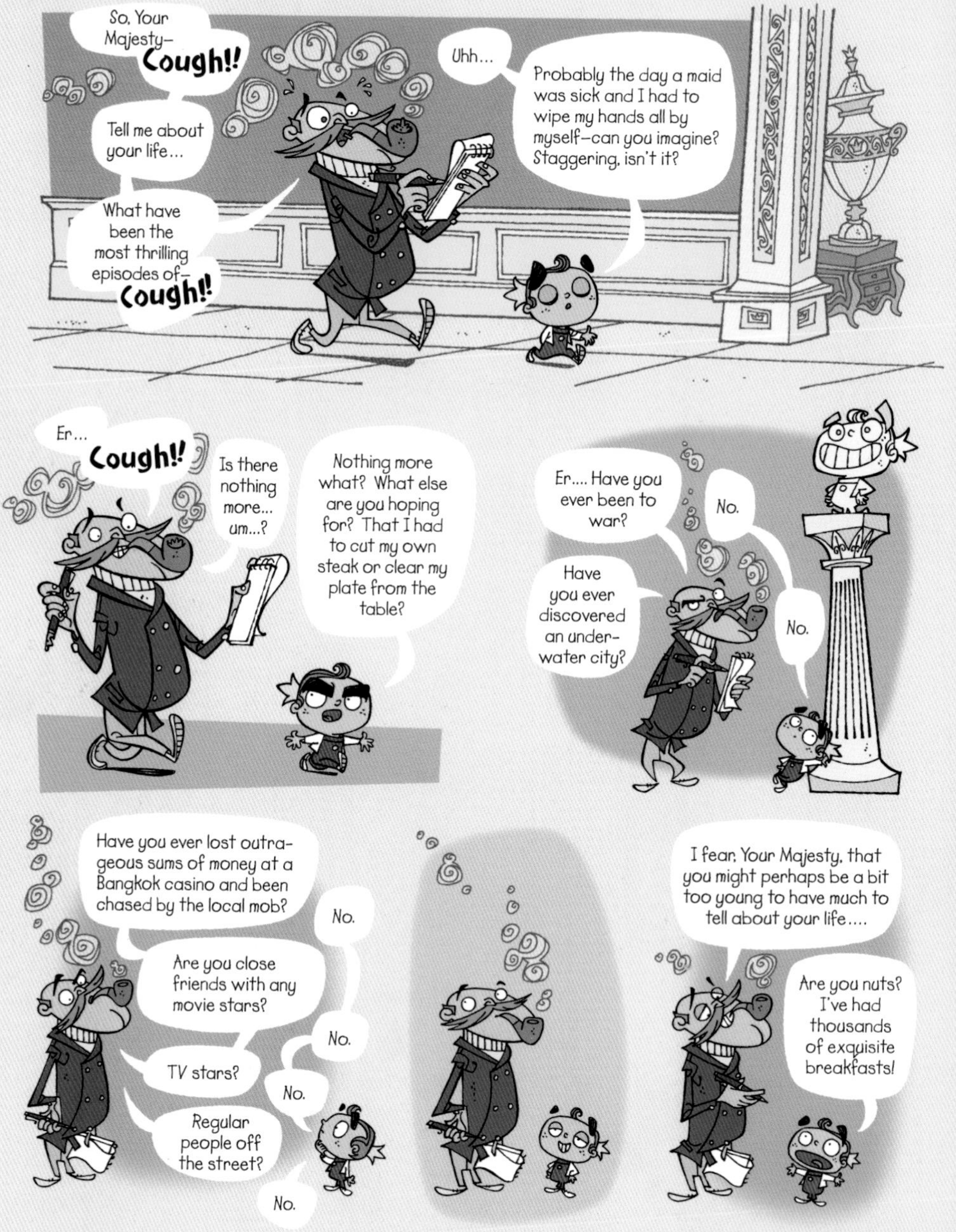
So, Your Majesty—
Cough!!
Tell me about your life...
What have been the most thrilling episodes of—
Cough!!
Uhh...
Probably the day a maid was sick and I had to wipe my hands all by myself—can you imagine? Staggering, isn't it?
Er...
Cough!!
Is there nothing more... um...?
Nothing more what? What else are you hoping for? That I had to cut my own steak or clear my plate from the table?
Er.... Have you ever been to war?
No.
Have you ever discovered an under-water city?
No.
Have you ever lost outra-geous sums of money at a Bangkok casino and been chased by the local mob?
No.
Are you close friends with any movie stars?
No.
TV stars?
No.
Regular people off the street?
No.
I fear, Your Majesty, that you might perhaps be a bit too young to have much to tell about your life....
Are you nuts? I've had thousands of exquisite breakfasts!

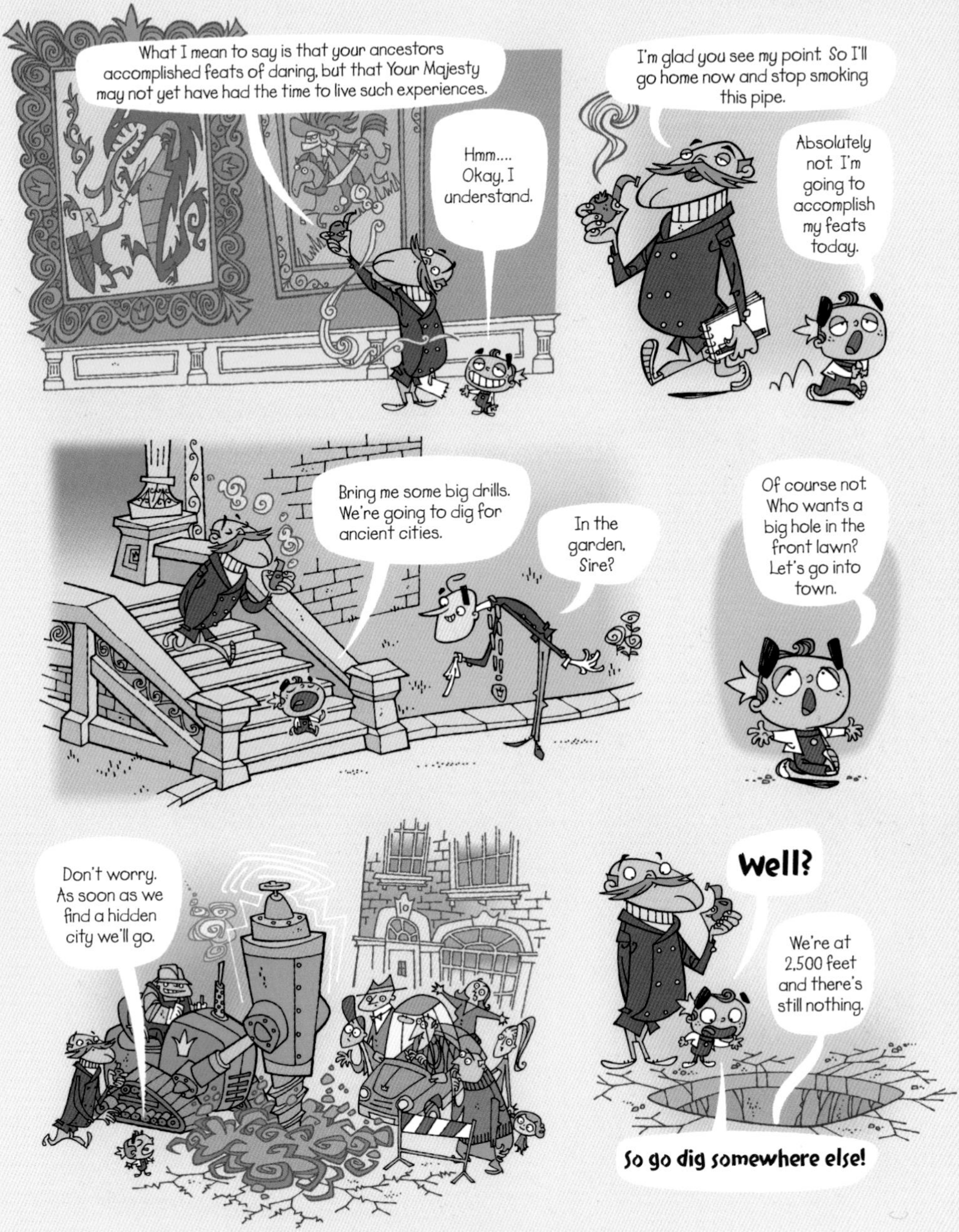
What I mean to say is that your ancestors accomplished feats of daring, but that Your Majesty may not yet have had the time to live such experiences.
Hmm.... Okay, I understand.
I'm glad you see my point. So I'll go home now and stop smoking this pipe.
Absolutely not. I'm going to accomplish my feats today.
Bring me some big drills. We're going to dig for ancient cities.
In the garden, Sire?
Of course not. Who wants a big hole in the front lawn? Let's go into town.
Don't worry. As soon as we find a hidden city we'll go.
Well?
We're at 2,500 feet and there's still nothing.
So go dig somewhere else!

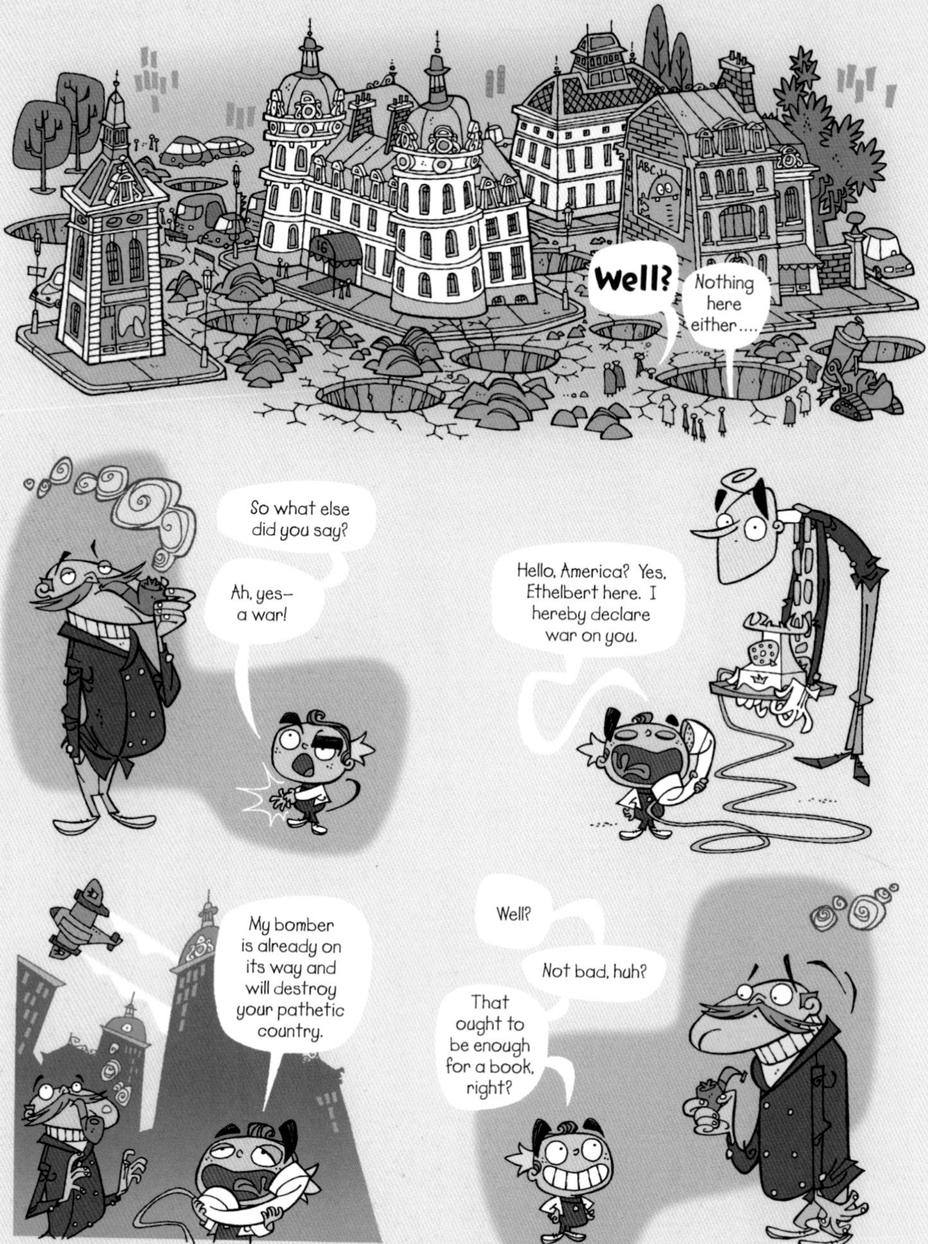
Well?
Nothing here either....
So what else did you say?
Ah, yes– a war!
Hello, America? Yes, Ethelbert here. I hereby declare war on you.
My bomber is already on its way and will destroy your pathetic country.
Well?
Not bad, huh?
That ought to be enough for a book, right?

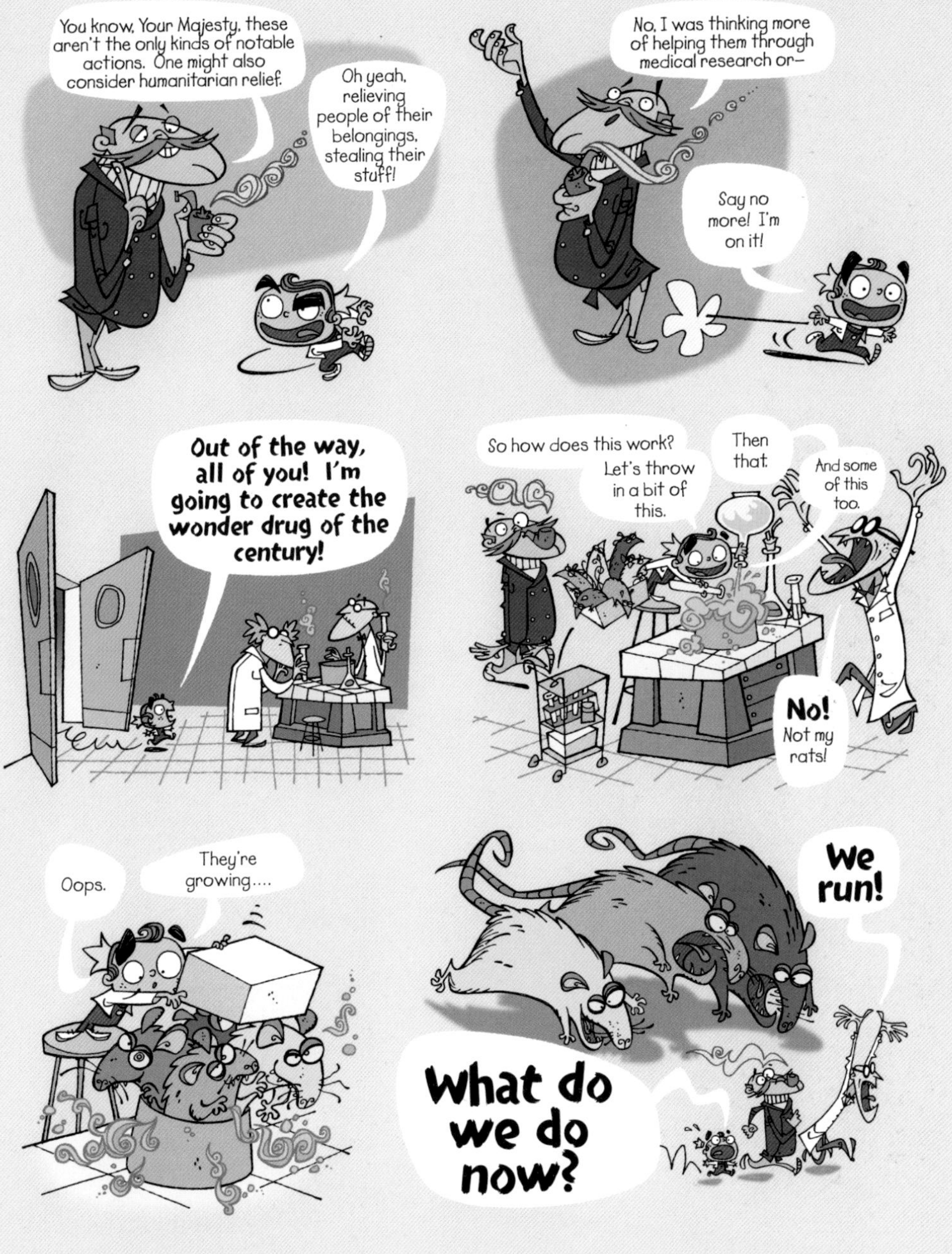
You know, Your Majesty, these aren't the only kinds of notable actions. One might also consider humanitarian relief.
Oh yeah, relieving people of their belongings, stealing their stuff!
No, I was thinking more of helping them through medical research or—
Say no more! I'm on it!
Out of the way, all of you! I'm going to create the wonder drug of the century!
So how does this work?
Let's throw in a bit of this.
Then that.
And some of this too.
No! Not my rats!
Oops.
They're growing....
We run!
What do we do now?

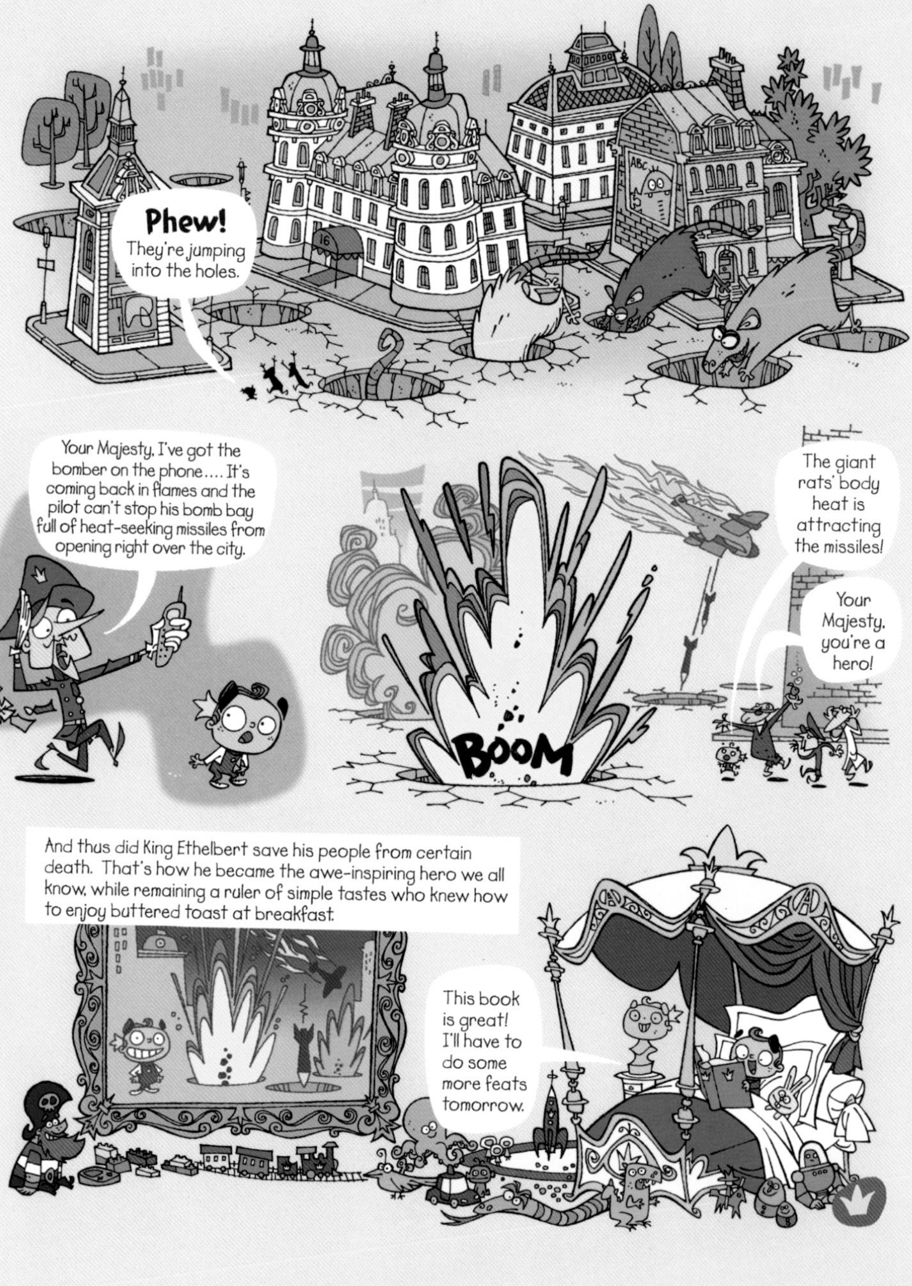
Phew! They're jumping into the holes.
Your Majesty, I've got the bomber on the phone.... It's coming back in flames and the pilot can't stop his bomb bay full of heat-seeking missiles from opening right over the city.
BOOM
The giant rats' body heat is attracting the missiles!
Your Majesty, you're a hero!
And thus did King Ethelbert save his people from certain death. That's how he became the awe-inspiring hero we all know, while remaining a ruler of simple tastes who knew how to enjoy buttered toast at breakfast.
This book is great! I'll have to do some more feats tomorrow.

Westfield Memorial Library
Westfield, New Jersey

First Second

New York & London

Copyright © 2001, 2002, 2003, 2004 by Guy Delcourt Productions—
Lewis Trondheim—Fabrice Parme
English translation copyright © 2007 by First Second

Published by First Second
First Second is an imprint of Roaring Brook Press, a division of Holtzbrinck Publishing Holdings Limited
Partnership
175 Fifth Avenue, New York, NY 10010

All rights reserved.

Distributed in Canada by H. B. Fenn and Company Ltd.
Distributed in the United Kingdom by Macmillan Children's Books, a division of Pan Macmillan.

Originally published in France in 2001 under the titles *Adalbert ne manqué pas d'air* and *Adalbert perd les pédales*, in 2002 under the titles *Adalbert a tout pour plaire* and *Adalbert s'en sort pas mal*, in 2003 under the titles *Adalbert plus que super* and *Adalbert fait du scandale*, in 2004 under the titles *Adalbert change d'atmosphère* and *Adalbert est trop génial* by Guy Delcourt Productions, Paris.

Design by Danica Novgorodoff and Tanja Geis

Library of Congress Cataloging-in-Publication Data

Trondheim, Lewis.
Tiny tyrant / by Lewis Trondheim ; illustrated by Fabrice Parme. --
1st American ed.
p. cm.
Translations into English of eight French stories originally published by Delcourt, 2001-2004.
ISBN-13: 978-1-59643-094-5
ISBN-10: 1-59643-094-X
1. Graphic novels. I. Parme, Fabrice. II. Title.
PN6747.T76T56 2007
741.5'944--dc22
2006021479

First Second books are available for special promotions and premiums.
For details, contact: Director of Special Markets, Holtzbrinck Publishers.

First American Edition May 2007

Printed in China

10 9 8 7 6 5 4 3 2 1

WESTFIELD MEMORIAL LIBRARY

3 9550 00400 8826

Westfield Memorial Library
Westfield, New Jersey

NOV 07

YAGN Tro
Trondheim, Lewis.
Tiny tyrant /